A Price
to Pay

Also by Angela Winters

No More Good

Never Enough

View Park

Published by Kensington Publishing Corporation

A PRICE TO PAY

ANGELA WINTERS

KENSINGTON PUBLISHING CORP.
www.kensingtonbooks.com

*This book is dedicated to the friends who
encouraged me to not stop at three.*

1

Thirty-one-year-old Carter Chase was standing impatiently in the foyer of his family's famous and often photographed home, the fifteen-thousand-square-foot Chase Mansion in View Park, a suburb of Los Angeles. He was impatient for a couple of reasons. First, his parents, Steven and Janet, were late. Church let out at eleven and it was twelve-thirty. They had promised to be home by noon at the latest. Second, he was always impatient to see his baby girl, Connor, especially considering he only had another eight hours with her before her mother would come pick her up from his house.

Connor Chase, the newest addition to America's wealthiest and most famous black family, was born six months ago and Carter's life was changed forever. Only a few months earlier, he'd been knocked in the face with the reality that her mother, Avery Jackson, the woman Carter loved and had wanted to marry, was married to another man, and pregnant.

He was only temporarily jealous of the other man, college professor Anthony Harper, because he had little right to be. Carter understood that he drove Avery away trying to control her and keep secrets from her. He was wrong and deserved to have his heart broken, which she did when she left L.A. to live in secrecy with relatives outside Miami. But he'd never stopped believing he would get her back. And as much as it hurt that she had been with another man, he wouldn't pass judgment on her. He'd been sleeping with any woman he could get his hands on in the six months after Avery left California, just to stop thinking about her for a few moments.

But the pregnancy was another thing. He was certain that Connor was his from the moment he saw Avery's belly, but Anthony had convinced Avery to lie and say the baby was his. He'd conspired with a local doctor who owed him a big favor to create medical records to support the lie. The idea that Avery, the woman he loved with all his heart, was having another man's baby had floored Carter.

Being a Chase, a member of America's black royal family, Carter had always gotten everything he wanted. He'd had a charmed life, always able to win any contest and influence or buy his way out of whatever he needed to. He was an heir to an empire, Ivy League educated and in charge of his own successful law firm; not to mention having that whole tall, dark, and handsome thing in his favor. He was six feet tall with chocolate brown skin and hazel eyes. His smile and style added to making him one of the most eligible bachelors on the market, with his pick of the best women. Which was why everyone was surprised when he hung it all up for a middle-class girl next door, Avery Jackson.

But they just didn't know. He hadn't expected to fall in love with her at all, but Avery quickly became everything in the world to him. She was perfect in every way that mattered. She grounded him, made him feel like a king regardless of his last name or his wealth. Carter felt a connection to Avery that he hadn't believed could exist between a man and a woman. But he'd made mistakes to get her away from her first fiancé, Alex, and even more mistakes to keep her. Unlike the other women he'd dated, Avery didn't care about the money, the glossy high-life or the power. She didn't care about all the things that came with being a Chase, so for the first time in his life a woman didn't put up with his crap, and she had left it all behind.

Like with any other obstacle, as soon as Avery returned Carter was determined to win her back, regardless of her marital and parental status. And he'd almost done it. He'd gotten her to the point where she admitted she wanted him—loved him—but there was one problem. Avery actually believed in fidelity and the sanctity of marriage. She wouldn't cheat on Anthony and she wouldn't leave him even after the truth of Connor's paternity came out.

But he was a Chase, so there was always a plan B. It would take a lot of patience, but he would get Avery back. And although he had been angry with her when she finally told him that Connor was his, moments after giving birth, it only made him more determined to get her back. Now it was about more than the woman he loved; he had a family.

So while it hurt to see Avery with her husband, Carter knew it was only a matter of time before he'd have her back. Meanwhile, he took every moment he could to spend with his daughter, whom he loved to no end.

That was, he took every moment that he could get Connor away from her doting grandmother, Janet Chase.

"They're coming." Maya, the caretaker of Chase Mansion, stood at the archway between the foyer and the great room.

She looked tired, although Carter never really saw her do anything but cook. She always hired contractors to do heavy work, but he knew his mother loved Maya, who had been taking care of the Chase clan for almost fifteen years.

"I can hear the car, Maya. Thanks."

"Are you sure I can't get you somethin'?" Although she'd been in the country for more than twenty years, Maya's Caribbean accent was still very strong. "You know how she likes to stall when she has the baby."

"Not this time," Carter said. "I have to get going. I'm meeting Julia for lunch."

"How nice."

Carter noted that Maya rolled her eyes like she did whenever the name of Julia Hall, Carter's current girlfriend, was mentioned. Maya had loved Avery because Avery was kind and warm to her, while Julia maintained a clear class distinction in the very few times she even acknowledged Maya was there.

Carter smiled at the sound of his baby's voice. Before the front door even opened, he could hear her laughter and cooing.

Janet Chase, a woman of the best breeding, class, and social mastery, had always placed her family first. She was the image maker of the Chase name, and tough as nails when it came to her family. She was also a sucker for a grandchild, and her only granddaughter simply brought her to her knees. She hated giving her up, but as soon as she walked into the house, she could see from the look on her oldest son's face, that she wasn't going to get away with her stall tactics today.

"Don't start," Janet said as she handed the baby bag to Maya. "We tried to leave, but they wouldn't let us. Ask your father."

"Who is they?" Carter asked, delighting at the squeal Connor gave as soon as she saw him and reached out for her daddy. She was so stinkin' cute.

"Everyone at church." Janet reluctantly handed Connor over. "I tell you, she looks more and more like Leigh every day. She looks ridiculously cute in her new dress."

Janet spent an obscene amount of money on dresses for Connor. There were two other Chase grandchildren, twins by second son, Michael, but Connor was a girl and that took Janet's indulgence to a whole other level.

"You're not letting people, strangers, hold her, Mom." Carter gave Connor a big, fat kiss on her lips.

"Of course not." Janet smoothed out her cobalt blue, Diane Von Furstenberg cashmere wrap dress. She was a very beautiful woman, who still turned heads in her fifties because she looked at least ten years younger than she was, and she had an air of unattainability about her that men loved.

She turned to Maya. "Can you please serve lunch in the Florida room in about an hour?"

Maya nodded, handing the baby bag to Carter before leaving.

"Hello, son." Steven Chase closed the front door behind him, greeting his son briefly before reaching down for his vibrating smartphone.

Carter would have replied if he thought his father was paying any attention, but he knew he wasn't. Steven Chase was head of a billion-dollar empire, Chase Beauty, and that empire came first. There was no ignoring him once he walked into a room. From even his youngest days, Steven had a presence that sucked up all the attention in the room. This included his own children, his sons especially.

Carter and his father had been at odds as long as Carter could remember, with brief periods of peace. Right now was a period of peace where they got along, but that still didn't guarantee he'd get any attention from his father.

"You're making me late for lunch with Julia," Carter said to his mother.

"Why didn't you tell me you were having lunch with her?" Janet asked. "I can keep Connor while you both . . ."

"No thanks," Carter said. "You'll see Connor again soon. We have to . . ."

"You know," Janet interrupted, "this wouldn't be an inconvenience if you actually came to church."

Carter gave his mother an annoyed glance. "You know that's not going to happen, Mom."

"You should open your eyes, son." Janet leaned forward to kiss Connor on her tiny, brown nose. "That God you've decided not to believe in gave you this blessing."

"Science and genetics gave me this blessing," Carter replied. In choosing to govern his beliefs by logic and rationality, he had made the decision while at Harvard as an undergrad to believe in evolution over creationism, and his mother had given him a hard time about it ever since. Avery gave him hell for it.

"Carter." Steven hung up his cell, getting his son's attention. His salt-and-pepper temples added a distinguished looked to his dark, masculine figure. "Come in the office. I need to talk business with you."

"I can't," Carter said.

Chase Beauty was the largest client of Chase Law, the small firm that Carter had decided to start instead of joining his father's company. This, in addition to his sense of entitlement and assumption of power and control over everything, made Steven expect Carter to jump at the snap of his finger.

"I have to meet Julia for . . ."

"Now," Steven said definitively. He was already walking down the hallway toward his office.

Janet joyously reached her arms out. "I'll hold her while . . ."

"Nice try," Carter said as he headed down the hallway with his baby in his arms.

"Close the door," Steven ordered without looking up from his desk.

"Dad, this has to be quick."

Steven looked up, ready to remind his stubborn son that a one-hundred-thousand-dollar-a-month retainer meant he could take as much time as he wanted, but thought better of it. They were getting along, as much as Steven and Carter could ever get along. These periods of relative peace between them never lasted long, so Steven let it go. "Did you read that Luxury Life report I sent you?"

"I read all the reports weeks . . ."

"No, this is a new one I had my marketing department put together. I sent it to your office Wednesday."

Carter shook his head. "I haven't gotten around to it."

"Dammit, Carter!" Steven leaned back in the detailed leather chair of his finely furnished home office, one of seventeen rooms in the house. "That's the only thing I asked you to do for me this week."

Carter pretended to bite Connor's tiny fingers as she put them over his mouth. She laughed as is if it was the funniest thing ever. "You know I have that big antitrust case right now, and two new clients."

Steven sighed. "As your father, I'm glad your firm is growing. As your client, I don't give a damn. Read the report by Monday."

That was a lie, Carter thought. He wasn't glad as a father either. Although he had interned in the Chase Beauty legal department during Harvard Law, Carter's decision to go out on his own instead of join the company, as expected, had always been a sore point between him and his father. A sore point was putting it lightly.

"I'll get to it tonight, after I drop Connor at Avery's . . ."

"Carter, I know you're happy you have a baby and all that, but you can't let it interfere with your work."

"Maybe I can do like you did, Dad." Carter's voice was laced with extreme sarcasm. "Just ignore my kid altogether. I'm sure she'll understand like we all did."

Steven sneered, wondering if Carter thought he was too old to get knocked upside the head. No, he hadn't been the best father, but he was building an empire and they had Janet. He still loved them all more than his own life.

"You've never appreciated the sacrifices I've made for this family," Steven said, "but you seem fine with benefiting from them. Read it. I need to make a decision now."

Carter wanted to ask why his father wanted to expand Chase Beauty, which had already added real estate and a chain of beauty salons to its hair-and-makeup product line, to include publishing, but he wouldn't. He didn't have the time for the answer.

"Look, Dad, I was supposed to meet Julia at Beso five minutes ago. I'll read it later."

"She can wait if you tell her to," Steven said. "She'll do whatever you want."

Carter frowned. "What the hell does that mean?"

"You know what it means," Steven answered. "Julia wants to be Mrs. Carter Chase. She'll put up with anything if she thinks it will get her closer to that goal. I'll call her if you don't have the balls."

"You know that's not going to happen." Carter's tone reflected his confusion. "Why would you even say that? You know that . . ."

"I know six months ago you said that Julia was just a temporary amusement until you could get Avery back. She was part of your plan to make Avery believe you were over her so she wouldn't be so cautious around you."

"She still is," Carter said. "But it's not as if I don't like her. You don't expect me to be celibate until I get Avery back?"

"Julia is in love with you. She's told your mother several times."

Carter believed Julia was more in love with the idea of being with a Chase than anything genuine. "I can't do anything about that. I'm going to marry Avery. That's it."

"Tell that to your mother," Steven said. "She's already picking out invitations."

"Mom doesn't need to know anything about this," Carter said with a warning tone. "Dad, you promised not to tell her."

"I haven't said anything," Steven said. "Now just read the report."

Carter got pissed off when his father acted as if he didn't understand the master plan, which was two-fold. Part one was to make Avery believe that he had truly gotten over her, had no intention of interfering with her marriage, and only wanted to deal with her in terms of being good parents to Connor. It was working. Carter even believed that Avery was a little jealous of his relationship with Julia at times. Because of their chemistry, Avery had previously refused to be alone with him. That was changing. Once her guard was down, she wouldn't be so reluctant to spend time alone with him. That was all it would take.

Part two was much more complicated. Carter had to create a situation in which Avery would be willing to leave Anthony and not hate herself for cheating on him. This had begun by completely emasculating Anthony at every opportunity possible without it seeming obvious to anyone but Anthony. When placed against Carter, very few men could measure up.

Steven smirked. "You remember, kid, it was my idea for you to crowd her husband out slowly, before I knew she lied to you about Connor not being yours. I'd prefer you be done with her. Julia is more suited to our circles anyway."

"You're starting to sound like Mom," Carter said. He placed Connor in the other arm. She was getting heavy.

Twenty-six-year-old Julia Hall came from a prominent Dallas family of doctors. She had made a departure and had gone into corporate finance, but this positioned her perfectly for a financial analyst position at Chase Beauty. Janet had intended for her to distract Michael from his wife, Kimberly, but Julia had wanted Carter from the start. She was a bona fide, black blue blood like his mother: those who had money, power and social standing dating back to the 1800s.

No one else belonged in these circles. New money, acquired in only a generation, didn't count. What was worse was money from entertainment or sports. They always wanted in, and people like his mother and Julia always wanted to keep them out.

"That wasn't your background," Carter reminded his father.

"This isn't about me." Steven was well aware that his middle-class background would never have gotten him where he was now if he hadn't married a woman like Janet. "This is about you wanting a woman that has rejected you countless times and . . ."

"You're exaggerating," Carter said. "Avery admitted that she wants me, but all that Bible blah, blah and . . ."

"Marital fidelity isn't Bible blah, blah, Carter. It means something to a lot of people."

"Well, nothing means anything to me except Avery and Connor. So, fuck her marriage and that teacher."

"You better watch it," Steven warned him. "If your animosity shows, it will force Avery to side with her husband.

"Don't worry about me." Supporting Connor had been the perfect excuse to make Anthony look inadequate. "I've taken every opportunity, and his growing frustration has only worked in my favor. I've undermined him without Avery catching on. She seems more and more annoyed with him every day. I've got her keeping secrets from him, thinking she's doing what's best for his pride. But it's only making him more jealous and possessive and when those secrets come out, he'll explode."

"Pitiful." Steven couldn't help but appreciate Carter's tenacity. He got what he wanted and that was what he had instilled in all his children from the beginning. The best education, training, and guidance had created four exceptional people. Well, at least three. Haley was something else entirely.

Carter felt no pity for Anthony. He was the one who convinced Avery to keep Connor away from him and guilted her into feeling obligated to him because he had been there for her when she ended her engagement to Carter. Avery was loyal and wanted to do what was right. Anthony was counting on that and Carter would crush him for it.

Steven chose not to press it any further. If there was one subject he couldn't change Carter's mind about, it was Avery. "Call me tonight after you've read it."

"It might be late," Carter said, grabbing the baby bag and turning to leave.

"I don't care," Steven answered. "And son . . ."

Carter turned back to his father, trying to move away from Connor's tiny hands that were blocking his eyes.

"Be careful with Julia. Women like her have one thing in mind: getting a ring on their finger. If she catches on that she's just a means to an end, you'll have trouble."

"She won't catch on." Carter really did like Julia. He just didn't love her. "I got it under control."

And Carter truly believed he did. In the last six months, he'd been as meticulous in his social life as he was in his professional life. Avery was just an inch away from him. He could taste her.

"Which one is it?" Thirty-year-old Michael Chase asked his seven-year-old son, Daniel, who was twisting and turning on his lap.

Daniel pointed to the computer, but didn't say anything. He was getting bored and Michael knew he should probably let up. It was good enough that, at seven, both Daniel and his twin brother, Evan, were acing educational software games aimed for eight-to-twelve-year-olds. But they were Chases, and doing better than expected was the least that was expected.

He'd had this conversation with his sons many times. Fate had them born into a family that lived under a microscope. The Chase family, in all their power, money, success and philanthropy, had become more than just a rich family. Their reign over the upper crust of black society, and powerful role in white society, made them unlike any other family of their kind, and the expectations would only rise with every generation. Carter was the Harvard lawyer. Michael was the Columbia finance whiz. Leigh was the Duke doctor and Haley . . . Haley was the spoiled socialite. Every rich family had to have one.

As the third generation of this dynasty, Evan and Daniel, now joined by Connor, would be expected to be at the top of their private schools, get into the Ivy Leagues, and project the appearance of perfection in career success, family, and commitment to the community. It was a lot of pressure, but it came with advantages too numerous to even mention; including a hefty trust fund.

"You're a Chase, Daniel. We don't give up. If you pick the right one, you'll get a card and can move to the next level."

Daniel sighed, lowering his head back to where it rested against his dad's chest.

"Jellyfish!" yelled Evan as he jumped around on the other side of Michael's desk.

"You can't even see it." Daniel sat up, seeming energized by the challenge of his brother.

"I already finished it." Evan jumped on the black leather settee nestled in the middle of Michael's home office, one of ten rooms in the six-thousand-square-foot, Tuscan-inspired house nestled in the ultra-lux Hollywood Hills.

"I told you about yelling the answers," Michael warned the son that was becoming more and more like him every day.

Daniel and Evan were fraternal, but looked almost identical. Both were a smooth, chocolate brown like their mother with dark, fierce eyes like their father. Daniel was reserved and thoughtful like his Uncle Carter. Evan was always on and eager, like Michael. Michael only hoped they would grow up best friends as he and Carter had. They certainly fought as much.

"They're all jellyfish, stupid." Daniel leaned forward. "It's a Bubbler Jellyfish."

Michael smiled. "You mean Blubber, right?"

"That's what I said."

"It isn't," Evan said without even looking up.

"Michael!"

They all looked up as twenty-nine-year-old Kimberly Chase stormed into the office. Despite wearing a T-shirt and jeans, no makeup, and her long hair in a loose ponytail, what always struck one first about Kimberly was that she was distractingly beautiful. Both men and women stared at her everywhere she went. The society papers gave her the title of "most attractive Chase."

"Mommy!" Evan jumped off the settee toward his mother. "I finished first. Daniel still takes forever."

"Did not!" Daniel yelled out in his defense.

"Go play," Kimberly ordered curtly. She was trying her best to hold her temper until the boys were out of the way.

Both boys looked at their father, which only made Kimberly angrier. Michael had always been the disciplinarian in the family, but in less than six months she had ceased to have enough authority over her own children to be listened to alone.

"We're learning," Michael said. "Play time will come later."

"Okay," Kimberly said, holding up a cell phone. "I just want to know who Shana is."

Michael reached for his pocket and felt that his cell was still there. He lifted Daniel off his lap. "Okay, you boys can go play."

Without hesitation, they ran out of the office. There was no glance toward their mother. Michael was all the authority they seemed to need anywhere. He was turning her own children against her and Kimberly wanted to kill him for it.

"Why is this bitch calling me?" Kimberly closed the door behind her.

"I don't know what you're . . ."

"Aren't you tired of that?" Kimberly asked.

"Tired of what?"

"Pretending like you don't know that I know you fuck anything that moves!" She tossed the phone at him.

Michael ducked to avoid the flying iPhone. When he looked back up, his dark eyes were intense. "I don't have to explain myself to you."

And he hadn't. Ever since Kimberly had done something that could destroy everything the Chase family had worked to create. That was six months ago. Since then, Michael never answered to Kimberly for anything, including his affairs.

"Besides," Michael said, "you don't fuck me, so why do you care who does?"

Kimberly was disgusted. "Don't flatter yourself, asshole. I don't care, but what I do care about is when one of those skanks calls me on my cell phone. How did this Shana bitch get my number?"

Michael wanted to know the answer to that too. "I'll handle it. Is there something else?"

Kimberly thought about the question. Yes, there was. He could give her a divorce and let her take her children as far away from him and his crazy family as possible. That's what she wanted, but Kimberly knew she wasn't going to get it. Michael wasn't going to give her a divorce unless she agreed to ask for nothing. And he would never let her take the kids. He told her she would never even see them again. She tried to leave with the boys six months ago, but he'd found her and gave her no choice but to come back to L.A. She couldn't be separated from her kids.

It used to break her heart that her husband had turned so cold to her. She used to worship Michael. He was her knight in shining armor. From an abusive, poor childhood to being a teenaged street hooker, meeting someone like Michael Chase just wasn't supposed to happen to someone like her. But then again, there was that beauty. She was modeling in New York when she had caught his attention the way she did every man that crossed her path. She was attracted immediately. He looked like a young Sidney Poitier, but it wasn't his good looks that got to her. It was his presence. There was a power about Michael that anyone would recognize. She'd had no idea who he was until after their one-night stand.

Her entire life, all the men Kimberly had known had treated her like a placemat. Michael was the first man who loved her and needed her. It didn't matter that she would never be accepted by his mother and they would have to lie to everyone about her past. Although she wasn't willing to get another abortion, she hadn't asked him to marry her when she found out she was pregnant. He asked her. And for almost seven years, he loved her and gave her the world.

Things began to change more than a year ago when Kimberly schemed to get rid of Janet Chase, the woman who made her life hell by reminding her every day she wasn't good enough for the Chase name. By dredging up a skeleton from Janet's past—an affair with another man after her engagement to Steven, which resulted in an abortion—she set off a chain of events that led to Janet's overdose on prescription pills and alcohol, while almost exposing the family for what it was: truly dysfunctional.

As with every other scandal, and there were too many Chase scandals to count, Steven and Janet's money and influence kept it a secret from the world. But Michael, who lived for his father's approval even more than his wife's love, hadn't been the same since. She had gone behind his back and almost destroyed his parents' marriage and his family's image.

But he still loved her and he did not leave her. He worked hard to forgive her, and even though the rest of the family had turned cold to her, Michael stayed. But his relationship with his father had taken a serious blow and Michael made it clear to Kimberly that she couldn't tip the boat again. He'd lose everything.

So when her old pimp, David Harris, came to California to blackmail her, Kimberly tried to handle it without telling Michael anything. But it wasn't money David wanted. He wanted revenge against Michael, who'd had him framed and put in a Mexican jail to keep Michael's parents, or anyone else, from finding out about his connection to Kimberly. David promised Kimberly he'd leave if she slept with him. She thought it was over when she complied, but it was only beginning.

Kimberly found out that David had taped their sexual encounter and was planning to post it on the Internet for the world to see. They struggled for the tape and David ended up dead. When she realized that someone else, hiding in the closet, had witnessed the accident and stolen the tape, Kimberly had no choice but to tell Michael, who had no choice but to tell his father and explain everything.

Kimberly's life had been miserable ever since. While he was eager to help her hide David's murder, when Michael found out she'd slept with David, he lost it. That, on top of the fact that his father now blamed him for almost destroying the entire family, was the end of their marriage. Michael made sport of humiliating her, isolating her from the rest of the world. He controlled every aspect of her life. She couldn't take a step outside the house or spend a penny without his knowing of it. He demeaned and degraded her when it suited him and still had the nerve to want sex.

Sex, she refused, but everything else she put up with. She didn't have much of a choice. Steven and Janet backed Michael's threat that she would never get the children. Kimberly wasn't just afraid for her own life. She was afraid of never seeing her boys, the only good things in her life.

"Yes," Kimberly finally answered. "I'm going out to eat with Avery."

"No you're not." Michael pressed the Exit button to release the CD-ROM.

"The boys want to see Connor."

He rolled his eyes. "Can you do anything but lie?"

"Can you be anything but a hypocrite? Your whole life is a lie."

Michael shot up from the desk and smiled when it caused Kimberly to jump. "I have you to blame for that."

It was Kimberly's turn to smile. "Which I take pleasure in every day."

Michael slowly came around the desk, enraged by the sight of her. Not because he hated her, but because he couldn't hate her enough to get rid of her. "The boys will see Connor at her birthday party next week."

"I'm going." Kimberly turned to leave, but Michael was at her side in a second, pulling her away from the door.

"I said no." Michael glared menacingly. "You walk out that door and you don't come back. Do you understand? You say good-bye to my sons and I'll let you leave with the clothes on your back. I'll even give you a few bucks."

After over six months of this, Kimberly had stopped falling to her knees in tears. She knew something, and that knowledge was giving her more and more confidence every day. "Is that so?"

"You heard me, bitch!"

"Yeah, I heard you now and when you said it last week and the week before. I still left, and you let me in when I came back. You even came looking for me when I didn't come back soon enough."

Michael let her jerk her arm free. "Don't push your luck."

"If I had any luck," Kimberly said, "you'd drop dead!"

When she opened the door to his office, Michael slammed it back. He leaned against her from behind, pressing her body against the door. He could hear her let out a gasp and it turned him on. Touching her always turned him on and he hated her for still having that power over him.

"Baby." He nestled his head into her neck, rubbing against her. "You have as long a leash as I want you to. You'll stay as long as I want you to and when I'm done with you, you'll leave; penniless and childless!"

Kimberly felt a shiver run down her spine. She wasn't a fool. There was no fighting the Chase machine. She'd seen what happened to anyone who thought they could. When David died, she'd seen how her DNA, which was all over David's hotel room, and her fingerprints, which had been in the system since she'd been arrested for prostitution at age fifteen, simply disappeared.

But showing fear only fed his sadistic torture of her, so Kimberly's elbow jutted back and hit him in the chest. "Unless you want me to throw up on you, you'll get off me!"

He leaned away, looking down at his watch. "Be back by five. I'm going out tonight."

Kimberly didn't care. He would go out tonight and sleep with some whore. At least he wouldn't bang on her bedroom door, demanding sex he wouldn't get, and wake the boys in the process.

Kimberly was shocked by what she saw when she opened the door. Her babies were standing there with a sullen look on their faces. They had heard them arguing . . . again. She took a step toward them, but they ran away in unison. Daniel would be silent for hours and Evan would cry. It was becoming the norm.

She had to come up with some way out of this. She had to get away from Michael and take her babies with her. It was the only way to save them.

Surveying another conquest, twenty-four-year-old Haley Chase looked down at the man she had just ridden to ecstasy, Garrett Collins. She had made him, a supposed cream-of-the-crop, cool stud, yell out her name . . . again. The best part was that he was mad she broke him down. That was Haley's pleasure; breaking a man down. But as he reached up to kiss her, she leaned back and rolled off of him. She wasn't a big fan of kissing. Besides, he was all sweaty.

She reached for her phone on the nightstand in the bedroom of his condo, in the rapidly regentrifying South Park, L.A. Flipping back her long, wavy, auburn hair, Haley knew his eyes were on her as she began texting her friends, making plans for tonight. As she lay back down, he stared at her glowing caramel-colored skin and firm, full breasts. His eyes veered down to her flat stomach and curving hips.

Haley was a temptress, and lived the part to the fullest. She had a smoldering sex appeal and the danger in her eyes was like a magnet. She was wicked to the core, and every man that chased her knew it. Still, they all wanted to be the one who softened her, tamed her. They all wanted to be the exception, but none of them ever would.

Then there were men like Garrett, who chased her for more than her body. He chased her for her last name.

"You could at least pretend to enjoy yourself," he said.

Taking just another second to finish her text, she turned to him and answered lightly, "I did."

It wasn't a lie. She'd had an orgasm. Only one, but he wasn't completely selfish. Garrett was handsome and very vain. He'd started balding his first year at Duke, so went the completely bald route and it suited him. He also wasn't as skilled as she'd hoped, but good enough for a twenty-six-year-old. Haley usually preferred older, richer men. She'd met Garrett on the UCLA campus, where he was attending law school and she attended graduate school. She had no idea who he was, but Garrett, like most black people from upper-class circles, knew exactly who she was.

"You sure don't act like it, girl." He sat up. "We'd make a great pair, Haley."

"What do you call what we just did?" She rolled over him to the other side of the bed and grabbed her panties. La Perla was too expensive to leave behind. "Please let's not turn this into another our-kind-of-people conversation."

"Your father likes me a lot."

Haley laughed as she got up in search of her other clothes. "First of all, trust me when I tell you that is not sweetening the pot. I hate my dad and him liking someone would be a big turnoff. Second, my dad doesn't like you because he doesn't like anyone but my mother."

"He will like me." Garrett placed his hands behind his head, leaning back as if he'd accomplished something.

"Well, I hope you two have a wonderful life together. For me, once I graduate from that damn school in May, I'm out of here."

"Why do you hate school so much?" He opened the nightstand and pulled out a case of cigarettes.

"Not while I'm here," Haley warned. "I hate the smell of those things. And I hate school because my father is dangling my trust fund over my head to force me to go. Not to mention I have to run into assorted Jacksons every day."

"Jacksons?"

Haley had hoped that her family was done with the Jacksons when Avery dumped Carter and ran off. But when Avery came back to tend to her father, who had been shot in the line of duty, a big fat belly got in the way. Now the Jacksons were relatives. This was compounded by Haley's regular run-ins with Taylor, Avery's social-climbing sister, who had transferred from Spelman to UCLA undergrad. To make matters worse, detective Sean Jackson, Avery's brother and Haley's ex-lover, the only man that had ever dumped her, decided he wanted to get his bachelor's degree at UCLA too.

"I've told you about them," she said in disgust. "The world is just against me."

"Where are you going to go?"

Haley grabbed her Gucci silver leather handle bag. "I have some unfinished business in Australia."

She'd spent the previous summer living the high life in Sydney, occasionally joined by her older sister, Leigh. It was a busy three months, but worth it. At least it would be in good time.

"Hey!" He crawled to the edge of the bed just as she headed out of the room. "Can I come to the kid's birthday party?"

"Are you kidding me?" Haley asked in disbelief. "It's a fuckin' party for a six-month-old. Who has a birthday party for a six-month-old?"

"I don't care about the baby," Garrett said. "I need face time with your brother."

Oh yeah, Garrett was also after a job at Carter's law firm. He hated where he worked and wanted out. "You already work at one of the top firms in L.A. What do you want his rinky-dink outfit for?"

"Chase Law is like the hottest and fastest-growing firm on the West Coast. And I want to work for a top outfit owned by a brother."

Haley leaned against the doorway. "I'll make you a deal. You find out everything you can for me about trust funds and you can come."

"Why do you want to . . ." He nodded. "You want to get control away from your parents."

"Right now, I get piecemeal. The trust says I have to wait until I'm thirty to get total control. I want to know if I can get it now. Because if I can't, I gotta make other plans. Do we have a deal?"

2

"This is completely ridiculous," thirty-six-year-old Anthony Harper said as he stood next to his wife outside the front door to Chase Mansion.

Twenty-nine-year-old Avery Harper looked at her husband, standing six feet tall and looking the role of college professor in his buttoned-up shirt and khaki pants. "Don't start, Anthony."

"You know I'm right."

He was, in a sense. Avery knew that to anyone who wasn't a part of the Chase social circles, all these get-togethers seemed excessive. But this was how it was with the ultra rich. They loved all the things their money could buy, but the one thing they loved the most was getting together to talk about all the things their money could buy. And the best part was that everyone else knew what they were doing and knew they weren't invited.

Avery shouldn't have been invited, but fate was funny that way. When Chase Beauty decided to go into the hair salon business almost two years ago, her two stores, Essentials and Essentials II in View Park and neighboring Baldwin Hills, were in Steven's sights. Despite her constant refusals to sell, Steven made certain that his oldest son, Carter, wouldn't give up. Everyone knew who the Chases were and what they were capable of, but Avery had no idea of what was coming.

She was almost killed. Carter's insistence that she sell struck a nerve with Craig, her dangerously-in-debt partner at the time who desperately wanted to sell, and all hell broke loose. Meanwhile, Carter pursued her and at the same time her fiancé cheated on her. It wasn't until she was head-over-heels in love and engaged to marry Carter that she'd found out that he had set up her last fiancé, Alex. It was all a game to win her over, and the lies and cover-ups to keep her from finding out gave her no choice but to leave him. He had completely broken her heart.

Leaving Carter was hard enough, but he was determined to get her back because Chases just don't lose. And when she found out she was pregnant, Avery got as far away as possible. But there was no escaping this family, and eventually she came back. Despite the fact that she had met and married another man and lied to Carter by saying Anthony was the father, Carter continued to pursue her. Despite a few slips, Avery had kept her vows and told the truth.

Now that Connor was here, she was tied to this family forever. Six months ago, Avery made it clear to Carter that Anthony was her husband and she loved him. He hadn't been happy, but to her surprise, he ended his pursuit. Or so she believed. There was no way to completely trust Carter. He was a Chase, after all.

And so was Connor.

Avery turned to her husband and reached out to touch his arm. "Please, Anthony. Can you just be civil for me, for a few hours?"

"It's always on me, isn't it?" Anthony asked.

"You're the one starting an argument all the time."

Anthony just shook his head, pulling his arm away. Avery knew what he was thinking. He wanted to point the finger at Carter, but the truth was, Carter had been great these past six months. He had stopped pursuing a romantic relationship with her and only wanted to be a good co-parent to Connor. Anthony's jealousy, something any man would naturally have of a man like Carter, made him see things that weren't there.

And then there were the things that were there. The things

Avery tried to hide from her husband and tried to deny she felt whenever she saw Carter. She had hoped that time would dim the fire she felt whenever he was within a mile of her, but it hadn't. Avery was certain Anthony sensed her feelings and that fueled his anger. But that wasn't Carter's fault. Avery knew it was her responsibility to manage her emotions and respect her vows.

"This family can be overwhelming at times," she said as she pressed the doorbell to the left of the wide, double doors. "But you and I both know that it could be worse."

When the doors opened, Maya stood before them with a wide smile on her face. "Avery!"

Avery reached out and hugged her. "How are you, Maya?"

"I'm as good as anyone can be, living in this house. Come on in."

As Maya stepped aside, Avery was stopped in her tracks by the first thing she saw. Carter was standing in the elaborate, marble foyer with Connor in his arms. Julia Hall, Carter's beautiful girlfriend, had one hand on Carter's back, rubbing it lovingly. Her other hand was holding onto Connor's as the baby, Avery's baby, smiled into her face.

Avery quickly composed herself, but couldn't shake off the effect of this happy little family scene. She had spent nights praying to God to help her get over her feelings for Carter and stop being jealous of his growing closeness with Julia. But something about seeing them both with Connor, as if this was Julia's family, filled her with resentment.

Then he turned to her and their eyes caught, locking onto each other. Could he tell she was jealous? Could he tell how attracted she was to him? He could read her so well, and his ego never failed to let her know. In the few moments she had allowed herself to be alone with him, Avery was always afraid he could sense it and would pounce. But he hadn't; pounced, that is. She should be happy.

Carter could see it. He hadn't planned on Avery stepping upon this little scene, but now that she had, he knew it only worked in his favor. And from the way she uneasily ripped her eyes from his and looked to the ground, he knew it had. When she looked up again, she had pasted a smile on her face and was walking toward them as if this was nothing.

Too late. Julia had served many purposes in Carter's life. She got his mother off his back, gave Avery a reason to let her guard down, and made Avery jealous. Although he hadn't been faithful to Julia since they started "officially" dating, he considered her his girlfriend. For now.

"Hello, Avery."

Julia, always perfect. She was mocha brown and as tall as a mile with long, shiny, wavy hair and a soft, full face with very little makeup. Her features were perfectly sculpted. She was Carter's type: beautiful but not flashy, sexy but not explicitly so. And as her saccharine smile lasted a few seconds too long to mean anything kind, Avery was reminded that Julia was a bitch.

Avery nodded her hello as she reached out for her baby. "How is my little love?"

"She was acting up a little bit," Carter said as he handed Connor to her. In the exchange, their fingers touched. He looked at her and could see the discomfort in her eyes, knowing that she felt the electricity he did every time they touched. He wasn't sure how much longer he could wait. "I think she was just missing her mama."

Avery focused all her attention on Connor as Anthony approached. "Let's go outside, Anthony."

Anthony paused for a second to give Carter an evil glare that made everyone uncomfortable. That was, everyone except Carter. He loved it. He politely said hello to Anthony, knowing the fool wouldn't say hello back. And the scene was set for the day. Carter was trying to be nice and Anthony was being the asshole. This guy was way too easy.

As they walked away, Carter's smooth lips curved into a smile. Anthony would be rigid and uncomfortable all afternoon. Everyone would be polite, but they wouldn't pay any particular attention to him. He would feel somewhat invisible and an overwhelming sense of being in the way. Since he was outnumbered at the party, he would wait until he was alone with Avery to vent his anger. She would get pissed and tired of him. Yet again.

"Carter?" Julia called, sounding farther away than she was.

When Carter turned to her his smile faded. Julia wasn't a fool. She had told him several times that she felt disconnected from him whenever Avery was around. He would tell her it was nonsense and buy her something expensive. Still, she caught the side glances and tension-filled stares between him and Avery. He imagined everyone did.

The look on her face and the question in her voice begged for him to remember she was there; to show her some attention and ease her insecurities. He leaned forward and kissed her on the lips. She wanted to kiss longer, but he pulled away. He was always the one to pull away. He wanted her often, but not when Avery was around. When Avery was around, Avery was all he could think of.

"Let's go outside." He took her hand and led her toward the family that she so hoped to be a part of that she was willing to ignore the fact that he didn't love her.

The Chase family held formal events in the immense great room of the house. Pictures of such events appeared regularly in society magazines all the way to the East Coast. However, when it was a family event, or just family and very close friends, they entertained out back by the pool.

The Chase backyard looked like a paradise. The Rainbow Stone deck was welcoming, with fluffy lawn chairs, tables, and a piercing blue vanishing-edge pool made of tumbled marble that looked magical at night with the shimmering lights along the edges. There was also a basketball court equipped with two official NBA basketball backboard rims, and baskets and a large garden Janet tended to that grew carnations, roses, daisies and orchids. Behind the garden was a two-thousand-square-foot guest house that Janet, drawing on her former life as an interior decorator, was changing from a Caribbean theme to an English cottage theme.

The fifteen-foot outdoor kitchen with a roof was made from red stone and equipped with everything from a refrigerator to a gas grill, rotisserie, wok, and barbeque pit/smoker. The area between the kitchen and the rolling, makeshift bar was where most of the family gathered.

The backyard was Avery's favorite part of the house. She felt less penned in there, and with the twins able to run around, the atmosphere was just lighter. That is, for everyone except for Anthony, who stood somberly at the bar making himself a drink.

"How many is that?" Avery asked as she reached him.

Anthony smiled. "I have a drinking problem now?"

"No, but I don't want you to develop one. Especially over nothing." She glanced back at Connor, who was being held by her Aunt Leigh, Carter's younger sister.

"What's nothing?" he asked sarcastically, putting the drink down as his wife wanted. "Being stuck with this self-important family of elitists for a few hours? It may be nothing to you, but not me."

Avery sighed. "Baby, I need you to be . . ."

"A good little boy?" he asked. "I've had the speech a thousand times, Avery. If this family was going to punish us for trying to keep Connor away from Carter, they would have done it by now."

"Don't be so sure," Avery said. "They're patient."

This was Avery's fear, even more so than her fear of giving in to her feelings for Carter. While living in Florida, hiding away from him, Avery married Anthony because he kept her from feeling alone and she didn't want to be unmarried when she had her baby. He was the opposite of Carter. He wasn't overwhelming. She could control herself when it came to Anthony. Most of all, she could trust him.

But Anthony's lie made Avery fear that Carter could use it against her if he ever decided to take Connor away. Every time she was around the Chases, she got the sense that they believed Connor belonged more to them than her. If Carter wanted to take her baby away, with all his family's money and power, Avery knew that she couldn't fight him.

Avery was the one who had exposed the lie. Once Connor was born, the love that she'd felt wouldn't allow her to continue such a lie. To rob Carter of this love was more wrong than anything he had done to her. So Avery told him the truth. Not everyone was as forgiving as he had been. He was blinded by his love for Connor, but Steven and Janet were very angry that she had attempted to keep "their" grandchild from them. This was the problem with the Chases. Everything belonged to them and anyone who might suggest otherwise would regret it eventually.

Janet had warmed to her again, but Steven barely spoke to her. He had never liked her since the poison of the way she was introduced to this family set her place in stone with him. They butted heads constantly and the effort to keep Carter from Connor was the last straw for him. This was why Avery needed Anthony to be . . . a good boy . . . whenever they were around.

"If he doesn't mess with me," Anthony said, "there won't be a problem."

She smiled, rubbing his arm in hopes of comforting him. Avery knew this wasn't easy on him and she loved him for trying, but he made it harder on himself, and everyone else for that matter, than it had to be.

"Hey, Avery!"

Avery grinned at the cute little face looking up at her. It was Evan, Carter's nephew, and she missed seeing him and Daniel regularly.

"Hey, honey." She ran her hand over his head. Both boys were getting big, but they still had a little baby in their faces; in those fat cheeks. "Where is your brother?"

Evan shrugged as he looked over at Anthony. "Hey, Mr. Uhm . . ."

"Harper," Anthony offered. "I told you you can call me Anthony, Evan."

"Daddy says no." Evan was shaking his head vigorously. "I should call you Mr. Harper."

"But you call me Avery," Avery said.

He looked at her, smiling wide. "But you're family. He's not."

"Great." Anthony turned and reached for the drink.

Avery knelt down to come face-to-face with Evan. "Did your daddy say that?"

Evan nodded, then his smile quickly faded and was replaced by an angry frown. "He makes me so mad."

"Why?" Avery had an idea why, but wanted to ask.

Evan leaned in to whisper. "He's so mean to Mommy. He yells at her and stuff and he never lets her come with us anywhere. She stays home and cries all day I think."

Avery sighed, trying to control her emotions for Evan's sake. "I'm sorry, dear. I'm sure things will get better. I'll go visit your mommy tomorrow, okay?"

"He doesn't let anybody come over to see her. Especially you. He don't even let her talk on the phone. He yells at her if he catches her."

Avery stood up straight. This was insane. Over the last six months, Kimberly had continued to tell her that things were getting better while still refusing to reveal what had made them worse. Kimberly had gained back some of the weight she'd lost over stress, but she was very depressed and withdrawn and no one stood up for her.

Sending Evan to go play, Avery searched for Michael. When she saw him, she started right for him. He was standing near the kitchen, leaning against a pole, chatting very nonchalantly with Carter. The two of them had a bond that Avery had tried, but couldn't, get her hands around. They shared everything, including all the bad stuff; the stuff neither of them ever chose to tell the women in their lives. They fought like hell, but stood up for each other without question. But Avery wasn't going to let that scare her.

Even though they were in the middle of a discussion, Avery didn't excuse herself. She lit right into Michael. "You clearly don't care what you're doing to Kimberly, but do you know what you're doing to your children by the way you treat her?"

Michael stood up straight, angrily. "What is your problem?"

Carter turned to Avery. "Avery, don't."

"Don't what?" she asked. "Stand up for Kimberly? No one else does. You get off on it, don't you, Michael?"

"Mind your own business, you little . . ."

"Hey," Carter warned sternly.

Michael looked at his brother and laughed. He knew Carter was still in love with Avery. He had seen through this whole farce with Julia a long time ago. He knew his brother better than anyone, and whatever hold this bitch had on him was still strangling him. She was the only woman that Carter ever sided with over Michael. That was part of the reason Michael couldn't stand her. Her nosy ass was another.

"Don't you have a husband to look after?" Michael asked. "Stay out of my marriage."

"Your son was near tears a second ago because of how you

make his mommy cry." Avery noticed that Michael swallowed hard for a second. This was getting to him. So why didn't he stop? "You may hate Kimberly for whatever reason I can't see, but they love her. She's their mother and everything you do to her, you're doing to them."

Michael took a step closer to Avery, hating her for telling the truth but respecting her for not taking a step back. "My family is none of your damn business. Carter, tell your baby's mama to get away from me."

"She's right," Carter said. He was a little shaken by the look of hurt on Michael's face as he turned to his big brother.

"You siding with her now?" Michael asked.

Avery was a little taken aback herself. Usually when she had a problem with Michael, Carter told her to stay out of it, refused to pick sides, or sided with Michael. Was he actually agreeing with her?

"I'm not siding with anyone," Carter said. "But Daniel has mentioned some things to me in the past couple of months."

"And you didn't tell me?" Michael's expression was taut and resentful.

"You blow up every time I mention anything about Kimberly. I'm sick of it and I don't have the time or patience for your blood-thirsty revenge against her."

"Revenge for what?" Avery asked. Although Kimberly would tell her nothing, Avery knew Michael had told Carter what had changed. But Carter would never betray Michael's secrets.

Carter turned to Avery, showing his discomfort. He couldn't tell her about the pimp, the murder, the witness, and the tape. That was a secret that had only been between him and Michael for the longest time and now included their parents. No one else could know. The price to the family was too high.

"Yeah, Carter." Michael folded his arms across this chest, daring his brother to betray him; to betray their whole family. He knew he wouldn't do it. "Tell her our secrets. Tell the woman who tried to hide your own baby from you."

"That has nothing to do with this," Avery said.

"You're both a bunch of hypocrites," Michael said with a laugh.

"You want to tell me about my marriage? Like you two wouldn't hit it if given the chance."

"Michael!" Carter warned.

"Everyone sees it." Michael shot them both a twisted smile. "So keep the self-righteous speeches to yourself."

After one last menacing glare at Avery, Michael shoved past Carter in search of a hard drink. This was none of that holier-than-thou bitch's business. He was in control of his marriage and he could take care of his boys. He'd thought he was in control of Kimberly's access to Avery, but he would have to work harder on that. That, and making sure Kimberly kept her mouth shut.

"Thanks." Avery felt guilty for the look on Carter's face now. He was in his worst moods when he and Michael were fighting.

"For what?"

"Backing me up," she answered. "I know its hard for you to go against . . ."

"You have to let it go," Carter said. "It really isn't any of your business."

"Kimberly is my friend and I love those boys. I thought you did too." As she saw Carter's frown deepen, Avery realized what she'd said and felt awful. "I didn't mean to . . . I know you love the twins."

Carter looked back at his little brother, who was becoming someone he no longer recognized. Michael hadn't been a perfect husband, but he loved Kimberly to death. She'd screwed up, more than once, but what Michael was doing now wasn't right.

"He's miserable," Carter said. "He's completely shut me out. I don't know how to make him listen."

"I'm sorry." Avery resisted the urge to reach out and touch him, to comfort him. He was a ridiculously handsome man, but was even more beautiful when he was sad. He very rarely showed any emotions. It touched her deeply when he did.

The soft tone of her voice made Carter turn back to Avery. Looking into her large, doe-like eyes, he saw the compassion that he had become so familiar with; had come to rely on to greet him when he came home at the end of the day or when he was stressed and angry over anything. Those eyes were so honest and empathetic. They reached inside of him and stripped him of any pretense; any need to protect himself. He got lost in those eyes.

"Avery." Her name came just above a whisper from his lips as he felt something just as familiar: the pull in his groin whenever she was near. He always wanted her.

She was in trouble, Avery knew it. The voice in her head was yelling, begging for her to turn and walk away. Even her heart was trying to whisper her away. But her body wanted her to take a step closer and touch him as the world simply disappeared around them.

Then she heard it. Her name was being called by . . . by her husband. She turned to look for him, but he was right there. He'd been standing right next to her, for how long she had no idea because she was so caught up with Carter.

Carter hid the resentment he felt at the interruption of this annoying man. He looked forward to the day when Anthony Harper would be out of their lives for good, but was actually happy he'd come just now. Another second and Carter was likely to have slipped up.

"Hey, Anthony." Carter reached out and patted Anthony's shoulder once before Anthony jerked away. Pleased that Avery noticed the gesture, Carter shrugged his shoulders at her and smiled before making a quick retreat. Let the arguing commence.

There he was.

When Haley finally found the disappearing boyfriend, he was in the kitchen talking on his cell phone. No, Garrett hadn't been around long and she probably wasn't going to keep him around much longer, but as long as he was with her, he had to learn the rules. Never, ever leave Haley hanging. He'd been missing for almost a half hour.

Haley was debating his punishment as she quietly snuck up to him, but just as she reached him, he quickly swung around to face her and the look on his face told her something was very wrong. His expression was tight with strain and . . . it looked like fear.

"Who are you talking to?" she asked, quickly placing her hands on her hips and assuming the pre-tantrum position. Haley gasped out loud as Garrett lifted his finger to gesture for her to wait. This boy must be crazy.

Without hesitation, she grabbed the phone from his hands. "No, I don't wait for anyone."

"Haley." Garrett reached for the phone and almost tore Haley's hand off getting it back. He put the phone to his ear and frantically said, "Hello? Hello? Mr. Bilton? Are you still there?"

He sighed, seeming satisfied with the response. Haley was ready to explode, but the nosy girl in her was more interested in what had Garrett looking ready to explode.

"Yes sir," he said, clearly flustered. "But I . . . I don't think it will come to that. Yes, I know I messed up, but Justin . . . Isn't that a bit drastic Mr. . . ."

He turned his back to Haley, but she wasn't having it. She stepped around to remain face-to-face with him, further intrigued by the pained expression on his face. She didn't need to rip him a new one because someone on the phone had just said something that made him look like he wanted to pee his pants.

"You can't mean that," he said flatly, as if he'd already known the answer to his own question. "Yes, sir."

He blinked, looking at the phone as if it would explain that entire conversation to him.

"Poor baby," Haley said with fake sympathy. "Your brown-nosing skills are pretty pitiful. You sounded like you were about to cry. I can't believe he didn't fire you. You were talking to your boss, right?"

Garrett appeared miles away as he attempted to place the phone in the side pocket of his pants, but missed and the phone fell to the granite floor. Haley was curious as to why he didn't even seem to care.

"Not exactly." Garrett ran his hand over his head, shaking it as if not believing something in his own mind. "Uhm . . . I have to go."

"What?" Haley asked. "You beg me to come to this thing, show up, disappear, and now you're telling me you have to leave? You must not plan on coming back here."

He reached down and grabbed the various pieces of his cell phone that had fallen apart. "Give me a break, Haley."

"I don't do that."

"I have to go." He shrugged. "It's out of my hands."

He was actually leaving, and Haley decided it wasn't necessary to see him again. "It seems like a lot of things are out of your hands, Garrett. Not impressive."

She was annoyed by the fact that he wasn't even listening on his way out of the kitchen, but as her mother entered, Haley didn't want to show it. She hated showing anything.

"What was that about?" Janet asked. "And why are you in here?"

"Don't I live here?" Haley opened the double doors of the stainless-steel refrigerator, peeking in for something; anything with chocolate.

"Is he leaving?" Janet waited a second, but realized that Haley wasn't going to answer her. "Well, he wasn't invited anyway."

Haley slammed the refrigerator door. "Is there something you want?"

"No," Janet said shortly. "There's something you want, re-member? You wanted me to tell you when your father was in a good mood so you can ask him about that condo in Sydney again."

Haley sighed. "Why can't you just make him buy it?"

While spending the summer in Sydney, Haley had gotten into her fair share of trouble, but had also found a reason to spend more time there in the future. She would have stayed had it not been for her father dangling her degree as a condition for getting access to her trust fund.

While there, she had stayed in the presidential suite at the Four Seasons on Sydney Harbor, but made friends with someone who lived in an exclusive condo building in downtown Melbourne. The second she entered the building, Haley knew she wanted to buy a condo there, considering that she would proba-bly need a place to stay in Australia for the future.

The problem was that it cost three million dollars, and she wouldn't have access to that much of her trust fund until she was thirty. She was barely getting by on the two hundred thousand she was allowed now. There was at least fifteen million dollars in there.

"I hate him," Haley said. "He's not going to do it, just to spite me."

"Your father has no need to spite you," Janet said. "And your attitude is not going to help. Why do you want this place so bad?"

"Why do I have to tell you everything?"

"Usually asking for three million dollars comes with more than *It's a great place and I have to have it.*"

"That's all there is to it," Haley answered, even though it was a lie. "Just tell him to buy it already. I'm sick of talking to him."

As her youngest daughter stormed out of the room, Janet knew something was going on. She could always tell when her children were up to something. Well, at least most of the time. She'd been caught off guard a bit too much lately, but she couldn't worry about that now. She had a little birthday princess to get back to.

When twenty-six-year-old detective Sean Jackson entered the living room of his parents' modest View Park home, he was looking for his father to help him fix his motorcycle, which had broken down again. What he found was his twenty-year-old sister, Taylor, lounging on one end of the sofa with her newest best friend, Claire, lounging on the other end. They were chatting while absorbed in their respective laptops.

Taylor was a pretty girl who had been a model while attending Spelman. Her skin was as smooth and glowing as chocolate milk, and she had an innocent beauty that was appealing, but not intimidating.

Claire was pretty, blond and not too smart. So why, of all the students in any of Taylor's classes at UCLA, did she pick Claire to hang with constantly? Claire's last name was Huffington. She was the daughter of the owner of Huffington's, the luxury men's shoe store chain. Taylor chose her friends carefully. Despite her decidedly middle-class upbringing, the daughter of an artist and a cop, Taylor only chose to socialize with the spawn of the rich. She had hoped a marriage between Carter and their sister, Avery, could get her in the circle. One couldn't get any better than being related to the Chase family. But that never happened.

It wasn't as if their parents were nobodies. Their father, Charlie, was the former chief of police of View Park, now retired after suffering an almost fatal gunshot less than a year ago. He was a local hero and many expected him to run for local office soon. Their mother, once a stay-at-home bohemian artist, was now the owner of HUE, a hot art gallery in View Park.

"What a whore!" Taylor laughed as she scrolled down her screen.

"I know," Claire added with a sneer. "She probably slept with both of them. I . . ."

Claire stopped talking and looked up when Taylor cleared her throat. Taylor nodded toward her brother, who was approaching them. Sean was dressed in a T-shirt and jeans, making him look even younger than he already did. He looked eighteen at best today, the poster boy for Boy Scouts. You could tell from a mile away, he was one of the good guys that the girls ignored when they were young, but wished they hadn't later.

Sean noticed the gesture. "What? Attempting to protect my delicate ears from sex talk?"

"What are you doing here?" Taylor asked.

"Nice to see you too, sis." Sean reached to push against her shoulder, but noticed that Taylor quickly turned her laptop so he couldn't see the screen. "What? What is it?"

"Nothing," she answered. She didn't want to get into it with Sean over Haley Chase. Even two years after their short, but extremely destructive relationship, Haley was still a sore subject with him.

"I'm a police detective," Sean said. "I'll find out."

"It's Haley," Claire offered with her chin lifted high.

Sean thought it was possible that girls like Claire had a hard time seeing a black girl elevated above them, no matter how wealthy her father was. Taylor might be a different case. Even if Claire and her set of friends let her "in" she still would be with them. They would never be with her. Haley was an altogether different story and Sean sensed that Claire was jealous. But Claire couldn't be too much of a snob if she was willing to hang out at their parents' very humble abode.

"What about her?" Sean asked.

Despite what his family thought, Sean was no longer upset at the mention of Haley's name. Two years ago, he'd fallen in love with her. He'd been protecting her from a drug dealer before she could testify to a murder she'd seen him commit while she was carrying on a secret affair with a married congressman. But he'd had to break it off with Haley. He could never make her happy enough on a detective's salary, and his pride was too strong to let her father take care of them both.

He'd regretted making the choice . . . for a while. Haley quickly turned on him and tried to ruin his life. He'd almost gotten fired from the police force because of her antics. Fortunately, her father sent her off to Europe to get her out of his hair. Even then he'd missed her. Until she came back and resumed her hell-raising tactics. This time she'd gotten Taylor involved and almost hurt him beyond repair.

Yes, he was over her now—mostly. After all, she was Haley Chase. "You don't have to hide it from me. I know how crazy she is. More than either of you."

Claire lifted up her laptop. "See for yourself. She started a fight at Club Villa."

"Haley got into a fight?" Sean asked. "She likes to decimate people with her words."

"She didn't get into a fight," Taylor answered, returning to her own screen. "She started one between two guys."

The headline on the black-celebrity gossip blog read PRINCESS CHASE SHUTS DOWN VILLA. Club Villa was the hardest-to-get-into nightclub of the moment, frequented by celebrities. Just another place where people stood in line for hours on end, weren't allowed in, but still came back the next night.

"I wouldn't really blame this on her," Sean said after reading the blog. "One guy was trying to talk to her and when he went to get a drink, another guy . . ."

"Still trying to defend her." Taylor shook her head. From the moment she'd met Haley, the bitch had treated her like dirt; the same way she treated everyone else.

"I'm not defending her." Sean handed the laptop back to Claire. He was a little concerned at how quickly he wanted to lay the blame elsewhere. He had seen a glimpse of a good Haley. It was only for a short while, but it had stayed with him.

"Well, have fun reading the gossip blogs," Sean said. "A good way to make up for lost time."

After getting herself into a little bit of trouble with a nightclub owner who had been sleeping with Haley, Taylor had made the decision to stay home. When modeling was her dream, Chris Reman, the manager at Pearl nightclub in L.A., promised her some local modeling jobs. He ended up trying to pimp her out. It was a nightmare, and even though she hadn't been harmed, Taylor wasn't interested in being too far from her mother. So instead of going back for her junior year at Spelman, she transferred to UCLA. In the process, she'd lost her scholarships.

"Nothing Haley Chase does even matters." Taylor clicked out of the site. "I need to be looking for scholarships anyway. If I get one, can I pocket it? I mean can I use it for everyday money?"

"I don't know," Claire said. "I've never needed one."

Taylor rolled her eyes. "Well, unlike you, I need the money. Bad."

"You don't really," Sean said. He knew that their parents had provided Taylor with enough spending money to get all she needed. Her definition of need had to be in order to keep up with the Claires of the world.

Taylor looked up at him. "And what did you say you wanted?"

Sean got the hint. "Fine, I'm out, but be careful with the money. If you get some extra ducats, you need to save them for your senior-year tuition."

Taylor didn't want to hear what she should be doing with it. She needed cash to buy new clothes. Things were too tight now that her father was retired.

"I know what you can do!" Claire started typing furiously on her laptop.

Taylor sat up straight, hoping that Claire's solution didn't involve some type of trust fund she would have to remind her again that she didn't have.

"Be an alibi!" Claire scooted close to Taylor on the sofa and showed her the web site she had found.

Taylor read it out loud. "Make money being an alibi. Whether it's a job reference, suspicious boyfriend, or a school confirming an unexcused absence, students will pay you to back them up."

She frowned suspiciously. "Is that legal?"

Claire shrugged her shoulder. "It has a web site, so doesn't that mean it's legal?"

Taylor couldn't believe she was serious. "No, and it's not a web site. It's a blog."

"I heard it pays pretty well."

"But is it legal?" Taylor was willing to do a lot of things, but not break the law. She was a cop's daughter and a cop's sister. She couldn't break the law.

Could she?

3

As Carter made his way to the roped-off VIP section of Sky Bar, the hot, outdoor nightclub in L.A., he heard a woman call his name. It was very vain of him, but he didn't always turn around. Women were always calling his name. They all knew who he was and came on to him constantly. Gold diggers came in every shape, size, and color, and he was an expert at spotting them.

But Carter chose to turn around this time, out of curiosity, because the voice sounded void of excited flirtation. From the tone of her voice, laced with demand, he expected to see someone he knew. He didn't expect who he saw: his sister Leigh.

"Dammit." Carter could foresee a big problem.

Twenty-eight-year-old Dr. Leigh Chase hardly went out to the clubs. She hardly went anywhere now that Hope Clinic, her free clinic for HIV/AIDS patients, had recently opened another branch in Compton. She traveled between this clinic and the original one in East L.A. constantly.

Despite graduating in the top five percent at Stanford, with a Human Biology degree, and the top ten percent at Duke Medical School, Leigh decided to forgo all the prestigious medical programs and private practices waiting in line to have her. She chose instead to travel to Africa and administer care to women and children stricken with HIV/AIDS. When she returned to L.A., much to the disappointment of her parents, Leigh poured a significant amount of her trust fund, with the help of donations, starting Hope.

The clinic was her life, and although there was a lot of tragedy connected to its beginning, it was her solace from the misfortune of being a poor little rich girl. She could forget everything when she was there, so she was always there, and couldn't wait to get back whenever she wasn't.

She was the embodiment of the image that their parents wanted to project for the Chase name. Leigh was sweet, smart, and pretty. She could be a little too soft in dealing with people, but was stronger than most expected. She was naturally feminine and men loved that about her. She was beautiful in a non-threatening way; more cute than hot. She wore no makeup and kept her soft, dark brown hair in a clip. When she dressed up, as she usually did for a Chase Foundation event, Leigh could look amazing. She looked like what their mother called, "a well bred woman."

Even when she wasn't working or attending a charity event held by the Chase Foundation, she didn't go out. She'd been unlucky in love and had pretty much written off a social life. She spent her time on more highbrow entertainment—operas and plays.

"What are you doing here?" Carter asked as soon as she reached him.

"Hi," Leigh responded. "Nice to see you too."

"I mean, yeah . . . well, I just didn't expect to see you here."

Leigh frowned suspiciously. "What's wrong?"

"Nothing. Why would you assume something is wrong?"

"After Dad," she answered, "you're the most confident man I know and you're nervous, so what's up?"

"You look great." He gestured to the peach, pleated cocktail dress she had on. "Got a date?"

"I'm here with my friend, Alicia." Leigh hadn't had a date since she ended it with her last boyfriend, Hollywood mega-star

Lyndon Prior. After Leigh was almost attacked by his best friend, Nick Gagan, Lyndon had chosen to protect his image rather than help her get justice. That was the end of their relationship, and thanks to her father's power and influence, the end of Lyndon's career. No one even knew where he was now. Certainly no longer in L.A., where he had shot off the A-list the second a manufactured gay relationship with Nick which resulted in a drug-induced assault was attached to his name.

"You don't usually come to the . . ."

"What is going on?" Leigh pulled on his shirt, determined to know now. "On the prowl?"

"You know I'm with Julia," Carter said with a mischievous smile.

Leigh tilted her head to the side as she smirked at her big brother. "And I know you slept with Jasmine Cobb last month too."

"How do you know that?"

"I introduced you at our spring charity ball, remember? You drove her home and she blabbed to everyone that she slept with you. Then she called me ten times every day asking why you hadn't called her back."

Carter shrugged. "Yeah, well it's complicated. If you ever got back in the dating game you might find out."

"Son of a bitch!"

Carter at first thought she was reacting to his playful brotherly insult, but she was looking beyond him. She was looking at what Carter hadn't wanted her to see.

"Do you see this?" Leigh grabbed her brother, swinging him around. "I can't believe him. What an asshole."

The asshole was Michael, their brother, standing in the VIP section with his tongue practically down the throat of a caramel-colored beauty in a tight black dress that showed her considerable, and probably purchased, assets.

"I have it under control," Carter said as Leigh was already starting for him.

"This is exactly what Mom was talking about," she said.

"It's not any of your business." Carter waved to the bouncer in front of the section and they were quickly let in.

Michael only had a second to prepare for Leigh's onslaught as she started in on him immediately.

"What are you doing?" she asked. She turned to the woman who looked none too happy to see her. "You know that he's married, right? Of course you do. The ring is right there on his finger."

"Who in the hell are you?" the woman asked, ready to defend her prey.

"She's my sister," Michael answered, half laughing. "Leigh at the club. Is this a special occasion or what?"

"Did you listen to anything Mother said to you?" she asked. "A picture of you and this . . . whatever, is going to be on the gossip blogs tomorrow if not ton . . ."

"Hey!" The woman, seeming a step behind, appeared to take issue with being called a "whatever."

Leigh ignored her. "If you don't have any respect for your own marriage, at least respect the family enough to keep your whoring out of the public eye."

"We're just talking," Michael said. The woman had sent him a drink and he had called her over as soon as Carter stepped away to take a call. He was going to take her home tonight, have sex and be home by morning.

"Yeah, right."

"That's enough, Leigh." Carter took her by the arm and pulled her a step away from Michael. "I have this under control."

"Do you?" she asked. "You're doing the same thing. May not be as bad because you're not married, but . . . Dammit, Michael. Why don't you get divorced already?"

This got Michael's attention and he stood up straight, leaning forward, practically pushing the woman out of his way with the force of his body. He didn't notice. He didn't care anymore. He didn't even know her name.

"I am fucking sick and tired of everyone sticking their nose in my marriage," he seethed. "Mind your own goddamn business, Leigh."

Leigh just leaned back, feeling pity for her brother more than anything. He was clearly miserable. "You're an embarrassment to this family."

She was already turning to walk away as Michael called after her, "Someone has to balance out your perfection."

Carter turned to the woman who was still standing there with a clueless expression on her face. "You have a nice evening."

She looked at him blankly for a couple of seconds before catching his drift. She turned to Michael in hopes he would keep her there, but Michael was already detached from her, searching for his beer on the table behind them. With a huff, she turned and walked away in search of another wallet.

Michael found his drink and turned back to Carter. "Don't you start in on me again."

"What is your fucking problem?" Carter asked, leaning in so those looking—and someone was always looking—couldn't hear. "You treat Kimberly like shit, but the second someone suggests you get rid of her, you blow up."

"You wouldn't understand."

But Carter did understand. Eight years ago Michael had called him up late at night to tell him he'd gotten a girl pregnant and wanted to marry her. Michael was in business school at Columbia and Carter was at Harvard Law. Their closeness had existed forever, only growing tighter when they were both sent off to boarding school on the East Coast. They were best friends who always told each other the truth, kept each other's secrets to the death, and occasionally tried to beat the living tar out of each other.

Carter helped Michael take painstaking measures to hide Kimberly's past from their parents. They had no choice. They were Chases. They weren't even supposed to marry outside of their social set, the upper crust of black families in America. Even a girl from a rich family didn't qualify if their money was only one generation on. A middle-class girl was out of the question. Someone like Kimberly, someone who was invisible to people like his parents, was a disaster in their eyes. And they hadn't even known about the hooker part.

Carter had kept that secret and Michael married Kimberly to protect the family name. If there was anything Janet wouldn't tolerate, it was bastard kids with the Chase name. So their parents swallowed their disappointment and Kimberly joined the family.

"I'm not done with Kimberly," Michael said.

"You sound like a fucking maniac." Carter grabbed his brother by the arm, pulling him closer. "You've overdosed on the revenge, Michael. It's killing you both and hurting the . . ."

"Stop." Michael jerked his arm away. "Leave my kids out of this. Jesus, Carter. I was just trying to have some fun."

Michael had never been completely faithful to Kimberly. It wasn't in his blood. He'd cheated on her twice during the seven good years of their marriage, before she ruined his life. That wasn't counting trips to Las Vegas. None of those women ever meant anything more than a boost to his ego. Sex had never been as good with anyone as it was with Kimberly. And he had never loved anyone as much as he loved her. Now, he knew he would never hate anyone more, either.

"When will you be done with her?" Carter asked.

Michael tried to keep control as he felt the rage building. Just above a breath, he answered, "When I stop wanting her."

Carter just shook his head. He didn't know what else to do for Michael. They had always helped each other out and backed each other up. "I know about Elisha."

Michael stared at him, trying to figure out what to say. Elisha Fisher was the broker working the deal that Michael hoped would get him back in his father's good graces: the purchase of a publishing company, expanding Chase Enterprises to luxury and private-wealth-management magazines.

Michael just smiled. "What can I say? She's a redhead. You know I have a weakness for those . . ."

"She's not just a one-night stand, right?"

Michael shrugged. "She's more like an extended one-night stand. As soon as the deal is done, I'll get rid of her. I have to make this deal happen."

Carter folded his arms across his chest. "If you really want to get Dad to talk to you, stop this self-destructive behavior. Anything that hurts Mom, makes him angry."

Carter knew Michael lived for their father's approval. It was a disease they shared, but Michael took it a level higher, to a form of worship. Michael lived for King Chase, as they had named him long ago. He'd chosen to constantly seek to please a man who was nearly impossible to please.

"He'd do anything for you," Carter added. "He's done that."

"And he hates me for making him," Michael said somberly. "This is all my fault to him. He says I should have never started this lie in the first place. If I had handled this whole thing right from the beginning, everything would be fine. Instead, you, me, Mom, Dad are accessories to murder. If only . . ."

"If 'if' was a fifth, we'd all be drunk." Carter saw the edges of Michael's mouth attempt to curve into a brief smile. "The truth is, if Mom and Dad weren't such snobs, you wouldn't have felt the need to lie to them in the first place. It's their unreasonable expectations that set this in motion. Dad knows that."

But Carter knew Michael couldn't hear him. Michael wasn't trying to hear any truth right now.

Carter knew he was wicked to find so much joy in ringing the doorbell of a house he was paying for. It was Avery's townhouse in View Park. It cost a measly six hundred thousand dollars and Carter knew that his child support checks of eight thousand dollars a month, were paying the rent and everything else. Anthony could no longer afford the mortgage now that he'd lost his job as a professor at Occidental College and was relegated to teaching in an L.A. public high school.

Carter loved it. He'd used his influence to get Occidental to offer Anthony a plush job as a statistics professor with a six-figure income plus great benefits. This contact also set him up with a real estate agent that showed him this townhouse in a neighborhood that Carter had already known Avery liked.

Carter knew Avery would want to stay home with Connor, so Anthony would be their sole provider. He refused to use Carter's money for anything other than Connor. But Carter was already providing everything for his daughter. So when Anthony lost his job only a few months into it, also through Carter's influence, Carter's child support was the only thing paying their bills.

Carter liked it best when Anthony got upset at an "innocent" mistake Carter made, just like he was about to do now. After dropping his drunk brother off at his home, Carter had headed right to View Park after taking a phone call from his mother. Janet was upset because she found that her day tomorrow with Connor was being intercepted by Nikki Jackson, Avery's mother. She told Carter that Nikki had Connor tonight so Avery and Anthony could have a romantic dinner at home, alone.

Not anymore. Trying to hold back his grin, Carter knew he'd probably missed the dinner, but had a chance to spoil the rest of the evening.

He heard footsteps on the hardwood floor coming toward him. It was Anthony, and Carter would have paid an endless sum to see the expression on his face when he looked through the peephole and saw him.

The door swung open and Carter was met with an immediate, "What do you want?"

Carter smiled as always, looking Anthony over. "How ya doing, Anthony?"

"I was fine until now." Anthony blocked Carter's view into the house.

"I came to see Connor."

Anthony looked amazed at Carter's arrogance. "You know you're supposed to call before you come over."

"She didn't tell you?" Carter asked. "I called Avery and told her. This seems to happen a lot. She doesn't tell you about our phone conversations anymore. I wonder why."

"Bullshit," Anthony spat back. "Avery would have never agreed to let you come over tonight."

"Why not?"

Anthony was about to speak, but held back. He studied Carter's expression and seemed to finally get what Carter had hoped he would. "How did you know?"

"Know what?" Carter heard Avery coming.

"You knew we were planning an evening together." Anthony's voice raised just enough to let Carter know this blow-up would come fast.

"How could I know that?" Carter asked.

Just then, Avery pushed her way to the front door. It was Carter.

He looked a little ragged and tired and she was angry that it bothered her to see it.

"What are you doing here?" she asked.

"I came to . . ."

"To ruin our evening," Anthony said. "He couldn't stand it that we're having a romantic night."

"What are you talking about?" Carter asked as he laughed innocently. "Can I at least know what I'm being yelled at for? I was just at my parents' house and this place is on my way home. I saw the lights on and thought I'd come by and drop off some applications for our daughter."

Anthony cringed, as he hated it every time Carter used the words "our daughter." Carter knew it reminded him of the bond he and Avery would always have.

"What applications?" Avery stood in front of Anthony, trying to defuse the situation. There was no way Carter could have known. The only person that knew was her mother and Nikki couldn't stand Carter. She'd never let him in on anything.

"For St. Anne's preschool." Carter handed her the folder that he had left in his Maybach for a week, waiting for the right time to use the applications to interrupt the married couple. "Can you fill these out and send them to the school?"

"You had to come by at ten on a Friday night to give us some paper?" Anthony asked. "Avery, you can't be fooled by this."

"I was expecting them." Avery turned to Anthony and gave him her look; the one that told him to slow his roll. Ten minutes ago he was laughing, talking about the crazy kids in his class. Now, he was acting like a sullen, spoiled child.

Anthony looked incredulous. "She's six months old. What would she need preschool applications for?"

Avery looked the sheets over. "It's true that we have to apply now for that school. It's the hardest to get into in L.A. and everyone has to do it early."

Carter wondered why Anthony was making this so easy for him. Maybe he was breaking down. It wouldn't be long now. "We have to get her into the right preschool if we want her to get into the right grade school that will get her into the right prep school that will lead to the Ivy Leagues. Mother is on the museum board with the principal's wife, so Connor is in the school, but we have to do the formalities."

"This is ridiculous." Anthony threw his hands in the air. "How much does this place even cost?"

Avery sighed, knowing her answer would evoke another outburst from her husband. "Twenty-seven thousand dollars a year."

"Are you kidding me?" Anthony asked. "How . . ."

"That's pocket change," Carter said, locking eyes with Anthony before adding, "Well, at least to me."

Before Anthony could start again, Avery said, "Honey, it's what's best for Connor. I promised Janet I would do this. It's okay. Carter is paying for everything."

"What a surprise." Anthony rolled his eyes. "Well, thanks for dropping off the applications. You can leave now."

"Wait," Carter yelled out as Anthony reached for the door. "I want to see her. Just to give her a kiss goodnight."

"She's not here," Avery said, touched at how Connor was able to bring out this softer side of Carter that even she hadn't seen before. "She's at my parents. You really need to call, Carter. This is a home with a family. It's not just a place where your baby waits for you to come and go. You have to respect that."

Carter nodded in understanding as Anthony smirked. It wouldn't be long before he knocked that smirk off his face.

"Let's go, Avery." Anthony, seeming satisfied, turned to leave.

But he shouldn't have left without his woman in hand. Carter wouldn't have.

"Avery," Carter whispered, gesturing for her to stay a while.

Avery leaned in with the door behind her. "This really isn't a good time."

"I didn't know she wouldn't be here. Why is he so pissed?"

"Just ignore him. He's in a bad mood."

"He's always in a bad mood." Carter knew the longer he could keep Avery at the door, the more suspicious and angry Anthony would become. "I'm sorry."

"It's okay." She waved a dismissive hand. Anthony would be a jerk for the rest of the night, but there wasn't anything that could be done about it now. "I have to go."

"I have to go away," Carter said quickly.

This got her attention. She turned back to him with her doe eyes widening enough to show she cared. "To New York," he continued. "I have to work with Michael on a deal for Dad. I just wanted to get a little bit of sugar for good luck."

Avery smiled. She couldn't resist. Carter could make her angry, crazy and confused, but he also made her laugh. "I'll kiss her for you."

"Can you kiss me for her?" Carter asked, making sure to sound in jest. "Because usually I kiss her and then she kisses me back, so . . ."

"Stop." Without thinking, Avery's hand reached out and touched his arm. In a second a bolt of lighting went through her. Inside she was begging herself to move her hand away, but she didn't. She only looked into his tired eyes, and smiled more.

Carter was amazed at his own self-control. He'd never before been able to do that where Avery was concerned, which was how he'd gotten himself into this mess. It took everything he had not to grab her and kiss those inviting, full lips. Her eyes were begging him to take her now. He'd never wanted anyone so much and it seemed like forever since they'd last had sex.

Hearing the clanging sound of dishes in the background, Avery finally realized who she was and where she was. She blinked, removing her hand and feeling guilty for not wanting to close the door.

"I'll bring her back a gift," Carter said.

After a moment, she spoke again, her voice somewhat uneven. "You always buy her things and she just ends up spending more time with the box they came in."

He loved Connor and spoiled her rotten with gifts she was way too young to appreciate. But what Avery hadn't caught on to was that he always made a point to buy Connor a very expensive gift that Anthony couldn't have ever afforded. Anthony caught on. Carter was spending twice on his daughter on very regular occasions what Anthony could spend on his own wife on special occasions.

"Just come back safe," Avery said with more emotion than she'd intended. "That'll do for now."

He smiled and winked at her, waiting for her to smile back. He stayed at the door as she went inside and closed it. He wasn't thinking of how angry Anthony would be that she'd stayed this long. He wasn't thinking about getting a gift for Connor. He was only thinking about Avery's smile just before the door closed. She wasn't just smiling with her mouth, she was smiling with her eyes; her whole face. He knew there was nothing Anthony could do to take that away. At least not tonight.

Room 555 was almost at the very end of the fifth floor of Reiber Hall, one of many UCLA dormitory buildings. When Taylor reached it, finally, the front door was open but she knocked anyway. She followed the lead from the web site Claire had shown her. It took a few days of asking around, but if she was right, this was ground zero for the campus alibi service.

Taylor was full of doubts, but she found herself here anyway. There was a Chanel dress on eBay that she wanted desperately, and the bidding was already at three hundred dollars. She needed cash.

"Come in!" yelled a voice from inside.

When Taylor walked in, she came face-to-face with a boy who looked more like twelve than eighteen. He wasn't quite white or anything else, so she figured he was biracial. He was about twenty pounds overweight with curly, out-of-control hair. She could tell right away the guy had money. His glasses were Emilio Pucci and he was wearing an Italian designed button-front shirt. And the decorations of his very humble dorm room included expensive bed sheets, an Acer Aspire notebook and a MacBook Pro notebook, each costing around three thousand dollars. Not to mention the large, flat-screen, high definition TV that was hanging on the wall in violation of dorm rules.

"Taking in the digs?" the kid asked with a strong Southern accent. He gestured for Taylor to sit down on the bed since he was sitting on the only chair.

She sat down unsteadily, glad the door was open. This kid looked shady.

He finished off the last of his Pepsi Max and tossed it in the garbage on the other side of the room. "School rules say fresh-men have to live in the dorm. No exceptions. But as soon as the semester is over, I'm out of here."

"I heard you own the . . . run that web site." She laid her purse on the floor after checking to make sure it was clean.

"Who told you?" he asked. "I'm Damon, by the way."

"Sorry." Taylor cleared her throat. "My name is Taylor Jack . . . Taylor."

"You're pretty." He said it as if it was just a fact that he thought he'd share, then swung around in his chair. "You go here?"

"Yes, I'm a junior. I was told that . . ."

"I ask because I've gone to pretty great lengths to keep my ownership of the site secret. I guess not enough."

"It was another student who told me, so I don't think it's off campus."

His expression was still as if waiting for her to say something that would ease his suspicion. He slid to the window and turned on his iPod deck, but it wasn't playing music. It was playing loud white noise and static.

"It's to drown out anything that might be picked up on a tape," he said in response to Taylor's curious expression.

Who did this guy think he was? "It's really not that serious, is it?"

"Gotta be safe."

"I'm not going to tell or anything," Taylor said.

"I'd deny it if you did," he replied, before a shrug of his shoulders seemed to indicate he was satisfied. "Besides, it's all legit. So, you need an alibi?"

"Actually, I need a job."

His eyes squinted as if he was trying to read her mind. "You know what we do?"

"You provide alibis. That's all I know. Do you have like a brochure or something?"

"Yeah, it's right next to the application form behind you." He laughed even more when Taylor actually turned around. "That was sarcasm, by the way. We are paperless, baby."

Taylor nodded, already knowing she didn't like this guy. "Do you do this all your . . ."

"I used to when it was just about alibis for absences from class, and then work. Certain times of the year we get a lot of excuses to delay midterms and finals, but that's getting a little dicey. Honor codes and all."

"Where do the other people work?"

"From their own rooms or apartments. I provide you with the phone. Each has ten lines, but I don't let people handle more than five at a time, unless they're good." His cell phone, on the desk in front of him, rang with the sound of heavy metal music. He leaned in to look and turned up his nose before turning back to Taylor. "Otherwise, they get confused and end up answering a line that was supposed to be a job reference and give a confirmation of a hotel guest having checked in.

"Hotel guest?"

"I've branched out beyond students," he said proudly. "People give their spouses a number to a hotel and we answer and confirm that the guest is there, but not in the room. We take a message. That's getting pretty weak lately, but the virtual seminar business is big."

"What is that?"

"I do those myself," he answered. "They're complicated. I usually start people off with doctor's excuses or make you just a buddy for some girl cheating on her boyfriend. If you're good, I'll bump you up to fake travel agency. My latest starter is the emergency phone call."

"What is that?"

"When people want to get out of a meeting or leave work early, at a specified time we call the front desk of his office and say there's been an emergency. You know. But not anyone can do this. Our clients pay a lot for confidentiality."

"What does it pay?" Taylor asked. "I mean for the people who work for you."

"I gotta train you first and you don't get paid anything for that. I will test you with phone calls and make sure you know how to handle it right. You know, sound professional; convincing. If you sound eighteen it isn't going to work. If you work out, I might pay you twenty-five dollars an hour."

"Serious?" Taylor could pay off that dress on her Mastercard in a couple of months; maybe less. "Because it's risky, right?"

"We are a perfectly legit business." Damon's expression held some caution. "There is nothing illegal about lying as long as it isn't to the police or anything like that."

"Police?"

"Yeah, we don't do criminal alibis. If we get a call from the cops, we don't know nobody. I'm learning a little about . . . hey, are you in law school?"

"No, undergrad."

"Well, we have a fax business and yes, some people still use fax machines. So, we accidentally on purpose fax a conference agenda for a meeting in Minneapolis for someone who is in the Bahamas with their girlfriend. The wife calls the number to tell us that her husband already left. We apologize and say we'll fax it to the hotel. Proactive stuff."

Taylor had to admit she was pretty intrigued at this point. "So are you . . ."

"Damon!" A kid with a buzz cut and thick glasses rushed into the room, ignoring Taylor completely. "Pizza is here. You're paying, dude. It's your turn."

Damon looked none too pleased. "Wasn't it my turn last time?"

"You doubled up. Come on, dude. The pizza guy is gonna leave."

Without excusing himself, or saying anything for that matter, Damon got up from the chair, grabbed his wallet from the desk and shuffled out of the room.

"Sure, I'll wait," Taylor said to herself after he was gone.

So the kid was rude. It didn't matter. She got the sense that he was raking it in and she couldn't get that twenty-five dollars an hour out of her head.

Her curiosity getting the best of her, Taylor got up and went over to the crowded desk. Only one laptop was running and it displayed a diagram of some sort with different hotel names and aliases. She imagined if she could have afforded it, she could have used one of these back in the day when she spent more time shopping, partying and modeling than going to class.

"Hi."

After almost jumping as high as the ceiling, Taylor turned around to see a guy that she immediately thought was one of the hottest brothers she'd ever seen. He had a superhero-type chiseled jaw and smooth, shiny skin. He looked young, but didn't seem like a student. He was dressed in a suit that was clearly expensive, but had a backpack.

"Is Damon in?" he asked.

Taylor noticed that his expression didn't change at all. She wasn't looking her best, but fortunately this guy seemed too distracted to notice. "He went to get pizza."

"Dammit." He took a few more steps into the room, reaching into his pockets. "I can't wait. I came all the way over here from the law campus and I'm already late for work downtown."

"Can I help you?" Taylor didn't know what she was doing, but she wanted to give this guy another chance to notice her. "I kind of work for him."

"I need an alibi." He opened his hand to her.

Taylor tried to pretend like it didn't phase her that he was offering her a wad of bills. They were mostly hundreds with some fifties. "Is that . . ."

"It's all fifteen hundred." He shoved his hand closer to her. "You have my info. I need a buddy to say we were hanging out tonight. Are you going to do it?"

"I . . ." Taylor was still looking down at the money in her hand.

"You probably won't have to do anything," he said. "In fact, I'm pretty sure you won't, but I have to have a backup."

"What for?"

"The usual." He waited for some recognition on Taylor's face. "You and I were hanging out at Lu Valle on north campus from like eight to eleven in the evening. I picked you up in my X5 at the student union and we went to Lu Valle where we ate and talked about politics and getting jobs in politics. Then I dropped you back at eleven. That was it."

"But how do we know each other?" Taylor was desperately trying to remember everything he'd just said. "Damon doesn't keep any paper. You know that."

He sighed impatiently, but quickly took a few seconds to tell her the scenario that usually played out. They also say they met a month earlier, hanging out at Jimmy's Café, and got into a conversation about internships. They can't have met too long ago because then they should know more about each other. He'd told her he had contacts through his law firm and could hook her up. They met for dinner to discuss those contacts, but never really got to any specifics. None that she would say she remembered. The key was not to be exact. Everyone forgets things. It just seemed so easy.

"What name are you going to use?"

"My name, I guess."

"Well?" he asked impatiently.

"Taylor Jackson." She held out her free hand to him and he looked confused before shaking it. His shake was firm and quick.

"So, what's your number going to be?"

Taylor knew she was crazy, but Chanel dresses and Prada shoes danced in her head. There were so many social events coming up. Yeah, she was crazy, but she tried to appear as sane as possible as she gave him her cell phone number.

"That doesn't sound like one of the regular numbers," he said. "Who did you say you were again?"

"Taylor Jackson." She looked around the room and, quickly pocketing the money, she grabbed a pen and ripped a piece of paper off a notebook. She wrote her name and number down. "You should call me to let me know whether or not I'll be needed."

He took the paper and stuffed it in his backpack. "Well, I don't know, but I don't think you'll be needed at all."

"Just call anyway."

"Here's my card," he mumbled as he handed her a thick, tan business card with red raised letters.

"You're in law school?" Taylor asked.

"I'm an intern at that firm. It's standard. Do you have one?"

Taylor laughed because she thought he was kidding, but his blank stare told her he wasn't. "No. I'm just undergrad. Communications major."

He snapped his finger. "Yeah, I'm supposed to ask that. Okay, I gotta go. I'm already late."

"Hey!" Taylor yelled after him when he'd almost reached the door. "What's the alibi for?"

He looked her up and down as if he wasn't sure he could trust her. "You're not supposed to know, remember? Plausible deniability and all that."

"Oh yeah," Taylor said, even though she had no idea what he was talking about. He was gone before she could say another word.

Taylor contemplated her options. She could stay, give the money to Damon, and the best she could hope for was free training. Or, she could take the card, the money, and do this one alibi, which was likely never going to happen, by herself. And maybe, if she was lucky, she'd run into . . . Taylor looked down at the card in her hand.

"Garrett Collins." As she hurried out of the dorm room, Taylor thought even the name sounded like he had money.

4

Carter turned up the volume on his bedroom TV screen as he passed by. He tossed a pair of underwear, two shirts, and pair of jeans in his Louis Vuitton Keepall Bandouliere travel bag. That should be enough. They were only going to New York for one day.

He could hear Julia calling his name from the hallway. She was on her way to the bedroom and for a second he regretted letting her move in with him. Unlike with Avery, whom he couldn't wait to get home to, Julia always needed something. Avery always gave when he came home. Comfort, conversation, a joke, a drink, food, or affection. Julia needed reassurance, commitment, promises, or attention.

But all he had to remember was the look on Avery's face when she found out that Julia had moved in and it was all worth it. It was just for a brief second, but her eyes widened and her lips parted a bit. She was jealous.

"Hey, sweetie." She smiled softly as she entered the room, tossing her Burberry leather tote on the bed. She wrapped her arms around his neck and leaned up for a kiss.

Carter enjoyed kissing her. Her lips were full and soft and she always smelled incredibly good. She was a very appealing woman in many ways and sometimes he really wanted her. This was not one of those times.

"What are you doing home?" he asked.

"Those bitches at work." She walked over to the TV, took a second to see the stock-market data flashing across the screen before reaching for the remote.

"Hey, I'm watching that." He hated Julia's television choices. She only wanted to watch celebrities.

Ignoring what he'd said, Julia turned back to him with a sigh that told Carter he was about to hear an hour's worth of complaining that would be followed by a need for reassurance about something.

"Those bitches hate me." She fell onto the bed, sitting next to his bag.

Carter wanted to turn and run, but he was getting used to this. She would follow him into the damn bathroom if she had to.

"They're all jealous because they know we're together. Like somehow I'm the bitch because I have a Chase." She flipped her hair back, talking in that superior tone that Carter was sure was the real reason they hated her. "Lisa Black, that damn project manager. A project manager, Carter! How can she be allowed to try and show me up? I'm a senior financial analyst."

"Julia, I have to . . ."

"She comes in the office this morning, walks over to me and starts going on about how she feels so sorry for me and hopes that you and I can work it out."

"Work what out?"

Julia spread her arms out. "Exactly. She wasn't going to give up until I asked that question. Despite the fact that she's right across from me, she's screeching about how she heard you were seen with some blonde at Nishimura the other night."

Dammit, Carter said to himself. Those nosy little bitches.

"She's totally lying and she knows it." Julia looked him directly in the eye, wanting reassurance. "Right?"

"Of course," he said as quickly and smoothly as he would have if it were the truth. In his own defense, he hadn't slept with the girl. Just sushi and drinks. "She's just trying to make you jealous so she'll feel better. You know all these bitter women. If they can make it seem like you're not happy, then it doesn't hurt so much that you have the life they'll never have."

Julia smiled, seeming to accept the reassurance, but only for a second. "But shouldn't we do something?"

"Just ignore them." After zipping up the bag, he reached for the handle, but she blocked him by placing her hand over it. He looked at her and saw that need again. It was exhausting.

"I thought that . . ." She frowned for a second as if contemplating what to say next. "Well, I actually told them that you and I were going to Dallas to visit my parents."

Carter tried to manage a kind smile. "I'm not going to Dallas, Julia. And I've already met your parents. They came up here three months ago."

"I'm sorry, Carter, but lunch at Dolce on Melrose doesn't constitute a meeting. You need a formal meeting. You need to be photographed playing golf with my father or something."

Carter could see Julia morphing into his mother right before his eyes. "You're looking for a photo op? No."

Her expression softened as she tilted her head to the side and smiled. "It would help me out a lot."

Carter shook his head. "This is the second time in the last month you've tried to manufacture a publicity event out of our relationship. I don't like it."

"You didn't seem to mind when the paps were taking pictures of you and Avery all the time."

Carter's eyes darkened quickly. Julia knew that Avery was a forbidden topic for her. "King Chase is waiting."

She grabbed his arm in a desperate move before he could walk away. "I'm sorry, Carter. It's just that . . ."

"Avery was my fiancée." He didn't like hurting her, but she had to learn that it wasn't worth it to bring Avery up. "You're not."

"I should be," she advocated.

Carter stood still and she pressed against him, her hands taking hold of his face to focus his eyes on hers. Hers were intent and fierce. "You and I would make a great pair, Carter. You know it. Everything about our families, our backgrounds, our best assets just work so well."

"I have to go, Julia."

She pressed her lips against his with a directness that he wasn't used to. He didn't move as her hands came behind his head, pulling him closer. He found this desperate seduction of hers somewhat arousing. He knew when she felt this way, she would do anything he wanted. Things, under a normal situation, she wouldn't even consider.

He reached out and placed his hand firmly on the small of her back, allowing his mouth to explore hers. Carter wouldn't allow himself to think of Avery in these moments, because he knew she was sleeping with her husband.

Julia let out a gasp as Carter grabbed her by the waist and lifted her body. He threw her back onto the bed, onto her back. There was a wicked smile on her face as her arms reached up to receive him.

He was unzipping his pants as Julia began hiking her skirt up and reaching for her panties. He wanted her now, but not enough to ignore the reporter on the television mentioning the word "murder."

"What?" Julia asked in a breathless voice.

"Watch." He slid away from her, focusing on what the reporter was saying.

"Cool, Bitton & Klein is one of the largest independent law firms in L.A. and has a reputation for dealing with not-so-reputable clients. The victim, identified as Justin Ursh, was reportedly shot point blank in the head, in the middle of his Beverly Hills living room. Ursh had been a partner at the firm for three years."

"Did you know him?" Julia asked.

Carter shook his head, his first thought going to Haley. As crazy as she was, he loved her and he was her big brother. It had been bothering him ever since she brought Garrett Collins to the house as her boyfriend. He worked at Cool, Bitton & Klein and that was never a good thing. Although Haley could handle herself with the best of them, it was better to be safe than sorry. He needed to do something.

"Julia, I've got to go."

Chase Beauty's executive offices held five floors in the 777 Tower building in downtown Los Angeles. It was here that Steven summoned his boys before sending them to New York. Sitting back in his leather chair, placed in the middle of his large corner office, he looked at both of his sons, each sitting in a chair on the other side of his new, oversized mahogany desk that Janet had purchased for sixteen thousand dollars at a Sotheby's auction, for his birthday.

"Just to repeat, I don't care what the situation is. We aren't going one penny over a hundred and fifty million for this company. Do you both understand that?"

Both men nodded, but they all knew he was really just talking to Michael.

They were on their way to New York to make the final decision on a deal to purchase Luxury Life Publishing Corporation, a formerly black-owned company that published five different magazines. Their biggest seller, *Luxury Life*, had the second-highest circulation of black business magazines; and they also published the best-selling ethnic women's upscale fashion magazine, *Sepia*.

"Seeing as how every takeover we try to execute, one of you two screws up," Steven continued, "I'm kind of skeptical about this."

"Don't be," Michael said. "This is a good investment. All of their products are popular despite practically zero marketing. We add the Chase name and market the hell out of them, especially the web sites, we'll be able to form partnerships with all the tech companies and dominate in no time."

Steven nodded. "I'm in this for the web sites and the possible partnership with *Robb Report* and *Forbes*. The other magazines, I don't know."

Carter chimed in. "The business magazine is catching up to *Black Enterprise*, and *Sepia* is unquestionably the leader. I think you might be able to hold on to that teen entrepreneur magazine too."

"What about the college mag?" Steven asked.

"There are an endless amount of possibilities there," Michael said. "Right now, they're focused on HBCUs. We can expand it into a basic college magazine for minority students in general, and create special quarterly issues for MBAs, law students, med school and tech students. Whatever. The options are endless with using the web site as a portal and social networking tool."

Steven had to hand it to Michael. He'd done his research and it sounded good. But he still had his reservations.

"I'm not crazy about this broker," Steven said. "She rubbed me the wrong way. I've had her background dug up. She's got some gaps in her history."

Michael sat up in his seat. "I told you I did a background on her before I brought her to you."

"And I did another one." Steven stared him down, letting him know that he wasn't going to explain second-guessing him.

Carter knew it was a good time to step in before things got ugly. Ever since the last fiasco with Kimberly, Michael and Steven's relationship had been tearing at everyone in the family. For Carter, it was the first time in his entire life when someone was more at odds with their father than he was. He enjoyed the respite, but didn't like seeing this.

"It doesn't matter." He stood up. "She's just brokering the deal. The publisher sold the business to her firm, but they're just holding it, not running it. All we need to know are the financials on the company and we have them."

"Yes," Steven agreed, "but we can't ignore the role she has played in making this happen."

Steven saw everything, so although his boys thought their quick exchange of glances had passed by him, it hadn't. These boys and their secrets were going to be the death of him. He appreciated their closeness, but he sensed there could be more Kimberly-like secrets between them that could hurt the family, the legacy. Steven had always assumed his power, money, and influence could take care of everything, but covering up the murder Kimberly had committed had been the limit.

"Is there something you want to say to me?" Steven asked.

Carter eyed him and Steven respected that. As crazy as the boy made him, even when he was wrong, Carter stood tall. He wasn't going to tell him anything. Michael was another story. He'd seen what keeping secrets from his family had cost him. Michael was further away from sitting in Steven's chair one day than ever before. He knew it was Michael's dream to take over Chase Beauty and it had been Steven's as well. He dreamed of Carter coming to the company and the two brothers running it together. But that was before.

Michael could feel his father's eyes boring into him, but he tried to hold out. "What?"

Steven reached into the folder on his desk and took out two large, glossy, black-and-white photos. He separated them and slid them across the desk, one facing Carter and the other facing Michael. Both boys leaned forward to look as Steven leaned back and waited.

Michael felt a little sick when he saw the picture of him and Elisha kissing outside The Plaza Hotel in New York. Without saying anything, Carter slid the other photo toward his brother. This was of Michael leaning against Elisha, in front of a restaurant, his hand on her ass, kissing her neck.

"I'll ask you again." Steven's tone held a wicked sarcasm. "Is there something you want to say to me?"

"What is there to say?" Carter asked once he realized that Michael wasn't going to say anything. "You obviously know that he's sleeping with her."

Steven looked down as his smartphone vibrated. "That's Chris. The jet is fueled and ready to go."

"You having me followed?" Michael asked.

"I was having her followed, you idiot." Steven grabbed the photos and stuffed them back in the folder. "Is this another woman who whispered to you in bed? Wasn't it Kimberly who urged you to convince me that we needed a fashion line so she could bring Janet's ex-lover back into our lives?"

"I didn't make you do anything," Michael said. He was never

going to let this go. "Can we just not do this? I'm not stupid enough to bring you another bad deal."

"Yes, you are." Steven said. He saw Carter open his mouth. "Shut up. This isn't about you. This is about Michael and his reckless behavior."

"It's a good deal!" Michael shot up from the seat and turned to leave.

"I'm not done talking to you, boy!" Steven yelled after him.

Michael stopped and turned around. "What's the point? A good deal, a bad one. What difference does it make? You'll still hate me. You'll still blame me for everything!"

If there was anything Steven couldn't stand, it was to see his sons feel sorry for themselves. He had taught them better. They were Chases. "I haven't blamed you for anything more than the part of all this that was your fault. And I don't hate you. I'm just sick of my business getting hurt by both of you, and your women issues."

"What did I do?" Carter asked, even though he knew what his father was talking about. From the moment Carter tried to buy Avery's two hair salons for Chase Beauty, it was a disaster. "Hold a grudge, why don't you?"

"Do I need to remind you two that I called in almost every favor I had out there to cover up a murder for you two!" He turned to Carter. "And yes, you too. You knew from the beginning all of the lies, and for almost eight years."

"Stop!" Michael couldn't stand to hear it anymore. "You covered that up for you. To save Chase Beauty, and for Mom, to save the family's image. You didn't do it for me and Carter had nothing to do with it."

"Let's go." Carter waved Michael toward the door.

"Wait." Steven called after them.

Carter turned back to him, holding his hand up. "The knife is deep enough for one day, Dad. We're leaving."

After they were gone, Steven felt regretful for how hard he came down on Michael, but he felt that he was doing what was best for both boys. They were already the target of envy and jealousy in the business world. They would inherit a billion-dollar empire, covering everything from cosmetics to real estate investments. Steven had spent countless hours, expending sweat and tears, to build something unprecedented by a black man in America, and he wasn't going to have it all go down over his sons' bad choices in women.

"Garrett Collins?" Claire stopped in her tracks and turned to Taylor. "Of course I know who he is."

They were walking toward the student garage after classes when Taylor decided to bring up the name. She'd been thinking about Garrett since she'd seen him a couple of days ago and was trying to come up with an excuse to call him.

Taylor smiled from cheek to cheek. "Well now I know him."

"He used to go out with Marian what's-her-name. You know, the ditz that was in political science. She graduated last year. She'd been in school for like six years."

Taylor did remember Marian and she wondered if Garrett was only interested in white girls. "What happened? Are they still together?"

Claire shrugged. "I don't remember why they broke up, but I think her dad hated her dating a black guy and he had just started law school. She said she never saw him anyway."

"Do you know who he's dating now?"

"Why do you ask?"

Taylor just shook her head nonchalantly. "I don't know. I just . . . He's gorgeous. And I'll bet he's connected."

"His family is rich or something. I don't know. I think he's seeing . . ."

"Rich?" Taylor smiled. "I knew it. He had money written all over him. Not the kind that is gonna get money, but the kind that already has it."

"Don't take this the wrong way," Claire said, "because you're totally hot. Your legs are like two miles long and all, but he seems like the rich girl type."

Taylor was getting angry. Claire had touched her weak spot, her economic status. "Well maybe his type has changed."

"Whatever." Claire rolled her eyes.

Taylor wanted to strangle her for making her feel like the help. She'd show her. "We've already hung out."

"When?"

"The other night." Taylor tried desperately to remember the alibi. She'd forgotten it almost as soon as Garrett walked away. "We kind of . . ."

"Taylor? Taylor Jackson?"

Taylor and Claire stopped as two men in gray suits approached them. She had no idea who they were, and something on their faces told her it wasn't good news. Immediately she thought of her father and panicked.

"What is it?" she asked. "What do you want?"

"I'm Detective Graves." This one was taller, looked younger and nicer. He was white with a sun-kissed tone to his skin and had bright green eyes. "This is my partner, Detective Falger."

"Is this about my dad?" Taylor asked. "Is something wrong?"

A year ago, Charlie Jackson, former Chief of Police of View Park, had been shot while trying to arrest a couple of car thieves. He'd almost died, but made it through. He had to quit his job due to stress.

"Your dad?" Detective Falger asked. "Who's your dad?"

"Former Chief of Police Charlie Jackson," she answered, then remembered she was in L.A. "Of View Park."

"That's your dad?" Detective Graves looked genuinely impressed. "Wow. Didn't know that, but no, ma'am. I'm sure Chief Jackson is fine. I've never met him, but I heard he partnered with L.A. cops all the time and he was well respected."

"This is on an unrelated matter." Detective Falger had a deep, gravelly voice and muddled features. He was clearly the tough guy. He glanced for a moment at Claire before turning back to Taylor. "Can we talk to you alone?"

"Just tell me what you want." Taylor was gripping the edges of the book in her hands so tight, her nails were making marks.

"Do you know a Garrett Collins?"

Taylor blinked, uncertain she'd heard right. "Garrett Collins? Is he okay?"

"He's fine. So you do know him?"

"What is this about?" Claire asked.

Detective Graves leaned in closer and lowered his voice. "You can imagine that we don't like questioning the former chief's daughter, but we're investigating a murder this past Wednesday. We need your help."

"Mr. Collins is a suspect," Detective Falger added, looking as if he didn't at all share Graves' discomfort. "But he says he was with you until about eleven that night."

Taylor's mouth dropped. She turned to Claire, who was looking straight at the ground. She looked back at Detective Graves, trying to think of something to say as her hesitation seemed to last hours.

"No, I don't know him." Out of the corner of her eye she saw Claire's head shoot up, but Taylor was more concerned with the skeptical look on both the detectives' faces.

"Are you sure?" Detective Falger asked. "I got the impression you know him very well."

"Well . . . I do know who he is," Taylor answered, gesturing nervously. All she could think of was Damon's words to deny anything if the cops came calling. "But we aren't friends or anything."

"So you did not spend time with him at Lu Valle on Wednesday night?"

Time was moving around Taylor in slow motion. Was this a joke? Was she dreaming this? He had given the cops her alibi. He had actually gone through with it. What was she going to do?

"No." She tried to answer as calmly as possible, but her voice gave her away. She was scared as hell and wasn't thinking.

They didn't believe her. Taylor could see from their expressions that they thought she was lying. She wasn't. She was telling the truth, but couldn't bring herself to disclose the whole situation. She had to talk to her brother first. Sean was one of the most respected young detectives in L.A.

"Thank you, Ms. Jackson." Detective Graves spoke slowly, not trying to hide his disbelief. "We might need to contact you again. You'll be around?"

Taylor nodded, feeling it better not to speak anymore.

"What in the hell was that?" Claire asked as soon as the detectives were out of earshot.

Taylor was speechless.

"Why did you lie?" Claire asked.

"I didn't," Taylor answered. She was shocked, but still aware of the embarrassment that admitting to Claire that she was lying about Garrett would bring. "It's complicated. Just . . . I have to go."

She was on the phone dialing her brother immediately, trying to reassure herself that she was telling the truth, so there shouldn't be anything to worry about. But just like the detectives, she wasn't buying it.

5

Avery was busy concentrating on two works of art, trying to decide which one she would place in the front of her mother's art gallery, HUE. Nikki Jackson was an artist who had given up her work to be a wife and mother. After Taylor entered junior high, Nikki found herself having more time on her hands. Having maintained her interest in art, she began putting on a few shows for local minority artists. They became so popular that she opened the gallery.

But since Charlie had been shot, Nikki had been focused on caregiving. When Anthony couldn't watch Connor, Avery brought her to the gallery, which allowed her to chip in more and more. Avery's problem was that she wasn't an artist and at times like this, she wished her mother was around more.

Avery leaned over the baby-blue-and-white bassinet where Connor was lying, trying to chew a baby ring. She was beginning to teethe. "Which one do you like better? They both look like a baby painted them anyway."

It was then that Nina, the young and always anxious assistant who had been working at the gallery since it opened, came to the back room with a concerned look on her face. She was always concerned about something.

"Avery, you should probably go out front," she said. "Your uhm . . . your friend is here and she looks very upset."

"My friend?"

"Kimberly Chase."

Avery grabbed the baby monitor and headed for the storefront. The gallery was empty, so it was easy to find Kimberly. Avery just followed the agitated voice. When she found her, Kimberly was yelling into her phone.

"So what you're saying is that you're scared, right? You're just another chicken-shit lawyer. You have no investment in that family!" Kimberly immediately hung up before bringing her hand to her forehead, as if to stave off the pounding.

"What's wrong, Kimberly?" Avery debated even asking the question because she had asked it so many times in the last six months, to no avail.

Kimberly turned around with tears in her eyes. "Malibu, Avery. I can't even get a lawyer in crappy Malibu to agree to represent me in a divorce. No one practicing law in the state of California is going to go up against the Chase family. They say it's because I signed a prenup and we've been married less than ten years, but that's bullshit. They're just scared."

"Scared of what?" Avery asked.

Kimberly waved a dismissive hand in the air. "It doesn't matter. I'm not going to get a divorce."

"You don't have to have a lawyer," Avery said. "You can just file for divorce."

Kimberly looked at her as if she was a fool. "So you expect me to go up against that family on my own? Tell me again why you ran away when you found out you were pregnant? Why you wanted to lie and say that Connor wasn't a Chase?"

Avery nodded. "I know. But so what if you don't get any money. Is holding on to money more important than your sanity?"

Kimberly's anger strengthened as she doubted Avery even listened to her. "It was at first. Not anymore. I told you this is about my babies. You know damn well if Carter wanted to take Connor from you he could. And you're as squeaky clean as they come."

Avery shivered at the thought and the fact that it was true. "What can I do, Kimberly?"

Kimberly looked around, her paranoia justified by Michael's admission that he had her followed sometimes. "I need a job. Here at the gallery. I need it to be a secret that I work here and I need you to pay me in cash."

Avery couldn't believe it. Michael had millions and he was keeping her on such a short leash she had to ask for money to spend on herself. "This is crazy. You aren't his child, Kimberly. Something has to be done."

Kimberly had wished she could tell Avery about David's death and the cover-up, but she couldn't. It was bad enough when Avery found out what Kimberly had done to try to bring Janet down over a year ago. But she had forgiven her for that. Avery was the only friend she had, the only person in her life that wouldn't bow to Michael's intimidation. She couldn't risk losing her.

"You can't tell Carter, either," Kimberly said.

"Of course not. I don't tell Carter my secrets anymore." Avery noticed the look of doubt on Kimberly's face. "What?"

"I see you two, Avery. You talk in the corner. The way you both look nervous when you walk by each other. I see the way you look when you don't know anyone is watching and you turn completely green when he kisses Julia."

"Stop it." Avery didn't want to hear any more of this. She could never deny to herself that she still cared deeply for Carter, but she wouldn't listen to this. "You're just emotional."

"I'm afraid," Kimberly said. "You can't tell Carter. He's on Michael's side. I know you think he's reasonable, but they are all evil. You can't . . . Jesus Christ!"

Before Avery could speak, Kimberly had rushed away toward the back room. Avery started to go after her until she realized who Kimberly was trying to avoid being seen by.

"Hello, Avery." Julia Hall approached her, looking almost regal in her purple Anna Sui shimmer lace dress. Her hair was styled in a fashionably messy do, and her flawless face wore nothing but lipstick.

Avery knew that most of the reason she didn't like Julia was because she was jealous of her relationship with Carter, but she could never admit it. She had no right to. It killed her to think of him making love to Julia, laughing with her, telling her his secrets, or at least his version of his secrets.

But there was also something beyond that. She was snobby, cold, and judgmental. Most of all, Avery knew part of Julia regretted Connor's existence. She intended to be Mrs. Carter Chase, and Carter having a child with someone other than her was . . . messy. The joy of Avery's whole world was nothing more than an inconvenience to this woman.

"What are you doing here, Julia?" Avery asked. "Looking for art work?"

Julia smiled, looking around. "Well, I am interested in redecorating the condo now that I'm living there permanently. Whoever decorated it last had horribly common taste."

Avery's smile never skipped a beat. She wouldn't give Julia the pleasure.

"But," Julia continued, "this modern stuff is not . . . well, it's a little too new money for my taste. I prefer classier, more cultured. No, Avery, I came by to talk to you."

"What about?" Avery reminded herself that she was a Christian. She had to stay calm even though she knew Julia was about to piss her off.

"Leigh's birthday dinner is coming up and she wants to invite you."

"And she sent you to tell me?"

Julia smiled sarcastically. "No, I sent me to tell you to decline the invitation."

"I wasn't aware you had the authority to tell me what to do."

Julia's eyes shrunk to slits. "You're not a part of this family, Avery."

"I don't claim to be," Avery said. "And just so you know. Just dating Carter doesn't make you a member either."

"I'm not just dating him," Julia said defensively. "We are living together and we are going to be married."

Avery turned away, pretending to look toward the front door for customers she knew weren't there. It took her a moment to let that pass before she turned back. "What does this have to do with Leigh's birthday party?"

"This is about you using that baby to . . ."

"That baby?" Avery asked in a warning tone. "Her name is Connor and she's Carter's daughter. If you plan on marrying him, you might want to at least remember her name."

"If?" Julia asked. "I will marry him and this isn't about her. It's about you using her to stay connected to Carter."

Avery wasn't going to let that pass. "I would never use my daughter for anything. I'm not like you, Julia. I don't have a plan. I'm not scheming for anything. Carter and I have a baby together, so we are connected whether I want it or not."

Julia let out a cold laugh. "You think so? Because I think it's you trying to keep that connection. Trying to keep him."

"If he's yours then what am I trying to keep?" Avery asked. She could see Julia's face redden in response. "This is not about me or Connor. This is about you and your lack of confidence in Carter's feelings for you. You should be talking to him, not me."

"Don't tell me what I should be doing with Carter! He loves me and I know it."

"If you believed that, you wouldn't be here." Avery felt a wicked sense of satisfaction at the look on Julia's face. "Don't explode, Julia. I wasn't going to come to the dinner anyway. Unlike you, I'm not desperate to stay in that inner circle."

Julia leaned in with a threatening glare. Her perfect face came closer to Avery's. "I'm not desperate for anything. I am in, Avery. I was born in. You may have slithered in through Carter during a moment of very bad judgment on his part, but it's time you realize that you are no longer welcome. And if you don't get out, I'll push you out."

Avery's fists clenched at her sides as she restrained herself. This woman was actually threatening her! Avery chose not to say a word, but she looked at Julia with an intensity that words couldn't have conveyed anyway. Julia paused a moment before leaning back. She took a deep breath, and without a peep, walked out with her nose as high as the sky.

As if on cue, Avery could hear Connor making cooing sounds from the monitor. She didn't know what she needed to do, but she was certain of one thing.

"I don't want that bitch around my baby."

* * *

Haley had had it. Garrett was on his last leg after leaving her at the party, but he'd made up for it by buying her a bottle of Bulgari Pour Femme perfume. She agreed to meet him for dinner at The Restaurant in the Hotel Bel-Air, but he had barely paid any attention to her at all. She wouldn't even put up with this from a rich man. She sure as hell wasn't going to tolerate it from some intern making only twenty-five hundred dollars a week. Dating him was charity in itself.

"Look, Garrett." She snatched her purse from the empty chair between them. "We need to talk."

"I'm sorry." Garrett looked up from his BlackBerry. His eyes were red, and although he looked impeccable, fashion-wise, there was a hint of raggedness about him. "I was expecting a call, but I won't look again."

"On the contrary," Haley said. "You can look all you want at your crackberry. I don't really care. I'm just gonna get out of this and head on home. No point in you paying for dessert if you aren't getting any yourself."

Garrett frowned as if he didn't understand. "Get out of what?"

Haley wasn't sure if he was serious or being an asshole. Either way she was finished.

Or maybe not. Because just as she slid her chair out, two men approached their table. Right away she knew they were police detectives. She had had more than her share of experience with law enforcement. Only this time, they only had eyes for Garrett.

"Hello again, Garrett." The older detective looked down at Garrett with a mocking smile.

Garrett rolled his eyes and turned away. To Haley, he looked as if he was about to throw up. "What in the hell is going on?"

"This has nothing to do with you, Haley." Garrett spoke as if he was attempting to reassure her.

"Hello, Ms. Chase." The younger detective flashed her a condescending smile. You might not know us, but we know who you are. I'm Detective Graves and this . . ."

"Do I look like I care what your names are?" she asked.

Detective Graves' expression was steeped in sarcasm. "Fortunately for you, this time we're here for your boyfriend."

Haley wasn't going to let the smirk on his face go. "I don't need fortune. I have money. More in my pocket than you'll ever see in your life. You can come for me all you want."

"Do you want this to be hard or easy?" Detective Falger asked Garrett.

"Now?" Garrett asked, pointing to the table to indicate he was in the middle of a meal.

"Then hard." The man shoved his hand inside his jacket and came out with a pair of handcuffs.

"Wait," Garrett pleaded, looking around. "Why am I being arrested? I have an alibi."

"No, you don't," Detective Graves said. "Ms. Jackson said she didn't even know you."

"Ms. Jackson?" All the hair on Haley's arms stood up straight. "Who are they talking about?"

Garrett looked as if he had to think for a second before saying, "Taylor. Taylor Jackson. We were hanging out. She told you, right?"

The older man flipped the cuffs in his hand. "She cut you loose, buddy."

Taylor Jackson! Haley couldn't believe it. "If you're sleeping with her I'll kill you here right now."

"Haley," Garrett pleaded. "Not now."

Detective Graves turned to Haley. "You sure can pick them, can't you, Ms. Chase? Your boyfriend here was the last person to be seen with a murdered lawyer. His car was seen leaving the lawyer's home in Beverly Hills just moments before the wife came home and found him shot right between the eyes."

For once, Haley was speechless. She looked at Garrett as he ran his hand over his face, stopping to grip his chin.

"He says he was with Ms. Jackson," the detective continued. "Says he has an air-tight alibi, but she says no."

Haley's mind was racing a hundred miles a second. There was a lot to digest here, but as she watched Garrett stand up and be handcuffed, Haley could only feel anger that that social-climbing pariah, Taylor Jackson, had found a way into her life again. So while Garrett was yesterday's news, Haley had bigger fish to fry and she would have to rescind her ceremonious dumping of him for the moment.

"She was with him," Haley said. All three men turned to her and Haley put on her acting face. "She threw it in my face earlier today."

"Did she now?" asked the younger detective. While he seemed curious, to say the older man looked skeptical was an understatement. "It appears to us that you seemed surprised she was even involved."

"I forgot. She is very forgettable." Haley maintained the "fuck you" expression on her face. If she acted as if she wanted to be helpful, she would give herself away completely. "I saw her on campus and she ran up to me with those chicken legs of hers. She wanted me to know that she had hung out with Garrett just to spite me. What she didn't know is that he had already told me he was going to meet with her about . . . what was it again?"

Garrett picked up on her nod toward him immediately. "Jobs. We talked about job opportunities."

"That's right," she said. "I remember now. Taylor wanted me to think they were on a date. I let her lay it all out for me just to make a fool of her. Then I put her in her place."

"See," Garrett said. "Can you uncuff me now?"

"It's not that easy," Detective Falger said. "Besides the fact that we don't believe her for a second, we have a warrant for your arrest, so we're executing it. If the princess here wants to make a statement, she can come too."

Haley was ready to plant her next seed. "Maybe she had something to do with this. Maybe she wanted to frame him to get back at him for turning her down. She hit on you, right? That night."

"Yeah," Garrett said.

"If you have any more stories to tell," Detective Falger said, "write a book of fairy tales. I think you're all lying. Maybe I'll be talking to you next, Ms. Chase."

"You wish," she said back.

As the men left with Garrett, Haley summoned the waiter. He cautiously came over, seeming almost frightened.

"Yes, ma'am."

"Put this dinner on my father's account," she said.

"Well . . . Ms. Chase. Your father's account with the hotel is for business lunches."

She looked at the man. His pale face went even paler as her expression darkened. "Do you want to keep your job?"

He didn't seem to hesitate. "On the account it is, Ms. Chase. Thank you."

Haley didn't know what in the hell was going on. Could Garrett actually be involved in a murder? She could see him doing something illegal, but imagined he was too much of a wimp to go that far. Whatever the case, somehow Taylor had injected herself into it and was trying to get out by denying she knew him.

Haley was going to make sure it wouldn't be that easy.

Michael watched with impatience as his brother sat across from him, looking over papers and contracts. He hadn't lifted his head in ten minutes and as every second passed, Michael felt it was a personal insult to him. They had spent the day in Manhattan poring over every minute detail of the publishing deal with the agent, Elisha Fisher. Michael was satisfied, but Carter continued to ask questions, turning what should have been a pre-celebration dinner at Jean Georges in Central Park West, into an inquisition.

The waiter waited for the garçon to remove their dinner plates and leave before approaching the table. "Will there be dessert for you tonight?"

Carter ignored the man, but Michael shook his head. "I think we're full."

"Shall I wait for the lady?"

"What lady?" Carter asked, laughing at his own insult. He looked up at the waiter, who seemed uncertain of how to respond. "It was a joke."

"It was an insult," Michael shot back, "to a woman who has done everything you've asked her to."

Carter waved the waiter away and he seemed more than happy to leave. "So you choose this woman to defend? Meanwhile you say ten times worse insults to your own wife, in front of me."

"Mind your own business." Michael leaned back on his side of the circular booth.

Carter placed the contract on the table. "When you make out with someone in public on a regular basis, you make it everyone's business."

"You just don't like her," Michael said. "Is this jealousy I'm sensing?"

"In your dreams." Carter took a sip of his Amuse Bouche wine, poured from a five-hundred-dollar bottle that Michael ordered as if the deal had been done. "Your eagerness is dangerous. I have to check it ten times over because I can see what you aren't willing to see."

"Since when did you get your psychiatrist degree?" Michael rolled his eyes.

"Sorry to take so long," Elisha Fisher said as she slid back into the booth next to Michael.

Elisha was a pretty woman by any standards. Her skin was alabaster white, which paired perfectly with her long, dark copper-colored hair. She dressed in colors that complemented her milky skin and brought out the light of her seductive green eyes. She carried herself as if she had all the money in the world. She wasn't very tall or shapely, but she was sassy, smart, and socially connected. The combination of these three qualities had gotten her farther than her Ivy League education and fortunate DNA pool could have alone.

"I saw the wife of a client in the ladies' room and had to do the kissing ass." She flipped her hair back and looked at Carter. "You know how it is."

"No," Carter said. "Actually we're the ones usually getting our asses kissed."

Elisha laughed as if she didn't notice Carter's cold tone. She leaned into Michael and kissed him on the cheek.

Carter didn't like this woman. Michael seemed temporarily enchanted with her, but despite not having a psych degree, Carter had become one of the best young lawyers in California by being able to read people without a word being spoken. The deal, if it could be worked out, would clearly be a win for Chase

Beauty, but it didn't change the fact that he didn't like this woman.

"You didn't miss anything," Michael said. "Carter is just being anal as usual."

He had stopped feeling guilty about liking the way Elisha felt next to him. He didn't love her by any standards and had originally only come on to her because of his interest in snagging this deal before anyone else could. They had only known each other for two days before they ended up in the Terrace Suite at The Plaza Hotel. Michael wasn't a fool. He knew that part of his affection for her was because she was a ticket to get back in his father's good graces, but that didn't mean he didn't like her. She did anything he wanted. And then there was that hair. He had a weakness for red hair.

Carter shot Michael a look that warned him against going further. "Elisha, I would like you to come back to L.A. one more time."

Elisha's practiced smile never faded. "What more is there to do?"

"My father isn't happy that we weren't able to meet with Alston Frist again. He seemed more than willing to meet with us the first time we were here, and he was speaking to Dad regularly in the beginning. What's changed?"

"He's moving on is what's changed," Elisha answered. "He sold the company to us because of personal matters that needed his prompt attention. He was eager to help in the beginning, but he's paying us millions to take it from here."

"And what exactly is this personal matter needing prompt attention?" Carter asked. "We've checked and there doesn't seem to be anything in his personal life going on."

"He told Dad it was a health issue," Michael said. "Dad seemed satisfied."

"A billionaire like Frist?" Carter asked. "If he's sick, we should be able to find out."

"Elisha, do you know what it is?" Michael asked.

She shook her head. "But I know that when I asked him for more specifics, his wife began to cry and ran out of the room. Either way, even though Steven Chase has a few billions, so does Alston. So whatever your money can find out, his money can keep hidden."

"You see," Carter said, waving his index finger at her, "that's what bothers me and I think my father is going to need some closure on that. You either get Frist to come to L.A. or you come and figure out how to assuage my father's concerns about him."

Elisha sighed, but never stopped smiling. She looked up at Michael and said, "Well, it isn't as if I won't love seeing you more."

Michael leaned down and pressed his lips against hers. Carter was only so patient. After a few seconds, he cleared his throat to get their attention.

"Do you mind?" he asked. "Cause I do."

Michael glared at his brother as he patted Elisha on her thigh. "Let's go. Carter will take care of the bill."

Michael thanked the flight attendant as she handed him a bottle of water. When they took off from LaGuardia, she introduced herself as Faith. She was the new flight attendant for the company that Chase Beauty hired to fly its Gulfstream IV private jet.

"Faith," he said as he accepted the bottle. "How far are we?"

"You're eager to get home to your family?" Her Texas accent matched her big blonde hair.

Carter laughed as he continued to look out the window.

Michael wanted to smack him, but he continued smiling at Faith. "Yes, I am."

"We're over Colorado right now. It will be less than an hour." She returned to the galley.

"You're such a damn hypocrite," Michael said.

Carter swung his seat around to face his brother. "Don't start with me on Avery again. You don't know what the hell you're talking about."

"Yes I do, but I'm not talking about your hypocrisy with Avery, which is still true. I'm talking about you cheating on Julia."

"Julia is not my wife," he said flatly.

"And she never will be," Michael added.

Carter gave him a sly grin. "You know something I don't?"

"No, we both know you're never going to marry her because you still think you're going to marry Avery."

"Everything comes back to Avery with you." Carter wouldn't deny it. It was the truth. "What is your obsession with Avery?"

"I never wanted Avery in your life to begin with, but let's face it, brother. If she could pick an unemployed school teacher over you, you might want to write this one off."

"Avery is the mother of my child," Carter said. "Our relationship is about Connor. That's it."

"You're a lying son of a bitch."

"Just handle your own . . ." Carter gripped the edges of the plush leather chair as the plane jerked hard. He paused a second before letting go. "Just handle your own shit."

"I do handle my . . ."

This time the jerk was so hard that Faith, back in galley, fell to the floor. Carter jumped up to get her, but she yelled for him to stop.

"No," she said. "I'm fine. Just sit down and put your seatbelt on. Now!"

Carter returned to his seat. Just as he tried to sit down the entire plane seemed to lurch as if it was going over a gigantic wave. Carter was lifted in the air and fell against the wall.

"Jesus!" Michael grabbed Carter's arm to keep him still. "What in the hell is going on?"

The captain came over the intercom trying to calm them down, but Michael and Carter weren't listening. The plane was shaking all over, and as soon as Carter was finally secured in his seat, it began to plummet.

Michael and Carter were looking at each other, but both were thinking of the women they loved and the children they lived for. They were beginning to lose consciousness as the plane continued falling. Anything that wasn't nailed down was flying around, glass was shattering into pieces and Faith began screaming.

6

Janet motioned for Maya to grab the pen and pad sitting on the granite-topped kitchen island while she instructed the caterer for Leigh's birthday event over the phone.

"I want to have the chilled, minted spring pea soup," she said as Maya nodded her understanding to write this all down. "The mini crab, avocado, and arugula crostini sound perfect."

The pasta pot on the stove began boiling over and Maya threw the pad down to tend to it. Janet reached for the pad herself, cradling the phone between her neck and shoulder.

"I also changed my mind and want you to bring back the Serrano-ham-and-tomato confit on olive bread, as well as the eggplant caviar with goat cheese and basil. That should be enough."

She blew a kiss to Steven as he entered the kitchen. He had forgone a round of golf with friends to be home with her and discuss the cruise they would be taking for their upcoming anniversary.

"Yes, that's about thirty people." Maya returned to help her, but Janet gestured that her help was no longer needed. "Please write that up and fax it back to me immediately. Thank you."

"Is the amazing Janet Chase losing her touch?" Steven said as he sat down at the table overlooking the back patio and pool. "Could you possibly be behind on your party planning duties?"

"Very funny." Janet came around the island and joined him at the table. "The party planner I hired backed out on me. She sold her business to a big company and I'm not dealing with some mass party producer. Maya, can you bring me that pitcher of lemonade in the refrigerator, and glasses? Thank you, dear."

"Trying to sweeten me up?" he asked. "There is nothing you can do to convince me to go on a cruise to Alaska."

"It's the only place we haven't been," Janet said. "It's a private line, ultra, ultra luxury."

"It's still cold. Cruises should be warm."

"We can talk about that later." Janet poured the lemonade Maya made extra sweet, just like Steven wanted it. "I want to talk to you about buying Haley the condo in Australia she wants."

"I'm not buying Haley anything," Steven said. "I just got a thirty-thousand-dollar bill from a catering company she hired for a party on the yacht that she didn't tell me about, let alone get my permission for."

Janet offered the glass to her husband. "She can pay that bill. I'll make sure she does. But she can't buy that condo."

"Why not?" Steven knew exactly what all his children were taking from their trust funds, each having several million dollars. Until they were twenty-five, it was one hundred and fifty thousand a year. After twenty-five, it was two hundred and fifty thousand. and after thirty, they could take whatever they wanted. "She has money and she never spends it," he continued. "She lives here rent free, drives a car I bought, uses our credit cards and takes every chance she can get to put her lifestyle on any account that comes back to me for payment."

"The condo is three million dollars, Steven. She doesn't have that. If she did, she would buy it. She wants it."

"She wants everything."

"True, but this is the first time she's wanted to own something that has value. Do we really want to deny her the privilege of owning property? I think we should support her."

Janet took a sip. "Or you can allow her a one-time withdrawal of three million dollars from her trust fund."

The phone rang and Maya left the stove to answer it.

Steven didn't enjoy being taken advantage of by Haley yet again, but he wanted to make his wife happy and he didn't want to spend the precious time he had with her, arguing over their daughter's constant demands.

"I'll make you a deal." He leaned in with a sly smile. "You tell Haley that I'll let her pay for that condo herself, as well as the upkeep, taxes, and management, with her own money. If she still wants to do it, I'll contact the trust."

He knew she wouldn't. Haley always complained about not being able to get enough out of her trust fund, but when it came down to it, she didn't want to spend her own money on anything.

"I'll do that," Janet said. "And I think she'll surprise . . ."

They were both jolted by Maya's blood curdling scream. Steven and Janet shot up from their seats. Maya's hand, holding the phone, fell limp to her side as a look of horror came over her face.

Taylor saw Sean hurrying up the walkway to the Jackson home and she knew he was going to go off. When she'd called him to tell him what had happened, there was a long silence on the other end followed by, "We can't do this over the phone. We need to be face-to-face. I'll check out what I can with the BHPD."

"Don't start on me!" she yelled as soon as he entered the living room.

"It's a murder case, Taylor!"

"Don't let Mom and Dad know," she pleaded, her hands entwined in prayer. "Just don't tell them."

"This is going to be a high-profile case." Sean sat down in his father's favorite recliner, trying to calm himself. "This guy was a rich lawyer with very rich clients. What in the hell have you gotten yourself into?"

"It's not my fault," she said. "Garrett tricked me. He used me as an alibi."

"How can he do that?"

"He paid me." Taylor could see her older brother's head about to explode. "It's a long story, but it makes sense."

"It better."

"Well, you know I've been looking for ways to make money and there is this alibi company." Embarrassed, Taylor couldn't look him in the eye as she spoke, so she looked down at her lap. "I thought I might get a job with them."

"Shut up, Taylor."

Taylor's head shot up. "I know it sounds crazy, but hear me out."

"No." Sean stood up, looking out the front window at the two detectives making their way to the front door. "I mean, shut up. Don't say anything until we can get you a lawyer."

Taylor felt a sense of panic press against her chest as she saw the same detectives that had approached her on campus. They were coming to her parents' house in Baldwin Hills? "We? You mean Mom and Dad? Do they have to know?"

Sean walked to the door. "I don't think you have a choice. Is there anything incriminating in this house?"

"What?"

"Answer me!" Sean grabbed the door handle. "We won't let them in if there is something . . ."

"No!" Taylor wondered if Sean actually thought she could be involved in a murder.

Sean greeted the detectives. He'd known Graves briefly from L.A. County detective training sessions. The older man was a complete stranger but he looked like all the other older detectives in the bureau: impatient, tired, and waiting to retire.

Detective Graves greeted Taylor and Sean and introduced Detective Falger to Sean, before saying, "I'm sorry to have to bother you again, Ms. Jackson, but we have a problem with your story."

"Story?" Sean asked. "Sounds like you're coming into this prejudiced."

"No offense, detective," Falger said in a fatherly tone. "But information has come to light that leads us to believe Ms. Jackson isn't being completely honest with us."

Taylor's stomach began to turn and she held her hands together tight, to hide that they were shaking. "I don't know what you're talking about. I told you that I . . ."

"We talked to Ms. Huffington," Graves said.

Taylor felt as if she'd been hit across the head. They went after Claire? The one person she chose to verify the lie!

"What does she have to do with this?" Sean asked.

"She was with Ms. Jackson when we questioned her before." Graves nodded toward Falger. "My partner here noticed that Ms. Huffington seemed uncomfortable about the whole conversation, so we thought we'd talk to her alone."

"How do you even know her?" Taylor asked.

"We took down the license plate of the car she got in on the campus lot." Graves began shaking his head as if he was genuinely regretting what he was about to say. "Your friend tried to lie for you, but she couldn't stick it out. She broke down and told us that you had mentioned you knew Garrett Collins and had recently spent time with him."

"I was ly . . ."

"Taylor!" Sean held up his hand to stop her. He turned to the detectives. "We're going to call a lawyer and get back to you."

"There's also the issue of Haley Chase," Graves added. He seemed amused by the widening eyes of both Sean and Taylor.

"What does she have to do with anything?" Sean asked.

"She says you blabbed to her about your relationship with Garrett too. That you admitted to being with him, to make her jealous."

"Why would she be jealous?" Taylor asked, thoroughly confused.

"Garrett Collins is her boyfriend."

Taylor's knees gave out on her as she fell back on the sofa. This couldn't be real.

"And Ms. Huffington told us that you and Ms. Chase hate each other." Graves said. "Is that true?"

Sean was shaking his head in disbelief. When he looked at the expression on his sister's face, he could tell that she'd had no idea. How could their paths cross again? Was this family cursed?

"She's lying," Taylor said. "I didn't even know she was . . ."

"Enough," Sean said abruptly.

"Out of respect for your father," Falger said, "we'll end this here and let you take the next step."

"Thank you." Sean motioned toward the door in a hint for them to leave.

They quickly followed suit after the younger detective gave Taylor a suspicious glare.

"I'm screwed," was all Taylor could say after Sean closed the door behind the detectives. "*Haley?*"

Sean suddenly felt a lot older than twenty-six as he turned to his sister and said, "From the beginning and don't leave anything out."

Avery could see through her husband's façade. It started in the morning, when Anthony got up and went running. He only did this when he was completely frustrated. This usually happened after an encounter with Carter, but that wasn't the case this time.

When he came down from a shower and joined her as she made lunch in the kitchen, he shared the good news. A possible research position in the statistics department of UCLA. It was the first good bite in a while, and Avery put on her best supportive-wife face despite knowing that the position was too junior for someone of his tenure, and Anthony wouldn't be happy doing anything other than teaching.

"There might be some possible speaking engagements." Anthony reached for the plates and handed them to Avery.

Avery placed the carrots on the plate and added the dip. "That sounds great, baby. You love speaking about stats."

"I know it bores you to death," he said.

Avery turned to him with a smile, showing the love she truly felt for him. "That's not true. I love it. I don't understand one word, but I can hear the pep in your tone. You're happy."

Anthony attempted a wide smile, but never quite made it. He sighed and leaned his head against the cabinet. "So why don't I want it, baby?"

Avery put her knife down and came over to wrap her arms around him. She nestled her head on his chest. "You don't have to take it if you don't want to."

"But that isn't true, is it?" He let her go and went over to the table in the middle of the modest white kitchen. Grabbing the opened envelopes on top of it, he said, "Because these bills keep coming and they're being paid by Carter Chase."

"Don't start that," Avery warned. "What should we do? Put all the money away and live on the street? The Chases would certainly try to take Connor away then."

"Why do I get the distinct feeling that losing Connor isn't the real reason why you don't want to make waves with Carter?"

Hearing Connor making loud noises in the living room was a welcomed distraction. "Anthony, we were having a good day. Don't ruin it, please."

Anthony shrugged like a sullen teenager as he made his way to the ringing phone on the counter top.

When Avery entered the living room, she saw that Connor had used her Cheerios to decorate rather than eat. She knelt down to pick as much of them up as she could. When she stood back up, she thought she heard the name "Chase," but assumed she just had Carter on the brain. Only when she turned to the television, pictures of both Carter and Michael were prominently displayed next to the head of a talking news reporter.

Avery rushed to the television and turned up the volume.

"The private jet was returning to Los Angeles from New York when it experienced mechanical problems and crashed in a town about two hours from Denver."

The Cheerios fell out of Avery's hand as she fell to her knees. Hysteria teased at the edge of all her nerves as she tried to comprehend what she was hearing.

"There are not a lot of details," the reporter continued, "but aviation officials confirmed that at least one person is dead."

Avery's mouth opened and she whispered his name. "Carter."

She grabbed her stomach and leaned over, feeling everything inside of her rip apart. In that second, she was faced with her complete and utter love for him, unable and unwilling to fool even herself.

Avery's breathing picked up pace as the reality set in. The reporter was talking about Carter! Her Carter! She felt her body shaking all over as a wickedly cold chill rushed through her.

The reporter continued. "The Chase family has been compared to the famous Kennedys countless times because of their wealth, power, celebrity, and philanthropy, as well as their various scandals. Unfortunately, it appears that they might also be resembling the famous Kennedys when it comes to tragedy. Both Chase brothers have children."

Avery gasped and swung around to look at her baby—Carter's baby. She couldn't stop the tears caused by her fear of the pain that this loss would mean to her child. To her.

Anthony came into the living room with the phone held up and a confused expression on his face. "Hey, it's Leigh and she's really upset. What's going on?"

When Sean turned the corner in View Park where the Chase Mansion spanned almost half the entire block, he hadn't expected to see what he saw. There was press everywhere, and a few police cars trying to control the reporters, cameramen and various on-lookers from the neighborhood. The press was always interested in the Chases, but this was mayhem.

He drove up to the spot where the police were trying to keep back the onlookers, and got out of his car. He saw all his old buddies at the View Park Police Department and gestured for Stewart Tillman, a beat cop who spent most of his time doing nothing but keeping up with the locals.

"What in the heck is going on?" he asked.

"You don't know?" Stewart asked, his hands stuck in the pockets of a uniform that was at least one size too small. "What are you doing here?"

"I have business," he answered. He didn't like discussing the Chase family with his former co-workers, because they all had temporarily lost respect for him when he'd let his obsession with Haley wreak havoc in his professional life.

"Carter and Michael Chase were in a plane accident. Their jet crashed in Colorado and somebody is dead. They haven't said who yet, but it's getting crazy over here."

Sean was speechless at first. The Chase family had been nothing but a nightmare for him, but he knew what this family meant to the black community. Not just the black community in California or the upper class—black people all over had an unexplainable admiration for the Chases. What would happen if both sons were dead? It seemed impossible, as if they were somehow exempt from this kind of stuff.

"I gotta get in," he said.

After making it through the press, Sean went through the black iron gates that kept the world at bay while offering a glimpse of the front of the massive red-brick, colonial-style house with its columned portico. When he got to the front door, he knocked, but no one came. He waited for a while, but reached for the knob and opened the door himself.

Once inside the expansive foyer, he called out again and this time Maya turned up from around the corner. Her face was haggard and her eyes bloodshot. She didn't ask him why he was there or how he got in. She simply said, "Haley is out by the pool."

When he reached the pool, the sun glared in his eyes. It took him a while to find her, but she was sitting in a lawn chair in a pair of cotton shorts and a T-shirt, with sunglasses covering her eyes. She was staring at the phone in her hand and didn't see him approach. She was in another world until he said her name.

Haley looked up, trying to come out of her haze. She thought she was seeing things when the image of Sean stood before her. She took her glasses off for a second to make sure he was really there. Yes, it was Sean and she, Haley, never thought she'd say it again, but she was glad he was there.

"Have you heard anything?" he asked as he grabbed another chair and slid it toward hers. She had only had her glasses off for a second, but he could swear she had been crying. Haley crying.

Haley shook her head as she held her phone up. "They won't say anything. They wouldn't let me come."

"Your Mom and Dad?"

She nodded. "They were already on their way to a jet someone let them borrow, before I found out. Then the press knew and all hell broke loose. But I'm supposed to just wait."

"Not just wait," Sean said. "Hope. You can hope, too."

She looked at him as if he was a fool, but she found comfort in his words anyway. There was a part of her that still cared about Sean. She hated that part, the weak part of her that had allowed her to fall in love that one time. But she hated Sean even more for dumping her. She would never forgive him for letting her mother convince him to let her go.

"Have you talked to what's-her-name?" Haley asked.

Sean looked confused for only a second before catching up. "Her name is Avery and no, I haven't. I just found out five seconds ago. I haven't been listening to the news. I've been busy, but I do need to call Avery. As a matter of fact, I'm going to do that right now if you don't mind."

"Wait a second." Haley sat up straight. "If you just found out about it, then why did you come here?"

"I needed to talk to you about something else. Taylor and this mess with Garrett Collins."

Haley's mouth dropped. She thought he was here to comfort her, but he was only here to bother her about his little skank sister? "Are you kidding me? Do you know what I'm going through right now?"

"I just told you that I didn't." Sean knew Haley enough to know a firestorm was coming. "I know now is not the time."

"But you still came, right?" Haley asked. "Fuck you and your little sister."

He was so used to her immature name-calling that it didn't even phase him. "Haley, whatever game you were trying to play, its getting serious and you . . ."

"Get out!" Haley reached for the first thing she could find, a half-empty bottle of water and threw it at him.

The bottle hit him in the chest and water splashed all over his face. "Dammit, Haley."

"How dare you!" she screamed. "My brothers could be dead and you're harassing me? How did you get in here anyway? No one is supposed to get in!"

She was getting louder and louder with each word. "I didn't mean to . . ."

"What are you doing?"

Sean turned around and stood up at the same time. Leigh had joined them and she was clearly distressed over the situation her sister was in.

"What are you doing to her?" Leigh rushed to Haley's side. "Calm down, Haley."

"He's harassing me over his stupid sister!"

"I'm leaving," Sean said, backing away. "I'm sorry. I didn't know until . . . I'm sorry. I'm leaving."

"Please do that," Leigh said.

Regretting that he even mentioned his sister, Sean rushed back through the house and out the front. He could breathe again. There was something about that house that cut off his oxygen whenever he was there.

Having borrowed the private jet of a close friend, Janet and Steven were able to arrive at The Medical Center of Aurora, in Colorado, within two hours of leaving California. Both had been on the phone the entire time. There was chaos at the hospital as the press got wind that the Chase men were there. Steven and Janet appreciated their status in America, but knew that the price was that there was no privacy in their lives, whether good things happened, or bad.

The only thing that kept Janet sane was the knowledge that both her boys were still alive. The hospital confirmed that the pilot had died due to internal bleeding and the flight attendant was in serious condition, but was expected to recover nicely. Both Carter and Michael had survived. They would not say more until the family arrived and Carter and Michael gave permission to release their information.

They were greeted by the president and CEO of the hospital, an attractive woman named Gloria Salves. She didn't hesitate to lead them toward the One North building where all the special suites for high-profile patients were.

"Your sons are being taken care of by our best staff," she reassured as she sprinted to keep up with them. "These are large, well-appointed rooms with upscale décor and treatments. The menu is gourmet and there are family accommodations as well."

She stopped outside a treated-pinewood door. "Here we are."

As Janet rushed past the two of them, Steven asked Gloria, "They're in the same room?"

Gloria nodded. "They were in separate rooms, but wanted to be here. This is our biggest room."

"Please get the doctor," he requested.

Janet paid no attention to the size and décor of the room. These were her babies. The first thing she saw was Carter, lying back in a bed, looking very tired. Already crying, she ran to him, but just before she wrapped her arms around him, she stopped.

"Can I hug you?" she asked. "I don't want to hurt you."

"I'm fine, Mom." Carter winced in slight pain as his mother hugged him tightly. He didn't care. It felt great. Just hours ago, he thought he'd never see her again.

Janet turned around and grabbed the divider curtain and flung it away, revealing Michael in a bed on the other side.

"Hey, Mom." Michael spoke in a low, slow voice.

"He's drugged up," Carter said.

Michael wasn't too drugged up to scream out when his mother hugged him.

Janet gasped and stepped back. "What did I do? What did I do?"

"Bruised . . . ribs," he answered. He lifted his weak arm and pointed to the glass of water on the tray next to the bed. "Thirsty."

As Janet rushed around the bed to retrieve the glass and straw and help Michael, Steven approached Carter's bed. Carter had rarely seen his father in a moment of weakness. To show emotions, for males at least, was considered a weakness in this family.

But Carter could see the emotion in his father's eyes and it triggered the little boy inside of him. King Chase was what all the children had named him; a dictator with a soft spot only for his own wife. But every now and then, Steven let the love they all knew he had for them, even though he didn't show it often, come through.

Carter reached his hand out and Steven placed his own on top. He leaned in and planted a very quick kiss on Carter's forehead like he always did when Carter was a child. The last time he'd gotten this much affection from Steven was the day he found out he was accepted at Harvard Law School.

"You okay?" Steven asked. "You had me scared there."

Carter smiled. "Sorry about that."

"You don't look so good." Steven could feel emotion welling

in his throat. These were his sons and he'd almost lost them. How would he have gone on?

Carter slid the bedsheet down, looking at himself. "I have some cuts from the broken glass that was flying around. Michael got the worst of it."

Steven made his way to Michael's bed only a few feet away. Janet was trying to give him the drink, but the straw kept falling out of his mouth and water was spilling all over. He looked like a child and it reached deep inside of Steven.

Michael had a glassy-eyed look as he smiled for his father. He could feel Steven's strong hand on his shoulders and the squeeze. "I'm all right. I really am."

Janet handed the glass of water to Steven and buried her face in her hands. She was sobbing uncontrollably now. Michael tried to reach out to comfort her, but he didn't have the strength.

Steven wrapped his arms around his wife comfortingly. "It's okay, dear. Look at them. They're fine."

"I know," Janet said. "It's just that . . ."

"I know," Steven said. The news that they were alive had sent a wave of joy over them, but the reality that it could've been the opposite still blew them both away.

There was a quick knock on the door followed by the entrance of a man in a doctor's white coat. He headed straight for Steven and held his hand out for a shake. "Mr. Chase, I'm Dr. Edwards. I'm glad you could get here so soon."

"Thank you for your help, doctor."

"I didn't do much," Dr. Edwards said. "Your sons were very lucky. Carter here has some cuts and bruises and a little whiplash that will go away in a few days. The concussion is a little more serious."

"Concussion?" Steven turned to Carter. "You didn't mention that."

Carter shrugged. "I guess I forgot."

"He's doing fine now, but was a little disoriented earlier." Dr. Edwards looked at the chart in his hand. "He might suffer some short-term memory loss until the swelling goes down, but the only real thing I think he'll have problems with are the headaches."

"What do you mean?" Janet asked, having recovered from her breakdown. "Like migraines?"

Dr. Edwards nodded. "He needs to be observed for twenty-four hours, but if he doesn't experience any blackouts or additional disorientation, he can go home."

"We want them transferred to Cedars-Sinai as soon as possible," Steven said.

Dr. Edwards didn't seem too happy to hear that. "I'll see what we can do. Michael here got the worst of it. He has a broken leg and bruised ribs. It's a clean, easy break, so I'm looking at six weeks with the cast. He's going to have some trouble moving for a while and will need to wear a pad around his ribs. He's on painkillers now and he'll likely need them for a few days, but I'd prefer no longer than that."

"Sounds good," Steven said. "Doctor, let's work on getting them to Cedars as soon as possible."

As Steven left with the doctor, Janet came over to Carter. "Are you having memory problems, sweetie?"

Carter shook his head. "I know everything I think I should know. You, Dad, Michael, Leigh and the kid. What else is there to know?"

"Good." She leaned in and kissed his cheek. "You don't need anything else."

"And there's Avery of course," Carter added. "We're engaged and we're going to get married soon."

Janet's eyes widened only briefly before she composed herself and spoke sympathetically. "Carter . . . I . . . You aren't . . ."

Carter laughed. "I'm just kidding, Mom."

Janet slapped him on the arm. "Don't do that. That isn't funny."

"Kimberly."

Janet turned around in response to Michael calling for his wife. She walked over to her son with a look of apprehension. "You're on painkillers, baby. Just rest."

"Where did she go?" he asked.

Janet's shoulders dropped in disappointment. "She's not here, Michael. It's just me and Dad."

"She was here," Michael said. He saw her face as clear as day just moments ago.

"It's the drugs, idiot," Carter called out. "The doctor told us twice only Mom and Dad were on the plane."

Michael was shaking his head, trying to come up with the right words to explain that he'd just seen Kimberly, but not finding them. "She's here."

"You can see her when you get to L.A.," Janet said, trying to hide the disdain she felt at his need for her. "She and the boys will be there waiting for you."

"I want to see her now," Michael said. "She's my wife."

Janet reached out to her son, placing a gentle hand on his arm. "She's not here, baby. You don't need her. I'm here."

Cedars-Sinai Medical Center in Beverly Hills is known around the world as being one of the best hospitals in America, and the hospital of choice for the rich and famous in L.A. Cedars is popular because it has the best doctors, the best security, and luxury suites that could rival a four-star hotel. And while Carter and Michael were being transferred into their own luxury hospital suites, Steven was on the Plaza level, where the press gathered to get the latest on who and what.

"My wife, Janet, and I appreciate the concerns of the many who have called Chase Beauty, the hospital, and have sent flowers." Steven didn't like to sit down at comfortable press tables. He stood tall and looked strong in a distinguished and expensive suit, looking directly in the eyes of the press, not even blinking as cameras flashed.

"Our sons are fine," he continued. "A few cuts and bruises, but they are only in the hospital for twenty-four-hour observation. They will both be going home tomorrow. My wife and daughter, Leigh, are with them now and my daughter, Haley, and I will be joining them shortly."

Haley was standing next to him. She didn't want to, but her mother made her. She'd taken advantage of a weak moment. Haley was so happy to see Carter and Michael when they arrived at the hospital, she was amenable to almost anything. She knew the script. Her entire life she had smiled for the camera and held her head high in the manner a Chase, even in the face of tragedy or pain, would be expected to.

"Right now," Steven said, "we ask that you all focus on Anderson Davis. He was a good pilot and a better man. He left a wife and son behind. His family needs our support and that is what we plan to give. That's all for now."

"Mr. Chase!" one reporter called out before Steven had a chance to turn away. "What about the crash? Do we know what happened?"

"Not yet," he answered. "There will be an investigation. We'll let you know. Thank you."

Haley was taught to stand until her father passed her and then turn and follow him. It was all a little show, but just as she turned, someone called her name. She looked into the crowd, barely able to see anything.

"Since you're here, can you answer a question about your involvement, if any, in the murder investigation of Justin Ursh?"

How in the hell did he know she was involved?

"No comment." She'd said that a million times.

"Is it true that your boyfriend is a person of interest?" someone else asked.

Haley didn't answer. She turned to leave but was halted by her father, who stood like a stone sculpture. His disapproving and damning eyes bore into her and Haley felt like screaming. He'd been looking at her like this her entire life. She couldn't stand this man who only chose to acknowledge that she existed in order to scold her.

"I didn't do anything," she said to him, even though she knew he wouldn't believe her. He never believed anything she said. She didn't wait for a response and she didn't care about press etiquette. She passed right by him and stormed into the hospital hallway.

Thinking she was escaping the fire, Haley felt a brick in her stomach when she saw who was waiting for her in the hallway. "What in the hell are you doing here?"

"I'm sorry about earlier," Sean said. "But I . . ."

"No, I'm serious. How in the hell did you get over here? There's supposed to be security."

"The security is on your brothers' floor, not here." Sean hesitated as he saw Steven appear from the press area. "And I have this, remember?"

Haley made a smacking sound with her lips as she placed both hands on her hips. "Do you think I give a damn about that badge?"

"What is this about?" Steven asked as he approached.

"I know your family is going through a lot right now, Mr. Chase," Sean said, "and I know we are all, especially my sister, happy that they're okay."

"Thank you." Steven took hold of Haley's arm to bring her along, but she jerked away from him.

"Don't touch me," Haley snapped.

Steven seemed unfazed by her reaction. "What do you want, detective?"

"I hate to bother you now, but Haley has gotten herself and my sister, Taylor, involved in a murder investigation and she's causing a lot of trouble."

"The murder of that lawyer," Steven said.

Sean nodded. "We know she wasn't involved or anything, but she has volunteered herself to be involved and, in effect, involved my sister."

"Your sister made her own bed," Haley said. "She lied first."

"We're aware of that," Sean said. "But your lie makes her attempt to tell the truth look false."

"What lie?" Steven asked.

As Sean told him about how Haley provided an alibi to back up Garrett at Taylor's expense, Steven's expression never changed, despite the fact that another emergency from Haley was not something he could deal with right now.

"Just tell me this," Steven said. "What do you want her to do?"

"Hey?" Haley said. "I'm right here, you know. I decide what I do. No one else, and I'm not going to bother with his little social-climbing sister."

"This isn't just about Taylor," Sean said, although she was all he thought about since their parents and the family's lawyer had escorted her into the police station only moments ago. "This is about your safety as well."

"Jesus Christ." Steven turned to Haley. "I'm going to send you to Europe again. I can't deal with this now."

"I didn't ask you for anything," Haley said.

"What danger?" Steven asked.

"I was able to get a glimpse of some of the file," Sean said. "The firm that Garrett works for is very shady and there is no doubt he is somehow involved in this murder. There are already signs of a cover-up, and the people the police suspect are criminals. They will do whatever they have to, to get rid of loose ends."

"She'll be down at the station tomorrow," Steven said. "Right now, we have family business. Come on, Haley."

Looking at Haley being ordered around like a child, Sean hated himself for feeling some compassion for this girl. Daddy issues were behind a lot of who she was, why she hated everyone and showed such disdain for men. Even though she knew that her father had broken every rule to protect her, she continued to hate him.

"This is serious, Haley." He looked into her eyes and was reminded of how beautiful she was. He remembered how he loved feeling her soft, auburn hair against his skin and hearing the sound of her sexy, raspy voice. "These people are dangerous, and if you don't do right by my sister I won't be around to save your ass a third time."

Haley rolled her eyes to give the impression she didn't care, but as Sean walked away, she felt a little tightening in her stomach. Sean had saved her life twice now. He killed a drug dealer just before the dealer had tried to kill her. Less than a year later, he shot her ex-boyfriend just seconds before that boyfriend was going to blow her brains away with a nine millimeter.

Was she going to need him again?

7

Standing right outside Carter's hospital room, Avery's heart was pounding so hard, she was sure it could be heard a mile away. The gamut of emotions she had been experiencing since that morning, had taken its toll. She wasn't sure she could survive when she'd thought he was gone. She could barely stand for the longest time. She wasn't hysterical, but she was devastated inside. All she could do for an hour was hold tight the baby, who was oblivious to the fact that the man who loved her more than any man ever would, could be dead.

But he couldn't be. Avery had imagined Carter being in her life forever, and not just because of Connor. She wanted him in her life. The thought of a life without him was too much to bear.

Avery was finally able to pull herself together when Anthony walked in on her in their bedroom in the middle of a prayer. It was a silent prayer and she hadn't even known he was standing there, but when she opened her eyes, he was the first thing she saw, and he knew she was praying for Carter despite the fact that she had told him her concern was only for Connor.

Nikki had rushed over and kept Avery calm until she got the call from Leigh that Carter was alive. She buried her face in her mother's chest and cried for a few moments before taking hold of Connor and kissing her incessantly. With every second that passed, Avery grew more and more anxious to see him, to touch him.

He called her just before getting on the jet to return to California. She could tell that he was still a little shaken and everything inside of her wanted to comfort him. Both Anthony and Nikki were standing next to her when he called, so she made it brief and agreed to get Connor to the hospital as soon as possible when he got to Cedars-Sinai. Nikki had taken her to the hospital because she couldn't concentrate well enough to drive.

And here she was, standing outside his suite, afraid of her own emotions in his presence. She took a few deep breaths, smiling at Connor, who was falling half-asleep in her arms. She felt titillating excitement creep through her unexpectedly, as she opened the door and saw him sitting upright in the bed. He was, as usual, looking down at his BlackBerry. Her heart screamed to her how much she loved him; how much she would have lost if she had never been able to see him again.

She started toward him, and when he looked up, she was frozen in place. Her breath caught at the sight of the bruise on his forehead. She hadn't realized she was no longer moving until he spoke.

"Do you expect me to kiss her from here?" Carter asked, all but ready to jump right out of this bed for his girls. Both of them.

Avery laughed as she approached the bed. She could see the bandages on his arm, but she was more focused on the bruise on his head.

"Does it hurt?" she asked.

Carter nodded. "But it's getting better. Especially now that you're here."

She looked into his eyes and remembered what it felt like to love him completely and feel no guilt or apprehension about it. Those were some of the happiest days of her life.

His eyes held hers, while his heart told him this was real. For seconds in that plane, this image of that nose, those eyes and especially those luscious full lips, had flashed before him and he'd wanted to reach for her. But she wasn't within his reach. Now she was, and for the first time since that plane started going down, Carter felt like everything was going to be all right.

Neither of them knew how long they stared at each other, but Connor's cooing and reaching for her daddy broke them both out of their trance.

"Is this my little princess?" he asked as he reached for her. She jumped into his arms and he immediately kissed her on both her cheeks. He held her out in front of him, looking at her and feeling himself overcome. His baby; his whole world and he almost . . .

Avery felt her breath being taken away as Carter's eyes began to fill with tears. When he held Connor tightly to his chest, Avery couldn't control herself. She reached out for him, placing one hand on his arm as she leaned in and whispered, "It's going to be okay."

Carter looked up at Avery, her face only inches from his. "I thought I would never see either of you again. Just thinking about it makes me . . ."

"I know." Her finger touched his cheek, wiping a tear away. She had never seen him cry before. "But I knew you had to be okay. I looked at her and knew you would see her go to school, fall in love, get married."

"Conquer the world," he added. "She is a Chase after all."

She smiled, letting her own tears fall to her cheeks as she enjoyed just feeling love and being so grateful. She gently took his face in her hands and felt the power of his presence engulf her. He always had that effect on her. She would get within feet of him and everything else disappeared.

Carter leaned forward an inch and his lips brushed against hers before kissing her. It had been so long since he tasted the softness of her lips, like sweet red wine, he imagined he would be rabid the moment he could drink from them again. But he wasn't. He was overcome with a sense of emotion and need that went beyond sex. This was reassurance that he was still alive, and she was the only person who could give it to him.

Avery felt a sexual sensitivity rush through her entire body as she kissed him. She felt herself dizzying, as if her feet had left the ground. It was so sweet and perfect, just as she remembered. She had missed this more than she could even comprehend. It had been a long time, but she had never forgotten the way his lips, and only his lips, could make her feel. No one else . . .

Suddenly remembering herself, Avery separated from him and leaned away. Her hands slowly left his face. Their eyes continued to hold each other as Carter leaned back. Avery couldn't hide that she was flushed. She knew her cheeks were so red it could be seen over her chocolate skin. Her hand went to her chest and she could feel her breathing.

And she could not tear her eyes away from his.

"I'm sorry," Carter said, even though he wasn't.

"It's okay," Avery said, her voice catching. "I . . . We're . . . How can anyone know what to do or say when . . ."

He held his hand out to her and she placed her hand in his. They didn't grasp each other or try to hold on. Her fingers merely trailed his palm before lifting away. She was too frightened to touch any longer.

"Ya!" Connor yelled as she reached out for her mommy.

Avery was finally able to turn away from Carter to focus on her little angel. "That's Mommy for now. I've noticed just in the past few days she says 'ya' and points to me."

"That's progress." Carter kissed Connor once more before handing her back to Avery. "I've still got a thousand on her saying 'daddy' before 'mommy.' "

Avery nestled Connor on her left hip. "You don't have a chance."

"You're probably right." He reached out and tickled the bottom of Connor's foot and she screamed in joy. God, he loved that sound. "I'd pick you first over me too."

"How sweet."

Julia's cold smile took the temperature in the room down about twenty degrees. She walked toward them, stopping at the end of Carter's bed.

Avery didn't care. She was too happy to let anything or anyone get to her. "Hello, Julia."

"Avery." She nodded a hello, before turning to Carter. "How are you feeling?"

"I'm great," Carter said, and he'd never meant it more. "I'm just great."

Julia's smile was having a hard time holding as she seemed to understand what he was saying. Avery didn't want to ruin the moment. It was too wonderful.

"I guess we'll get going," Avery said.

"You just got here."

"Visiting hours are almost over anyway," Julia said. "Besides, I'm sure Avery's tired. She certainly looks like she's had a hard day."

"We all have," Avery said, not bothering to look in Julia's direction. "We'll come back tomorrow?"

"He's leaving in the morning," Julia said. "I'll be here to take him home. To our home."

Avery continued to ignore her, staying focused on Carter.

"Why don't you come over tomorrow in the afternoon?" he asked. "Everyone's going to be there in the morning but they're all going over to Michael's in the afternoon. I'll be able to spend a little bit more time with my angel."

"Yes," Julia said. "We'll be happy to see Connor then."

Avery took Connor's arm and waved it in the air. "Say ' 'bye Daddy.' "

Connor said nothing, seeming bored with the situation. It was definitely time to go. Without a nap today, she was about to get extremely cranky.

Avery never glanced at Julia as she left, but she felt Julia's eyes on her. She wondered exactly when Julia had joined them and what she'd seen and heard. But she felt no guilt. It was natural for her to kiss Carter. He was the father of her child, and she had thought he'd died. They were both overcome with emotion for their baby. It was nothing more than that.

"I've looked over your X-rays." Leigh sat on the end of Michael's hospital bed, her hand on his cast. "I told them I was your doctor. It's a good, clean break. You'll be fine."

"I'm already fine," Michael said. "I wish you'd tell her that."

He was talking about their mother, who was sitting in a chair at the side of the bed, still looking apprehensive.

"I'm fine," Janet said. "I'm just worried about you moving, with that big thing around your middle."

"It's just a standard pad," Leigh said. "It's the same thing he wore when he was a little kid in Jujitsu class."

"Daddy!" Evan ran over to the bed and began jumping in place. "Can I break my leg so I can get a cast too?"

Michael laughed. "No, buddy. One broken leg in the family at a time."

"I'm next then." He rushed away to the window to rejoin Daniel, who was playing with his action-figure toys.

"On that note," Leigh said, standing up, "I have to go. The clinic needs me."

After Leigh was gone, Janet suddenly remembered she had forgotten to update her on the plans for her birthday dinner. She promised Michael she would be right back and went after her daughter. The last thing on Janet's mind when she exited the room was what was before her. If she hadn't looked up in time to stop, she would have run right into Kimberly.

As both women eyed each other, there was no misreading their reactions. Janet had hated Kimberly from the start because she was ghetto trash, and Kimberly had hated Janet from the start because she had done everything she could to remind Kimberly that she didn't belong, every day since they'd met.

Then there was all the other stuff. Kimberly had tried once to tear Janet and Steven's marriage apart by bringing back an ex-lover of Janet's and with him, very bad memories. But Janet had prevailed, and found some joy in the fact that it had fractured Michael and Kimberly's marriage.

Janet had hoped that Michael would tire of Kimberly and the iron-clad prenuptial agreement would assure she couldn't take his money when he got rid of her. But he wouldn't get rid of her. He was completely taken in by her exceptional beauty, and Janet would always blame Kimberly for almost bringing the entire Chase legacy into the gutter with her.

And yet, she was still here. For some insane reason, Michael would not divorce her. He seemed to hate her, clearly hate her, but she was still here.

Most encounters between Janet and Kimberly began and ended

with insults and threats. A few times, they'd ended with straight fighting, hair pulling, and slapping. But Janet didn't have the energy today. She had almost had her entire world destroyed.

Kimberly caught Janet's eyes just for a moment before looking past her and continuing into the room. In her dreams, this woman would burst spontaneously into flames. Janet had made her life a living hell, and every time Kimberly tried to break free or enact her revenge, she only made things worse for herself.

Kimberly used the distraction of her sons running to her and pulling at her legs, to avert her gaze from Michael as she entered. But ultimately she would have to look at him and when she did, damn if she didn't feel something.

Seeing him there looking weak and vulnerable, she should be happy. She should want to take advantage of this. It wasn't as if he didn't do it to her every chance he got. The hate and resentment that had built up in her heart for this man over the last six months frightened her at times.

"Daddy said I can break my leg next." Evan took his mother's hand and led her to the bed. It was as if he could sense she was reluctant to approach.

It was moments like this, when she walked into that hospital room and he first laid eyes on her, that Michael was reminded of how devastatingly beautiful Kimberly was. He resented that beauty because he wasn't sure he could live without seeing it.

He smiled at her as she sat in the chair that Janet had previously occupied. She didn't smile back. She just sort of looked at him with a kindness in her eyes that he hadn't seen in what seemed like centuries. Or was it pity?

"It's nice to finally see you," he said.

"I'm here to pick the boys up," she answered in a flat tone. She felt somewhat compelled to touch him, but resisted. She begged herself to remember how he treated her. "They have swimming practice in an hour."

"They can skip it today, can't they?" he asked.

"They're competing in a few months, Michael. They have to practice now more than ever."

Michael nodded, not wanting or willing to resist. "I thought maybe when I come home tomorrow, we could have a nice family dinner out on the patio. Marisol can make one of her Mexican dishes and . . ."

"What are you doing?" Kimberly asked.

Michael tilted his brows, looking at her uncertainly. "I'm just trying to spend time with my family. I almost died, Kimberly."

"Don't talk to me like I'm your wife."

"You are my wife," he responded angrily. "Jesus, Kimberly. For one second can you just . . . I don't know, pretend? I need to . . ."

Kimberly was touched by the sense of disillusionment in his voice and regrettably found no joy in his pain. But she wouldn't fall for it, either. He had made her cold and emotionless in his presence.

"So you want me to pretend like we are happily married because you got a little boo-boo?"

Michael leaned forward and looked into her eyes earnestly. "When that plane was going down, I thought of you and them. I was filled with regret and I . . . I know I can't erase what I've become, but I just . . . You're my wife, Kimberly."

Kimberly took a deep breath and looked away. Her eyes fell on her boys, who had stopped playing and were standing together at the end of the bed, watching them with blank expressions on their faces. Kimberly slowly reached out and placed her hand on Michael's. When she turned back to her boys, they were both smiling now, and she smiled back. She would do this for them.

But she still hated him.

"Garrett. Garrett." Haley pushed him away as his body pressed against her. "Stop."

"What is it?" he asked in between deep, quick breaths.

He was on top of her and had been trying to get something going for some time. It was clear to Haley that he wasn't going to get it done, so this was a waste of time.

"Just get off," she ordered.

"Dammit." He stopped moving and slid out of her before rolling onto the bed, by her side. "Dammit!"

What is he mad about? Haley asked herself. She was the one whose time had been completely wasted. They were in bed at the Hotel Bel-Air in one of the suites where Chase Beauty placed investors and other visitors to L.A. Garrett had called her as soon as he left the police station. His wealthy parents in North Carolina sent one of L.A.'s best lawyers to represent him, and in the end, they didn't have enough to hold him.

Frustrated after her conversation with Sean and the whole ordeal with her brothers, Haley needed to have sex to release some tension. So she had agreed to meet him at the Bel-Air because he refused to go back to his apartment.

"I'm sorry," he said after a few minutes. "I wanted to, but . . ."

"Let it go." Haley sat up, looking for her clothes. "You're gonna have to leave."

"Why?" he looked up at her with childish confusion.

"Because I'm leaving," she answered.

"Are you sure I can't just stay here one night?" he asked. "What's the big deal?"

Haley started getting dressed. "Do you think the place is bugged or something?"

Garrett look worried. "Partly, but there are other reasons."

"You're scared," she said, finding his lack of composure disappointing. "Of who?"

Garrett opened his mouth as if to speak, but instead just sat up with a pout on his face. "Just let it go."

"Fine, but you're not staying here."

"I'll get my own room, but I don't want to pay with my credit card. Can I have some cash?"

Haley almost stumbled at the words. She placed a hand on her hip and looked down at him with scorn. "No, you didn't just ask me for money."

"I didn't ask you for money," he countered. "I asked you for cash. You know I have money."

"I don't know anything about you anymore," she answered. "From what I hear, you're a murderer. So why wouldn't you lie about everything else?"

"I'm not a murderer!"

Haley's caution antenna went up. "Don't get your panties in a twist, boy. I'm just saying what I heard. And that alibi of yours is total bullshit."

"If you just stick with your story, I'll be fine."

"Do you think I did that for you?" She laughed. "Don't flatter yourself."

"Just stick with it," he called after her as she went into the bathroom.

"I did it to stick it to that bitch." She was brushing her hair into a ponytail when Garrett showed up at the door. "Not for you."

"All that matters is if you keep to yours, I keep to mine, and Taylor tries to cover up her lies, it will at the least be confusing enough to keep me out of the fire."

"I can't take any hassles from the cops." She brushed past him on her way into the bedroom. "My dad is mad at me because of this. It's bad timing. If this starts to cost me more than it's worth, which it clearly is about to, I'm out."

"I need you to help me," Garrett said. "I'm not a murderer. I just . . . Look, the alibi is a lie. I paid Taylor to provide an alibi for me."

Haley wondered if Garrett thought she had bought his alibi before now. Was he that stupid? "How do you even know her?"

"She works for the alibi guy," he said. Garrett paused for a second as if he was suddenly remembering something. "Dammit! The alibi guy. If Taylor connects me to him, then . . . they'll see my file in his system. He said it's all encrypted, but . . . Dammit!"

"Can you get dressed a little faster?"

"This is all very complicated."

"But you know who murdered the guy, don't you?" she asked.

"I was there," he said, plopping down onto a walnut-brown chaise. "You don't want to know any more."

"For once today, you're right." Haley crawled across the bed to reach her vibrating phone on the nightstand. It was her mother, no doubt demanding she come home and play her role in the manufactured image that is the Chase family. "I don't care what you did or didn't do. I just care about it not getting connected to my family. My shit in Sydney isn't tight yet and until it is, I need access to that trust fund."

"What shit in Sydney?" he asked.

She looked him up and down with a smirk on her face. "You

have your secrets and I have mine. Now get dressed and get out of here."

Michael was fuming and Marisol's picking at him didn't make things any better. The second he had gotten home, Kimberly disappeared. He was coming down from the pain medication and the boys were driving him crazy. Marisol finally showed up and tried to help him get back into bed after changing into his bathrobe and night shorts.

"I'm fine," he said, holding his hand up to stop her.

"The sheets," Marisol said. "I will just pull the sheets up and . . ."

"It's enough." Michael hadn't intended to yell, but could see that Marisol was offended. "I'm sorry, Marisol, but I'm fine. Go look after the boys."

"They're asleep." She stood up, hands on her hips, surveying him as if he was a project that she was unsatisfied with. "I can . . ."

"Just tell me when my wife gets home," he interrupted.

As if on cue, Kimberly showed up in the bedroom carrying at least five bags with designer names on them. Both Michael and Marisol stared at her as she sauntered casually across the massive room and placed the bags down on the plush settee. When she turned to face them, she smiled as if the world was grand.

"You've been shopping?" Michael asked incredulously. "You've been shopping?"

"Just in time too." She placed her Prada bag on the bed and sat down leisurely on the window seat pillow. "Sergio Rossi almost turned the lights off on me."

"What the fuck, Kimberly?" Michael hadn't expected all hugs and kisses, but this was some bullshit.

"Marisol, can you place these bags in my bedroom?" Kimberly kept a smile on her face as her maid picked up her bags and left the room.

"I thought we . . ." Michael was seeking the right words. They hadn't had a civil conversation in so long. "I thought we had an understanding."

"Thanks, by the way," Kimberly said, leaning back. "Since you canceled all but one of my credit cards and put a five-thousand-dollar limit on the only one you let me have, I used your credit cards. Expect a bill for about seventy-five grand next month."

She stared at him, waiting and daring him. He wanted to be angry. She could see him on the edge of explosion. She was calling his bluff.

Michael wanted to strangle her. He knew what she was doing. She was forcing his hand. "I don't give a shit about the credit cards. You should have stayed home."

"Oh yes, that's right. You had planned a dinner. Just the two of us. Where's the candlelight?"

"You enjoy mocking me," he said with a nod. "So yesterday was bullshit."

"Yesterday was for my children," she snapped. "You think I don't know what you're doing? You're weak right now, physically and emotionally. So you have to pretend to be nice, so I'll take it easy on you until you get your strength back. When you do, you turn into the bitch of the century again."

"I almost died, Kimberly!" He placed his right hand on his left rib as he winced in pain.

"I'm going to hire you a nurse." Despite the sharp tug at her heart at the sight of him in pain, Kimberly's expression remained cold and untouched. "Between her and Marisol, you should be fine."

"I don't need a nurse," he argued. "I need a wife!"

Kimberly leaned forward with a frank expression. "Well, you should have thought about that before you threatened to never let me see my children again."

Michael wasn't buying it. "I know you, Kimberly. You still care about me. Somewhere in there you do."

Kimberly swallowed the emotion that tried to convince her it was there. "There was a time when I would do anything for you. You were my king; my savior. But you killed everything."

Michael felt desperation rush through him as she stood up and turned to leave. "That's impossible! This is never going to die."

She turned back to him. "Everything dies."

He shook his head. "Not us. I felt it when that plane was going down. We can still . . ."

"Shut up!" She came to his bed, leaning down toward him. "You don't get to destroy my life and get your wifey back when you're feeling a little vulnerable. You have treated me like a prisoner."

"You made my father hate me! You knew what Chase Beauty meant to me and now it will never be mine, because of you!"

"Poor baby," she mocked. "Daddy doesn't wuv me anymore, so . . ."

He reached out and grabbed her, pulling her closer. "You'd better shut up."

Kimberly fell onto the bed, but was so consumed with anger she didn't care. "What are you going to do? You can't even walk. Look at you now. You're cringing in pain."

"I don't care." He endured the excruciating discomfort he felt rip through his body as he grabbed her shoulders and pulled her to him. "Everything about you is pain for me."

Kimberly tried to push away when she realized he was going to kiss her. "You disgust me."

With one hand, Michael grabbed her by her hair and turned her face up to his. "I know you feel something."

"I hate you!" With her free arm, she reached up and slapped him across the face. "I hate you!"

"I hate you too!"

His mouth came down hard on hers. As he tasted her bitter lips, he only became more determined to have her. Michael lifted her up a bit to put her on his lap. It hurt, but he didn't care. Nothing, not even a broken leg or a bruised rib could keep him from having her. For so long, despite how he felt about her, he never stopped wanting her; he never stopped wanting to feel the way that only she could make him feel.

Shocked at first, Kimberly was frozen when he kissed her. He'd tried to kiss her many times, but she'd always seen it coming and got away. But this time it seemed different. He wasn't begging her. He was demanding and Kimberly was caught off guard by how much it reminded her of the good times; times when she ached for him to devour her, with no limits.

She didn't make the decision to kiss him back. She just did, and when she did, her body began to ache for him in the way it hadn't for so long. She was hungry and grabbed at him, pulling him closer. She heard him wince in between moans and Kimberly found a sadistic satisfaction in causing his pain. She pressed harder and harder, her excitement only growing.

Michael's heart sounded like a freight train inside of him as it picked up its pace. Feeling her respond made him lose it. He reached for her blouse and ripped it open. Lifting her body a little, he brought her chest to his face.

Kimberly grabbed at his bathrobe, pulling it down to reveal that dark chocolate body and those perfect muscles. She felt herself quivering all over as she lowered her head to kiss him on the neck.

"Kimberly," he moaned as he reached back and removed her bra. He tossed it aside and smothered his face between her warm, firm breasts. His need was urgent and the fire in him was about to explode into an inferno.

Kimberly moaned with pleasure as he teased her left nipple with his wet tongue before taking her breast in his mouth. He reached under her Juicy Couture high-waisted skirt and ripped at her panties. They came apart and immediately Michael thrust his fingers inside of her. She made a sound that told him how good it felt. There was something about it that made him feel powerful; that told him she was all his.

Her hips moved as she felt the stimulation reach every inch of her body. Only he could make her feel this way.

"Now," she ordered.

Michael heeded her call and knelt up to move his underwear down his legs.

"Come here," he said, grabbing her thighs, squeezing them tight and pulling her closer. He could . . .

"Wait!" Kimberly stopped just as she was about to come down on him.

"Baby, please." Michael couldn't wait one more second.

She could see he was hard. Large and hard, but she had to set the record straight.

"You need to know," she said, speaking with the intensity of her feelings, "this means nothing. I still hate you."

Michael yelled out as Kimberly lowered herself onto him with full force. The pain, the ecstasy, combined for the perfect storm inside of him. He looked up at her as she took hold of his shoulders. He could feel her throbbing around him as she moved up and down at a steady pace.

Michael gripped her tight, making her stop. When she looked at him with surprise, he could see she was just as lit as he was.

"Don't stop," she whispered between heavy breaths.

"I'm not going to stop," he said. "I'm just warning you."

"Warning me?"

Michael smiled wickedly. "To hold onto something."

Kimberly moved forward, pressing herself against him as she reached for the headboard. She gripped the top just as Michael began to thrust faster and faster.

She was screaming now because she was gone. He was grunting wildly with every move. He would do this until she climaxed and she loved it.

But she still hated him.

"What are you doing?" was the first question Avery asked Carter after he opened the front door to his downtown L.A. penthouse.

"You want to come in, don't you?" Carter stepped aside to let them in. As they passed, he reached out and pinched Connor's fat cheek. "How's my little spoiled princess?"

"You shouldn't be up, Carter." Avery made her way down the rose-red-colored walls of the hallway to the living room.

She looked around the apartment, noticing that her little touches were gone, and that Julia had already begun leaving her scent around the home. It was difficult for Avery, being there. They'd shared so much in the short time she'd lived here. And when he touched her . . . They had christened each of the six rooms in this home as well as the hallway several times over. And every time she came here, Avery remembered every moment. That was why she was always so eager to get out.

"Where is Julia?" she asked. "She should be here taking care of you."

Carter held his hands out to Connor, but she didn't move from her mother. He could tell she was getting tired. When that happened, she didn't want anyone but Avery. "What about Julia gave you the impression she was the nurturing kind?"

She turned to him with a smile. For once, Avery had actually hoped that Julia would be there. She needed the buffer. "I'm surprised Janet even let you both go home. I would have assumed she would make you come back to Chase Mansion so she could fuss over you."

"Don't think she didn't try."

Carter knew what Avery was doing. She was engaging in small talk to avoid an awkward moment or a silence. She didn't want to do anything to bring up the kiss they shared yesterday. But there was no avoiding it. He had tasted the sweet nectar of those lips he had known were his from the first moment he touched them. He had been unable to sleep or concentrate at all, unable to think of anything since that moment and he knew Avery was in the same boat.

"Mom has put Julia on double time, planning the Museum Ball." Carter tried again to get his daughter's attention. This time she responded and held her arms out. "That's my girl." He looked at Avery. "At least sit down."

Avery gave up her baby, although she didn't want to. She felt too vulnerable without Connor in her arms.

It was bad enough that she had been unable to sleep or eat, thinking of coming here today. She'd found herself alone in the bathroom last night, daydreaming and softly touching her lips. And then again that morning in the shower.

"I'm fine." He sat down on the sofa with Connor on his lap. She wrapped her arms around his neck as far as they could go and leaned into him. "Is she okay?"

"She had a bottle earlier and was sleeping in the car on the way over here." Avery turned away from him, focusing her attention on the bookcase against the wall. The way she felt whenever she saw Carter playing with Connor scared her. She enjoyed it too much. It made her think things, imagine things that she shouldn't.

Carter looked in the baby bag Avery had placed on the coffee table. "A lot of bottles in there. Have you stopped breastfeed-ing?"

Avery shook her head. "I'm mixing it up. The doctor said it was okay that I do some breast milk and some formula."

"But you're expressing it," Carter said. "You're not breastfeed-ing her anymore."

"Sometimes. Are you questioning me? I know what's healthy for my own baby."

"Take it easy," Carter said. "I know you're a great mother. I was just curious. You know I like breastfeeding because . . . well, your breasts are pretty huge."

Avery couldn't help laughing, but she still kept her back to him. "Shut up."

"I heard you laugh," Carter said. "You can't hide it from me."

"I see Julia has already started redecorating." Avery walked over to the bookcase, needing to keep her distance from him. With every passing second, she was becoming more and more alert, aware of her body's reaction.

Carter leaned back, cradling his baby in his arms. "Is that what you want to talk about, Avery?"

Avery turned back to him, knowing now that ten feet wasn't nearly enough distance. "What do you mean?"

Carter had thought long and hard about what he would say when he saw her again. He didn't want to risk all the work he had put into the last six months, but hadn't everything changed? A few days ago, he'd felt invincible. He was the great Carter Chase. He was gifted and privileged, smart and a winner. He was special by blood and lucky by chance and he had a plan to win back the woman he loved. That was a few days ago.

"We should probably talk about that kiss."

"No," she said. "It didn't mean anything."

He stood up. "You know me to be a lot of things, Avery. But stupid isn't one of them."

"Fine," she agreed, repeating the assurance she had given her-self over and over again. "It was a product of the moment. I was only happy to see you alive. You're Connor's father and . . ."

"I'm going to put her down." Carter started for the bedrooms. "Then we'll really talk."

"Carter, don't make it more than it is." Avery knew now she was going to have to leave. She would come back for Connor after a few hours, but she couldn't stay. She was feeling all the hair on her arms stand up straight, just from the idea that they might have to talk about that kiss.

There were three bedrooms in the condo. Carter's master bedroom, one he had converted to a home office, and a third guest room generally kept empty except for Michael's occasional drop-ins. Six months ago, to Michael's disappointment, Carter had the room transformed into a baby's room. He and Avery had agreed that he would have her every other weekend and Carter wanted everything to be perfect. The truth be told, Connor had spent more nights at his parents' house when he had Connor than here, because Carter needed the help. Babies were a handful.

"Here we go, sweetie." Carter gently lowered her into the bassinet.

When her body softly hit the sheets, she let out a yawn that was bigger than she was. Her arms and legs stretched out in four directions as her mouth opened wide.

"You take a little nap while Daddy . . ."

Carter felt the buildup just one second before the bright lights flashed in his eyes and his head began to pound. His hands went to each side of his head as he felt like something was trying to push his eyes out from inside. The pain was unbearable and he didn't even notice that he was making so much noise.

Avery panicked at the sound of Carter yelling. The first thing that entered her mind was Connor. She reached the room in less than a second to find Carter leaning away from the bassinet, letting out a pain-filled moan as his hands gripped the sides of his head.

Avery rushed toward him, taking a second to look in the bassinet. Connor was already sleeping peacefully. It wasn't her. It was Carter. She grabbed him just before he almost fell over. He was heavy and she almost fell under the pressure, but managed to lift him upright.

"What is it?" She grabbed his face with her hands and lifted it to hers. His eyes were shut. "Carter, tell me."

When he opened his eyes, the suffering she saw in them ripped her to shreds inside. She was helpless and felt as if she was going to panic if she didn't do something soon.

"Migraines," Carter was finally able to say, feeling as if someone was punching him in the head. His vision was blurry as he looked at her. "In my bedroom. My pills."

"Come on." Avery manufactured enough strength to help him down the hall into the master bedroom.

She sat him on the bed and ordered him to lie down. He wasn't moaning anymore, but he was still holding his head.

"Where are the pills?" Avery asked, looking around. She felt her heart beating madly in her chest. "I don't see anything."

Carter pointed at the dresser near the door and Avery rushed to it and grabbed the bottle. She ran into the bathroom to fill a cup with water. Carter had already sat up when she returned to the bed, and he swallowed the pills quickly. The pain, which had seemed as if it would kill him, had lessened to just terrible at the moment.

"Lie back down." Avery sat on the bed and tried to physically make him lie back, but he refused. "Carter, please."

"No, I'm fine." Carter squeezed his eyes shut and opened them a few times until his blurry vision began to clear up. "I need to sit up."

"You need to lie down," Avery said. "This is horrible. It's because of the accident, isn't it?"

Carter wanted to nod, but he didn't dare move his head. "It feels like someone is jabbing me with a pick all over. Shit."

"I'll call Dr. Adams," Avery said. "He's still your doctor, right? Or should I call Leigh?"

"Neither." Carter could feel the pain subsiding, but he was still a little dizzy. "I'll be fine in a moment."

Avery didn't take her eyes off him, for what seemed like a full ten minutes before he lifted his head again.

Carter finally looked up at her and was touched by her concern. "Really, it's not as bad as the last two times."

"The last two times?" Avery was angry now. "Why didn't you tell me you were having migraines?"

"Why would I tell you?"

"I have a right to know if you're in pain," she argued, unable to catch herself before letting it all out.

Carter knew from her expression she hadn't meant to say that. "You're not my girlfriend anymore. I don't have to tell you anything."

Avery tried to swallow the pain with a diversion. "But if you had been holding Connor, I . . ."

"I would never hurt her!" Carter's own voice ended up ringing in his head. He knelt forward, placing his face in his hands.

"Carter!" Avery leaned over to him, placing one arm around his back and the other hand to caress his head. "I'm sorry. I know you would never let anything happen to her. I'm just . . . What do I need to do?"

"I'm going to be all right," he said. "I'm sorry I snapped at you. It's just these migraines hurt like hell. I never thought the most pain I would ever experience would be in my head."

"Is this permanent?" she asked.

He was just beginning to realize that she was holding him. Her arm around his back, her hand on his head. As the pain subsided, it was being replaced with something more dangerous.

"No," he answered. "Just for a while."

"What's a while?"

He shrugged, realizing how close she was to him, her face only inches from his. Her loving, caring eyes stung him. There was such a softness, tenderness in every inch of her face that just looking at her made him feel better. "A few more days. Maybe a week."

"What can I do?" she asked. "Please, Carter."

He smiled at her tender plea. There was no way he could refuse her anything. And he didn't even want to. "Can you rub my temples? It helps."

Avery didn't hesitate, ignoring all those distractions she had trained herself to feel and do to avoid being close to him. She positioned herself behind him and he leaned into her. As her fingers gently massaged his temples, she found herself loving the way his heavy body pressed against hers. She loved the way he smelled.

Carter didn't think to hold back as her fingers went to work.

He let out a moan of pleasure, feeling his own arousal from the feeling of her breasts against his back. He closed his eyes, ignoring the training he had given himself over the last six months to avoid these moments for fear of giving away his feelings for her and scaring her away. He didn't care anymore. Being near her felt good and he was going to enjoy it.

"Are those pills addictive?" Avery asked, unable to stand just the sound of Carter's quiet moans. Part of her enjoyed making him feel good while the rest of her knew she was in danger.

"Of course," Carter finally answered. "That's what makes them so good."

"Stop joking," she ordered. "I don't want you to become addicted to them."

Carter let out a quick laugh. "You don't have to worry about me, Avery."

"But I do," she said. Avery stopped massaging his temples as she sat back on the bed with a sigh that gave away the overwhelming emotion she was feeling. "I can't help it."

Carter turned around to look at her and he could see she was about to cry. "It's okay, really."

"I thought you were dead!" She felt a rage engulf her and without thinking, she punched him in the chest. "Dammit, Carter."

Carter grabbed her arm and pulled her to him. He wrapped his arms around her and she laid her head on his chest. "I know you were scared. I was too, but I'm fine, Connor is fine and you're fine."

When she looked up at him, Avery opened her mouth, wanting to say something, but she was feeling too much to even begin to express it. She knew he was going to kiss her and there was nothing in this world she wanted more.

To hell with his plan, Carter thought to himself as his lips came down on hers. This was his woman and he needed her. She needed him and there was nothing that would stop him from making love to her now.

When his lips met hers, Avery felt the electricity of one thousand volts jolt through her system. The shock made her shiver in his arms as he pulled her closer. His lips pressed harder and she opened her mouth. When she felt his tongue enter her mouth, she responded as her body told her to. She grabbed him by the shoulders and pulled him to her as she fell back on the bed. Her hunger could not be satiated fast enough.

The lust that Carter felt for Avery exploded inside of him as he lowered himself on top of her. He only wanted more and more as he kissed harder and deeper. The taste of her mouth intoxicated him and he could not control himself. He had waited so long for this. His hands greedily ran up and down her body, pulling at the clothes that were in his way.

Their lips separated only because neither could breathe, but Carter didn't hesitate to taste her again. His mouth sizzled down her neck as he reached down and unbuttoned her silk blouse. Her skin was as he remembered it, soft and firm. And warm.

Avery felt his hands stroking her and her body began to writhe back and forth. The mastery with which he did everything to her made her insane. She wanted him desperately and had never stopped, but feeling so clearly his desperate desire for her only stoked her fire more.

She began to moan in response to every kiss he placed on her body and as she felt his tongue trail the space in between her breasts, Avery felt a fire rush through her veins and into her soul. The combination of the urgency of his movements and the intimacy of his mouth was drugging her with pleasure. Nothing in this world existed but her body molding into his.

Carter loved the taste of her, and the way her body was moving in response to his demanding caresses made him crazy with wanton lust. It had been awhile, but he had never forgotten the way Avery made him feel. He heard her call his name softly and he could barely breathe. He grabbed the top of her jeans and slid them down with her panties, tossing them off the side of the bed.

Looking down at her while he hastily removed his clothes, Carter admired this body that he had come to know so well. He had tasted, delighted and ravished it many times and it had never been enough. Having Connor had made her breasts fuller, but nothing else had changed. She was perfectly curvy and feminine everywhere, and Carter could no longer wait for the reward of being inside of her.

Avery's body had never stopped moving, but when she felt Carter touch her again, his tantalizing mouth teasing her flat stomach, traveling to her belly button, she was again overcome with the need to possess every bit of him. The anticipation built inside of her as she felt him grip her thighs and move lower. When his lips gently kissed the top of her sweet center, Avery's head begin to spin. When his tongue entered her, searching deeper and deeper inside of her, Avery began to moan louder and louder. Her hands went to her own breasts, cupping them roughly as everything inside of her was focused on her growing desire.

When Carter finally looked up again and, saw Avery caressing her own breasts it turned him on beyond his own comprehension. He had been hard for a long time and seeing how ready she was, was all he needed.

Avery screamed out loud in painful pleasure as he entered her. He completely filled her, and she was transported into a cloud of torturous lust. She winced and called out his name and loved every second of it. His thrusts began slow, but she dug her nails into his back, the way she had always told him that she wanted it harder and faster.

The intensity of being inside of her left Carter with a sense of reckless abandon. She was tightly gripping him as he plunged in and out of her, making him feel frantic. Their bodies reacquainting with the perfection of their chemistry, remembering everything. He lowered his head and nestled it into her neck, saying her name over and over again. When he felt her nails dig into his back, Carter lost it.

He was moving inside her with a savage intensity as they both moaned louder and louder, their bodies rubbing against each other. Avery felt the spiral of pleasure begin to tease at her nerve endings; her fingers, her nipples, her toes. She wrapped her arms around him tightly as he thrust harder and harder. When the sensation took her, Avery yelled in ecstasy that vibrated through every inch of her. Her body began to quiver all over and her head fell back. She was in heaven and couldn't imagine that it would ever end.

* * *

As soon as the post-love-making euphoria was over, their bodies separated, Kimberly and Michael immediately returned to reality.

"We've never had a problem there," Michael said as Kimberly sat up in bed, her back to him. He looked at the curve of her spine, her back wet from perspiration. Every inch of her drove him crazy.

"Just with everything else," Kimberly said as she scooted off the bed in search of her clothes. She found her skirt bunched up at the end of the bed, but her shirt was torn. She grabbed her bra and put it on.

Michael was trying to find something to say to negate her response, but he couldn't. She was right. "This is a mess. We used to be . . ."

"That was lifetimes ago." She turned to him, hating herself for being so weak for him.

The day she knew he would hate her forever was the day she and Michael were in Steven's office at Chase Beauty. Michael had explained her past to his father and how everything culminated in David's death. Once she realized that both he and Steven thought the sex tape of her and David, which David had threatened to put on the Internet, wasn't from when she was a teenage hooker, but from the day before, Michael lost it.

She knew that he would never tolerate her cheating, even if it was an attempt to make David go away. But that it was with David, had made it a point of no return. Michael had never judged her for the life she had before she began modeling in New York, but she knew he was always uncomfortable about the hold David had had on her as a young woman.

"Everything doesn't have to be lost." Michael wasn't sure of what he was saying. He only knew that she was a second away from leaving and at that moment, he would do anything to keep her there and back in his bed.

"It was lost six months ago," she answered, her voice wavering and weak.

"But what if we can . . ." Michael doubted his words even before he said them, but he felt a desperation inside that only Kimberly could bring out in him. "What happened on that plane . . ."

"Stop." She held up her hand, unwilling to listen to this and not trusting herself to maintain even what little shred of dignity she had left. "We've gone too far in the wrong direction to ever turn back. No matter what happened to you, this . . . this won't happen again. Ever."

Michael felt his heart harden toward her, urged on by his ego. He swallowed his pain, feeling a white-hot hatred for her that consumed him.

"Then what are you standing there for?" he asked. "Get out of my room."

Kimberly didn't give him a chance to tell her to leave again. She was gone in a second, slamming the door behind her. She was a fool; that much was clear. She'd been a fool forever, but she wouldn't be again. She wouldn't even allow herself to consider a fresh start with him.

Would she?

8

Carter was in the main conference room of Chase Law watching the presentations of his recruiting director, Rachel Dawson. She had laid out all the credentials, experience, and pros and cons of this year's top law-school-graduate applicants for Chase Law. He was trying hard to concentrate because he knew how important this was. But somehow a group of twenty-six-year-olds, eager to make six figures for working ninety hours a week, didn't interest him.

He was thinking of Avery; only Avery. Part of him was very upset that she left, taking Connor with her, while he was in the shower. But most of him was just happy that he had made love to her again . . . and again. There was a lot of time to make up for and he couldn't wait to be alone with her again.

Yes, he contemplated the Pandora's box he had opened, but nothing mattered. Except of course the fact that Avery hadn't returned his calls and that was two days ago. He knew not to push it too much. She would only use it as an excuse not to see him.

"Mr. Chase!"

Carter blinked, coming back to reality, realizing that Rachel had called his name three times. "You were saying?"

Rachel was standing in front of the whiteboard that was attached to the wall of the cherrywood and gray marble conference room at Chase Law.

"I was saying that if we're only going to hire three," she said, "we should decide between candidates C, D, and F. They all have Ivy League top-fifteen-percent academics, but based on his postgraduate clerkship with Judge Marble, candidate E is a forgone conclusion."

Carter nodded. "Let's put together an offer with all the bells for him immediately. Do we know who else C, D, and F are interviewing with?"

Rachel nodded to her assistant, Sammy, who nervously typed at her laptop.

"Yes," Sammy said. "F is Charlotte Peretti and she's interviewing with Ismen, Smith and Prescott and . . ."

The buzz came from the conference phone in the middle of the long wooden table everyone was sitting at. Everyone knew to stop talking because the only person that was allowed to interrupt sessions in the conference room was Patricia, Carter's assistant, a middle-aged woman who had been with him since he started the firm.

"Carter."

"Yes, Pat?"

"Mrs. Harper is here to see you."

It took Carter a second to realize she was talking about Avery. He had blocked her last name from his mind. To him, she would always be Avery Jackson until she was Avery Chase.

"She's here?" Previously leaning back in his leather seat, Carter sat up straight.

"Yes, sir. I asked her to wait since she doesn't have an appoint . . ."

"I'll be there in a second." Carter leaped up from his seat, looking at the other five people in the room staring at him. "This is fine. I want to see the offer for E on my desk by the end of today. Put together a report on our competition for the top three by tomorrow. I'll decide then."

He was out of there and down the hall to his office within seconds. Telling Patricia to hold all calls and not let anyone in,

Carter rushed into his office and looked to his right. Avery loved the ceiling-to-floor window wall in his large corner office. She could look out over downtown L.A. and beyond. That's usually where she had waited for him in his office when they were together. He would come up behind her, wrap his arms around her, and they would look out the window together, talking.

But could he do that again now that they had slept together? He wasn't hers . . . yet, and the way she stood with her arms crossed over her chest told him she was upset. "Avery."

When she turned around, Avery saw Carter coming toward her and she was struck with the desire that immediately took her over. She had stopped wishing he wasn't so ridiculously handsome, especially in those expensively tailored suits. Despite the flush she felt, she held out her hand to stop him before he reached her. He looked upset as his arms, which seemed poised to hold her, lowered and flattened to his sides.

"We need to talk." She stepped away to create more distance between them.

Seeing him now only made her feel more conflicted inside. The last two days she had been in a haze. All she could do was think of making love to him. It was more like a dream than a memory. It was mind-blowing perfection and she hadn't been able to think of anything sense.

But her guilt had gotten the best of her. Once he had gone to the shower, she was overwhelmed with shame and could barely breathe until she got her clothes on, grabbed her sleeping baby and left. When Anthony had come home, she told him she wasn't feeling well and just wanted to go to bed. She couldn't even look at him.

"That doesn't sound good." Carter contemplated her morality causing them problems, but there was no going back now.

"You can't tell me you don't feel any guilt about yesterday."

"None at all." He took a seat in his chair. "Everything about us making love, was right. I know you felt it."

Avery walked over to the side of his massive desk, placing her purse down. She began wringing her hands together, trying to maintain the courage to say what she'd come here to say.

"I felt horrible."

"You can't lie to me," he said. "I felt, tasted, every inch of you and I made you feel great."

"All of your arrogance aside, I wasn't talking about us making love." She turned to take a seat on the black leather sofa a few feet from the desk. "I was talking about afterward. I was too ashamed to look at Anthony."

"Were you too ashamed to look at Connor?" he asked. "She was what we made the last time we made love."

Avery's heart warmed at the thought, but she quickly composed herself. "No, Carter. This can't happen again."

"Are you going to start quoting the Bible?" Carter stood up and made his way to the sofa. "Because I would prefer we move past that."

"You can mock my faith all you want," Avery said. "But I broke my vows with you. Do you understand what that means?"

"You want to know what I understand?" He slid so close to her that their knees were touching. "I understand that the second I kissed you, the entire time we'd been apart disappeared. I know that no matter what definitions of good or bad exist, what we felt was nothing other than right."

"We can't . . ."

"We can." He reached up to touch her face and was glad she didn't turn away as he ran his finger softly against her cheek before urging her toward him. "We can and we will."

His lips on hers sent Avery under his spell. He was so masterful and seductive in every move of his tongue inside her mouth. He would stoke her fire with every kiss and make her want him more than what was right.

"Do you remember what you told me six months ago?" he asked, still holding gently to the side of her face. "About how you knew you would give in to me if I pursued you?"

Avery nodded. "I said I would give in, but I would hate myself."

"And if I had pursued you, that would have happened."

"But . . ."

"But I didn't. We kept our distance, Avery. We did what was right and what happened?"

"We ended up together anyway," she answered. "But this wasn't an ordinary circumstance. So much has happened to spur this on."

"Exactly." Carter held back nothing as he looked into her eyes. He wanted her to see how weak he was for her, and how unashamed he was of loving and wanting her. "What happened was life. All those things we think matter, things we'll get to in time and plans we make for some reward later in life, mean nothing. All that matters is what is deep in our guts."

"Wanting you is deep in my guts," she responded, knowing there was no sense in pretending anything else. "But so is wanting to be a good wife and a good example for my daughter."

Carter let her go as he stood up. Looking down at her, he asked, "You don't want this to go any further?"

"No," she answered, unable to look up at him. "I don't."

"I'll leave you alone, Avery." Carter paused for a moment. "I don't want to put myself through this and I don't want to hurt you. So, even though it will kill me, if you look me in the eyes and tell me you don't love me, I'll leave you alone."

Avery felt weak in her knees as she slowly stood up. She tried hard to think of everything she believed in; her faith, her vows, her husband. It had to be enough to give her the strength to do what was right.

She took a deep breath and looked into his intense hazel eyes and opened her mouth. Nothing came out.

Without another thought, she reached out for him and pulled his head down to hers. She kissed him with all the possession of a woman kissing her man; the man she loved. Only a week ago, she'd thought she'd lost him forever and now he was wrapped around her. She couldn't bear to let him go.

When Michael used one of his crutches to kick the door open and stormed into Carter's office, Patricia was right on his tail, but he didn't care. "None of those rules apply to me! Ask Car . . ."

He was stopped in his tracks as he saw the end of Carter and Avery's kiss. They quickly stepped away from each other, with the look of perfect guilt on their faces.

"I'm sorry, Carter." Patricia stood at the door with her hands on her hips, looking ready to hit someone. "I didn't expect him to be so fast on those crutches."

"I broke my other leg skiing when I was twenty-two . . ." A smile spread across Michael's face as he took a few hops toward the love birds. "Well, what do we have here?"

"None of your business." Carter stepped in front of Avery as if to shield her from his brother. "Wait outside, Michael."

"What for?" he asked. "I saw you. You can't put this toothpaste back in the tube. Besides, it's too much labor for me to walk out and come back."

"This isn't what you think." Avery avoided eye contact with Michael as she rushed to the desk to grab her purse.

"No," Michael corrected her. "It's exactly what I think, and that halo over your head looks a little crooked."

"Hey!" Carter eyed his brother as his lips pressed together. "Not another word."

Leaning into his crutches, Michael lifted his arms in the air in surrender and made his way to Carter's chair behind his desk. He slammed his crutches on the edge of the desk before sitting down.

Carter caught up with Avery as she passed Patricia and started down the hallway. He took hold of her arm and turned her to him. "Where are you going?"

"I have to get out of here." Avery felt ready to panic. Having this between her and Carter was bad enough. Now Michael, who never liked her, knew. This could only get worse. "What if he tells Anthony?"

Although Carter wanted to tell her that Anthony was going to have to find out sooner than later, he knew she needed to be reassured right now. "He won't."

"He can't," she said desperately.

"You know that Michael would never betray me." Without thinking, he noticed a couple of lawyers walking by and removed his hand from her. He took one step back and kept silent until he was sure they were out of earshot. "You have nothing to worry about. All that matters is when I'm going to see you again."

Avery couldn't believe she was doing this; thinking of a way to see Carter behind Anthony's back. Who was she? What was going on?

"Avery." His tone hinted at his impatience, but he wasn't going to test her again. "When?"

"Call me later today at the gallery," she answered after a while. "I'll know better then."

She rushed away, feeling both dread and excitement in the pit of her stomach. Since the day she left View Park, after finding out she was pregnant with Connor and fearing what a vengeful Carter might do, she'd had dreams of being with him again. In her dreams, they were married and happy. They were a family. The lies and deceit had never happened and life was perfect. Then she woke up and realized that this life she dreamed of would never happen. She had made her choice. She loved Anthony and he had sacrificed so much for her and Connor. She had made vows and thought nothing could make her do what she'd done yesterday.

She felt angry at the weakness of her own faith. Where was that strength in the face of temptation? Where was that horrible guilt that would kill her inside and give her no choice but to end this affair now? She had come to Carter's office with it, but it wasn't even strong enough to last five minutes. And she left with a schoolgirl-like sense of eagerness about seeing him again.

Carter slammed the door behind him when he entered his office. "Get the hell out of my chair."

Michael didn't move. "I'm a cripple, man!"

Carter approached the chair, his hands gripped into fists at his sides. "Get up."

"So how long has this adulterous relationship been going on?"

"Get up."

"I want an answer to my question." Michael swiveled around once, stopping by grabbing onto the desk. "I'll count to five or . . ."

"I'll count to three." Carter took hold of one of the crutches. "Then my fist goes through your face."

Michael and Carter argued almost every day, but as they grew older, those arguments rarely turned into physical fights. Yes, a fist flew every now and then, but they were averaging a drawing-blood type of fight once every couple of years. Sensing another one coming on, Michael grabbed his crutch out of Carter's hand and got up from the chair as quick as he could.

"Your hypocrisy is astounding," he said.

"What are you doing here?" Carter took a seat. "I thought you were bedridden with broken ribs."

"Bruised ribs, and they're already feeling better." He lifted his arms. "See, no pad."

"Did you come here to show me that?"

"Check your BlackBerry, asshole. We're having lunch with Elisha and Dad at the country club. My driver is waiting downstairs. So how long, big brother?"

"Just a few days ago," Carter answered.

"You lying son of a bitch!" Michael laughed.

"You'll tell no one," Carter ordered. "And I'm not lying."

"I could tell no one," Michael countered with a quizzical tone. "Or I could tell everyone."

"You owe me, little brother. All the secrets I've kept for you."

"You're making a huge mistake," Michael said.

"Need I remind you, that's what I said when you planned to marry Kimberly?"

"What you said was I should make her get an abortion," Michael answered. "But that can be a little difficult for those of us who actually believe in God."

Carter closed his laptop and stood up, grabbing his keys on the edge of his desk. "My point was, you didn't listen."

"Touché," was all Michael could respond. Kimberly had destroyed his life, but she had also given him some of the happiest years ever and the two sons he valued most in the entire universe. "Besides, it appears we're making the same mistake."

"How do you figure that?" Carter asked as they headed for the door.

"You're sleeping with someone else's wife and I'm sleeping with mine." Michael smiled at Carter's confusion.

"If you had any real morals," Carter said, "you'd let Kimberly go so you can both get on with your miserable lives."

Michael's smile faded as he looked Carter dead in the eyes. "Morals or not, that is the one thing I will never do."

When Sean looked through the peephole of his apartment door, he was taken aback by who he saw. When was the last time

Haley Chase had come to his apartment? The day he broke up with her and she set his living room on fire. What was he in store for now?

Sean opened the door a crack and looked out. "What do you want?"

"Are you going to let me in or not?" Haley asked. "The commonness of this hallway is upsetting my allergies."

"Yes, I forgot that the smell of the middle class can make you sick." He stepped aside. "My shift starts in two hours, so can you keep your foolishness to an hour or less?"

When Haley walked inside the apartment, she was glad that she felt nothing. She was afraid she might. Haley always excused her falling in love with Sean with some kind of victim's syndrome. Several attempts had been made on her life because she had agreed to testify against Rudio, the drug dealer she witnessed murdering one of "business partners." She'd felt as if her parents had turned on her after forcing her to go into hiding. Sean was all she'd had and what had begun as a game, trying to seduce a little Boy Scout into breaking all his own rules, turned into a dependency that she thought she was too strong to fall into. She had loved him and paid the price. She hadn't let any man do that to her before and she never would again.

"I'm not here for foolishness," she answered. "I'm here about Garrett. You're right. He's in this knee-deep, and I need to cut him loose before my asshole of a father ships me off to Europe again."

"Are you ready to tell the cops you lied about my sister?" Sean asked. "If not, then we have nothing to discuss."

Haley intended to do no such thing, until it served her purposes. "Of course, but I have to talk to my lawyer first. My mother's orders. Can you tell me what you know?"

Sean didn't trust her for a second. "Have a seat."

Haley looked around, not wishing to sit anywhere. "Didn't you get a raise transferring to L.A.? Get a maid or something."

"Sit down or get out," Sean ordered as he retrieved a can of pop from the refrigerator. "You need to talk to me first."

"You don't believe me?" Haley asked as she finally sat down in a chair at the dining room table. This place was terribly small and made her uncomfortable. She couldn't believe that he had expected her to live here instead of the million-dollar condo her father was going to buy for them.

"Is that a serious question?" Sean asked. He leaned over the counter that separated the kitchen from the dining room. "What do you know?"

"I know he's involved," Haley answered. "He was at the murder, but says he didn't do it."

"He says."

"Garrett's not an idiot. If he thought a murder was going to go down, do you think he'd use some stupid college alibi service as his backup?"

"Who does he say did it?"

"He was too scared to say, but he was there and he admitted to lying about his alibi."

"He told the truth?"

"He paid her, Sean. He said she works for this alibi guy and . . ."

"Taylor told me about him, but I can't find him. He's just disappeared. Does Garrett know how to contact him?"

She shrugged, looking away. "Before I answer any more questions, I want to know what you know. What am I . . ."

That was when she realized what was lying right there on the dining room table next to her. Police files. "Is this it?"

Sean hurried over to the table, grabbing the papers up. "I'm not even supposed to have this."

"Why can't you get on the case?"

"I'm not Beverly Hills PD, and there's no way I'd be let in on a case where my sister is involved." He stuffed the last paper in the file and placed it inside the top drawer of the curio cabinet against the wall. "It wouldn't matter anyway. The FBI came in and took over. This was all I could get before all the files and evidence were taken away."

"I'm not going to tell anyone," she said. "What is it?"

"Bits of the case," he answered. "It's all I could get my hands on."

"When did you steal them?"

"Last night," he said. "It's incomplete and I'm still trying to figure some stuff out."

"What do you plan to do with it?"

"Once I know what it means, I'm going to use it to help Taylor get out of this mess."

"What have you figured out so far?" Haley saw the skeptical look in Sean's eyes. "I came over here, didn't I? Can you imagine how hard that was for me? I want to end this so I can move on. Tell me what you have."

For the next several minutes, Sean explained to Haley what was general knowledge at the police department. Cool, Bitton & Klein was notorious for taking on criminal syndicates as clients. L.A. detectives had been able to tie at least forty murders to their various clients, but had only been able to nab a few of them. The firm's criminal defense practice was top notch.

Justin Ursh joined the firm five years ago from a small practice on the East Coast. Based on files the police had, he was a trouble-maker from the start. Sean imagined he was a brash young man who allowed the lure of a two-hundred-and-thirty-thousand-dol-lar salary and eighty-five-thousand-dollar bonus to blind him to his ethics. Once on board, he had mentioned to more than one friend, all from different firms, that he regretted his choice.

Justin had been placed on the Velez Holdings account, owned and operated by reputed gangster-turned-business-man, Roberto Velez. By all accounts he was a good lawyer. He'd defended them against a number of RICO charges, as well as two murder charges and one attempted-murder charge. He had gotten two acquittals, a hung jury and a jury nullification. But Sean deduced that the guilt was getting to him. A little over two months ago, Ursh con-tacted the FBI. He'd thought it was anonymous, but the FBI used the surveillance they had set up to track the tips that were lead-ing them to Velez's criminal enterprises, to the pay phone in a coffee shop two miles from where Ursh's nanny lived. Ursh used to drive her home often.

"What did he tell them?" Haley asked.

"I have no idea," Sean answered, "but I think if I can decipher these FBI notes, I can find out. My suspicion is that the informa-tion had to be good enough for them to want to take his murder off BHPD's hands."

"That would be breaking the law, right? Telling his client's secrets."

"Not breaking the law, but breaking his confidentiality. He would probably be disbarred if it came out. He was trying to do what was right, but someone found out."

"Where does Garrett fit into all of this?"

Sean shrugged. "One of Ursh's neighbors said they saw someone matching his description get in a car that looked like his, moments after they heard a gun shot."

"That's weak."

Sean nodded. "They need more. Garrett joined the firm a year ago as an intern and now works as a clerk part time. He was assigned to Ursh's cases. It's possible that Garrett found out about Ursh and the FBI, and told."

Haley shook her head. "But that doesn't mean he did anything?"

"That's what I need you to tell me." Sean sat in the La-Z-Boy facing her. "I need your help, Haley."

Haley offered the softest smile she could manage. "Of course I'll help you, but why do you need my help? The FBI is on it."

"Loose lips are all over this thing." Sean shook his head in frustration. "Taylor has agreed to help the FBI all she can, but even with what little she knows, she's at risk. Maybe you can help me with what you know."

Haley stood up and walked over to him. She grinned at the look of surprise on his face as she sat down on his lap.

"What are you doing?" Sean asked. There was no way he wouldn't be affected by this. Haley was an incredibly seductive, sexy woman. Her devilishness only made her more appealing. No good could come from being this close to her.

"You're a great brother, Sean. I doubt my brothers even know what's going on with me, but you . . . you stole those files. You risked a lot to get any information you could to help Taylor."

"I love her." Sean felt his body react as Haley wrapped her arms around him. He knew the girl was from hell, but she smelled like heaven.

"You did it for me too." Haley leaned in. "Didn't you? With Rudio and again with Chris. You were willing to do whatever it took, at whatever risk to you, for someone you cared about. You do care about me, don't you?"

"What are you doing, Haley?" Sean could feel his arms slide over her thighs despite wishing they wouldn't. She was wearing short shorts, and the feel of her soft thighs made him unable to hide his attraction to her.

Haley knew she was shameless, but the second she sat on his lap, she wanted him. She could at least say that. "I guess I'm getting emotional."

"You don't get emotional," he countered.

She rolled her eyes. "So what is this, then? What am I feeling now? I'm remembering how you saved my life and what it was like before . . ."

"We both agreed that breaking up was for the best."

Although he said it was because he wasn't interested in a real relationship at the time, Sean had really broken up with Haley because Janet had made clear to him what he already knew, but ignored because he was in love. Haley would never be happy in a life with a cop and he would never be able to live a life on Steven Chase's bankroll. Once he'd revealed the truth to Haley, they'd spent one second considering what could have been, before agreeing that there was no real hope for a future together.

Haley offered a reassuring stroke of her hand over his head. "Sean, don't get your hopes up. I'm not asking for anything other than right now. I can admit to you I'm scared, because you are the only person I've ever admitted it to before. You're the only person that can make me feel safe and I need to feel safe right now."

Everything inside of him told him to pat her on the leg and tell her to get up. But he didn't. He let her kiss him once and then again, reacting to Haley the only way a man could.

"I think that went well, don't you?" Elisha closed the door to Michael's office after she stepped inside.

Michael turned to her, watching as she casually tossed her purse on his desk and sauntered toward him. He tossed his crutches on the floor and backed into his chair. "You're very good. Setting up a conference call with Alton Frist clearly made Dad happy."

"How can you tell if he's happy?" She grabbed the arms of his chair and leaned in, giving him ample view of her modest cleavage.

Michael smiled at her advances, but didn't take the bait. "You can't. I've spent thirty years deciphering that man's face and I can barely tell. But I think he was happy. He wants this to happen."

"What is he afraid of?" she asked.

"He's not afraid of anything," Michael corrected. "He's just excessively cautious. It's made him a billionaire."

"And you will reap all the benefits when you take over." She positioned herself on his lap.

"Easy," he said. He really didn't want her on his lap or in his office. He had work to do.

"This deal will make you king," she said. "Don't you believe it?"

Michael would never tell her how much he hoped that was true. With everything that had happened, he feared he would never be CEO of Chase Beauty. This was especially so after Carter joined the board of directors last year. His father had threatened Michael countless times with his belief that Carter would eventually join Chase Beauty.

"It better," Michael said, looking away.

"So where is my reward?" She leaned in for a kiss.

Michael turned his head away. "Not right now, Elisha."

"Why not?" she asked suspiciously.

"I have work to do before we go to the pilot's funeral." He grabbed her at the waist and began to lift her off of him. He was still in pain from sex with Kimberly the other day. "I'm not in the mood."

"So maybe you aren't as grateful as you should be." She had a sinister look on her face as she refused to budge.

Michael saw that look on her face, the one that came before she had a fit. "Grateful? Don't act like you're doing me a favor, sweetie. I've worked my ass off on this one."

"But you don't know everything," she said with a sly smile. "For instance, East Coast Publishing just put in a bid for half a million more than you're offering."

He did know, and it made him angry that she thought she could use this against him. "But they don't want to continue the product line. They only want the properties, advertisers, and subscription list. Frist clearly said he wants the publications to continue."

"Look, baby, I get paid either way." She placed her hand gently on his head. "And since Frist put me in charge, Steven Chase isn't the only person you need to keep happy."

Michael assumed she was bullshitting. Elisha wanted this deal to go through almost as much as he did, but he couldn't take any chances. This deal was his redemption and there was nothing he wouldn't do to make it work.

"Then let's see if I can make you happy." He grabbed her hair and brought her face to his. He didn't want her and he would get rid of her after the deal was done. But for now, he would give her what she wanted.

When Kimberly approached Michael's office, she assumed his executive assistant looked at her the way she did because it had been an eternity since she had visited her husband at work. Kimberly used to show up at least once a week in that past life; the one where she was happy.

But it wasn't that at all, and Kimberly realized as much when she opened the door to Michael's office without knocking. She should have known better. Both Michael and Elisha, sitting on his lap, turned to face her with a look of surprise on their faces.

"Isn't this pretty," Kimberly said.

Michael felt a brick in his stomach. He didn't need this. He wanted to push Elisha off his lap, but seeing Kimberly, he was immediately reminded of her recent rejection of him. He certainly wasn't going to risk upsetting Elisha and hurting this deal.

Elisha slowly got off of Michael's lap, never taking her eyes off Kimberly. Kimberly wanted to slap that thin-lipped smirk off her face. It wasn't out of jealousy. She was just angry and sick of it.

"Is this your newest slut?" Kimberly asked, smiling at the angry expression on the woman's face in reaction to her insult. "Vanilla is your flavor of the week I take it."

Elisha looked at Michael as if she expected him to defend her, but he didn't acknowledge her. He kept his eyes on his wife. "Gutter talk doesn't flatter you, Kimberly. Or then again, I guess it does."

"Well that certainly didn't last long." Kimberly knew he knew what she was talking about.

"I never promised you anything." He thought this whole situation was totally fucked up, but Michael tried his best to act as nonchalant as possible. The deal was what was most important now.

"Actually you did." Kimberly was surprised by the softness in her own voice. "Once, seven years ago, but who's counting? It was only a wedding vow."

She got her hit in, Kimberly could tell from the reaction on his face. He was trying to hide it, but she stuck him and that would have to be enough. For now.

As she slammed the door behind her and started down the hallway of Chase Beauty's executive offices, Kimberly knew that she didn't have to worry about ever hoping or believing again. All she had was hate and this was war.

As he emerged from his bathroom, Sean expected to see Haley still on his bed, where she was when he left. But she wasn't. He assumed that she had gotten tired of waiting. Haley didn't like to wait for anyone or anything and he had taken longer than usual, trying to wash away his sins with this woman.

In a way he was happy she was gone. He wouldn't have to deal with what came next. After spending twenty minutes in the shower chastising himself for making such a stupid mistake, he imagined Haley had done the same and had gone about her business.

"Haley?" Wrapping the towel around his waist, he made his way down the hallway into the front of the apartment. She was nowhere.

He sighed, relieved that he wouldn't have to deal with it now. After all, if he didn't hurry he would be late for work and now that Haley was going to help with the investigation, maybe the FBI would let him . . .

Panic hit Sean as he noticed out of the corner of his eye that the top drawer to his curio cabinet was slightly open.

"Dammit!" He rifled through the drawer, but he knew it was a waste of time.

Everything he had on the case was gone. He had nothing. When he saw Haley Chase, this time, after all she had done to him, he was going to kill her.

9

Carter wasn't really sure why he got a five-hundred-dollar-a-night Crown suite at The London West Hollywood hotel. It was habit, he guessed. He liked the modern look of the place, it was easy to get to from both View Park and downtown L.A., and there was something about the interior of the room that made him think it would be a good place to meet Avery. The decorations lent a sensuality and sophistication to its colors and textures.

It seemed appropriate. This was mostly about sex. He couldn't wait to get his hands on Avery again, and ever since she agreed to meet him there, he'd been aroused. He was starving for her and imagined he always would be. Yes, there was something very exciting about the secrecy, but he didn't need anything to get him excited about Avery.

Still, despite the sex, he wanted to be with her. It was the one thing he shared with Avery that he had hardly shared with any other woman; an enjoyment in just being with her. Whether they were dining on a yacht in Nice or hanging out on her parents' back porch eating hot dogs, her presence soothed him and he loved talking to her.

Things were different now.

Avery hadn't even finished knocking on the hotel room door before Carter opened it. All the butterflies in her belly disappeared at the sight of him. She had tried to ignore what she was doing as she showered, shaved, put on her silk panties and her mid-thigh pleated summer dress. She had tried to ignore what she was doing as she left Connor with her mother to "run some errands." She tried to ignore what she was doing as she drove her car to the hotel and into the garage.

But there was no ignoring it now, and her body didn't give her any time to care. The second she stepped inside, Carter grabbed her by the waist and pulled her to him with one hand while he slammed the door shut behind her with the other. Her purse fell to the floor and she felt an animal hunger surge through her as her hands went to his chest.

Their lips devoured each other as they stumbled against the door. Carter felt on fire as Avery frantically undid his buttons and lifted his shirt up. He separated his lips from hers for only a second before reclaiming them. Avery felt herself going insane as Carter's hands greedily moved up her legs, squeezing her soft, creamy thighs and pulling on her panties.

Avery inhaled sharply as Carter lifted her into his arms and carried her over to the sofa only a few feet away. He kicked the wine stand out of the way and ice went everywhere. He couldn't wait the five extra seconds it would take to get to the bedroom.

Having discarded her dress, Avery was now in her underwear, and as she ran her hands up and down Carter's strong arms, she felt waves of pressing need begin to smother her. His mouth kissed her chest just above her breasts, then her neck and then her chin. When he took her mouth again, it was too much.

"Oh God, Carter," she pleaded. "Please wait."

"For what?" he asked.

"A condom," she answered, turning her head away. They hadn't been safe the first time, but she wouldn't be that stupid again. She spoke to him between leaving kisses on his neck. "Do you . . . have a . . . condom?"

Carter wasn't sure why that bothered him. He was a strong believer in safe sex. He even used a condom when he slept with Julia, mostly because he was sleeping with other women. The only time he'd gone uncovered was when he knew he fell in love with Avery. He'd thrown away his black book and he knew she would never cheat on him.

"You want me to wear a condom?" he asked, sitting up.

"You have to." Avery didn't like the look on his face. He was upset, and that was the last thing she wanted. She reached for him as he lifted off of her to sit beside her. "Don't, baby. I just . . . Anthony and Julia. If we're going to do this, we have to think about . . ."

"About Anthony and Julia?" Carter turned his body so his back was to her.

Avery sat up behind him and wrapped her arms around his bare chest as she leaned into his back. "It's only safe. You know that."

Carter nodded. "For now, I understand. But you'll be leaving him and I'll be breaking up with Julia, so . . ."

Avery gasped. "What?"

Carter turned to face her and the look on her face told him that she had no intention of leaving her husband and he was too angry to be hurt. "What did you think this was? An affair? A fling?"

"No, no, no." Avery was shaking her head, not certain of what she thought this was. It was wrong and so right, horrible and beautiful at the same time. "You could never be that to me. I just . . ."

"Did you really think I would be your kept man?" he asked. "For how long?"

"Don't let your ego ruin this moment, Carter."

"You can blame this on my ego all you want, but there is no way I'm going to be your man on the side while Anthony plays the husband."

"He isn't playing the husband," Avery said. "He is the husband."

Carter ignored the pain of those words by not responding to them. If he said what he wanted, all hell would break loose. "I understand that this might be difficult and complicated, but . . ."

"Might be?" Avery asked. "He's my husband!"

"Stop saying that word!" he demanded. "He never should have been that and now that I have you back, I won't stand for it."

"Stand for it?" Avery's eyes widened in response to his arrogance. "You're already trying to take control of my life? Tell me what I can and can't do?"

"You can do whatever you want, Avery. But you can't do it married to Anthony. I can be patient enough for you to break it to him as best you can, but I've wasted too much time sitting on the sidelines watching you married to another man."

"Carter." She waited for him to turn back to her, but he didn't. She reached out and placed her hand on his shoulder. His skin felt soft and hot. She squeezed, and then harder, before he turned back to her. "Please, baby. I need you to understand. Everything has changed so fast. A month ago we were just friends, connected by Connor. We were both in love with other people and . . ."

"Were we?" Carter asked. He didn't think it was necessary to tell her all he had planned these past six months. None of that meant anything anymore. "I know I've always loved you, Avery, and I got the distinct feeling that you've always loved me."

"No matter what our feelings," she said, "we weren't together. Then you almost died and all these feelings just took over. Now we're together and . . . it's just so much."

Carter took her hand off his shoulder and brought it to his mouth. He kissed it gently, knowing that he should be grateful that she was handling their affair this well. He had so much to be grateful for now that she was back in his life.

"I know what you're saying, but I can only be so patient when it comes to you, Avery."

She leaned forward and hugged him tightly. "I know. But I'm just getting my head around this. What about our families?"

As his blood pressure lowered, Carter could better understand the delicacies of what she was saying. Her parents hated him, and then there was his family.

Avery leaned away, taking his face in her hands. She kissed him on the lips twice. "No matter what we do, they're affected and it won't end there. You're a Chase and everything that everyone in your family does becomes public. We have to be careful and not act too quickly."

Carter nodded reluctantly. "But not too slowly, Avery. I want my family; you and Connor."

"I know what you want," she said. "I want it too, so much it makes me want to scream. But I have to think of Anthony and the sacrifices he made for me. What this would do to him. He has no one but me here. I care too much about him to just slap him in the face with this and walk away."

Carter didn't give a damn about Anthony, knowing it was his idea to lie about who Connor's real father was. Because of Anthony, if Chief Jackson had not been shot, compelling Avery to come home, Carter might still not know Connor existed. Anthony Harper could go to hell.

"But you will walk away," Carter said. "You will leave him and be with me."

Avery knew she should nod to appease him, but it would be a lie. No matter what her heart told her she wanted, there was something inside of her, ingrained in her soul, that told her she had no right to turn her back on her husband.

"He's so weak right now, Carter. He's been beaten down and most of it's to make me happy. I won't . . ."

Avery was startled by the force with which Carter grabbed her and threw her down on the sofa. His mouth slammed down on hers with a power that overwhelmed her. She thought at first to push away, but the taste of his hungry lips reignited everything inside of her.

He kissed her again and again on her lips, her face, her neck and her chest as his hands caressed her breasts. He was moaning his hunger; his angry passion. He wanted to devour her, to keep her with him so she couldn't go anywhere.

Avery felt waves of insanity rush through her as she yelled out his name over and over again. She wanted him inside of her now.

"Carter, please!" she begged, her nails digging into his back. "Now, baby."

"Do you love me?" he asked, kissing her frantically.

"Carter!" The delay was becoming too painful to bear. "Please."

"Do you love me?" he repeated, his voice sounding like a guttural groan.

"Yes," she screamed out loud. "Yes, I love you!"

Then suddenly Avery felt him let go of her. It was like a slap in the face with a cold brick. She opened her eyes and in the haze of her passion she reached for him, but he pushed her hands away.

Carter waited until she was looking right in his eyes, and with the coldest stare he could manage, he said, "Go home, Avery. Your husband's waiting for you."

Avery was paralyzed with intense astonishment as Carter got up and zipped up his pants. She thought she called out his name once or twice as he grabbed his shirt off the floor and his keys off the console table, but she wasn't sure. She couldn't think clearly as her body was still taken by desire. She had been on the edge of a cliff, ready to completely descend into madness and then ripped back to reality with an icy rejection that made her feel angry, ashamed, and hurt.

She started crying the second she heard the door slam behind him. This was unworkable, she knew that now. She was living in a fantasy world where she could have everything she did want and keep everything she should want. Not with Carter. God had cursed her to fall in love with a man who was simply unable to be anything other than everything to a woman.

Could she choose him over everyone else? Anthony would be heartbroken and her parents' disappointment couldn't be quantified. Avery's mother was her very best friend and she couldn't imagine what she might say, not to mention the fact that Nikki never liked Carter even when it wasn't a sin to be with him.

And what would she gain in exchange for all that she lost? The chance to once again live a life in the public eye and be surrounded by that dysfunctional freak show he called a family? Was he worth that?

She refused to answer that honestly, because she was completely devastated by what her subconscious told her that answer was. Yes, Carter was worth anything.

As she watched her sons with their trainer in the twenty-five-meter heated swimming pool at the Beverly Hills Country Club, the last person Kimberly expected to see was Elisha Fisher, but that was exactly who approached her at her patio table. Kimberly didn't get a chance to speak before Elisha sat down across from her at the table.

"I thought it was time we meet," she said, never looking away from Kimberly as she waved away the waiter on his approach. "Don't you?"

Kimberly offered a smile that could win her an Emily Post award as she gently placed the book she was reading on her lap. "I hope you're wearing sunscreen. That painfully pale skin of yours won't last a second in this sun. And I wouldn't want anything to happen to you."

Elisha's smile slithered across her face. "How kind you are. So much more civilized than Michael described you to be."

Kimberly laughed sarcastically. "Look lady . . ."

"My name is Elisha Fisher."

"Do I look like I care what your name is?" Kimberly asked, satisfied by the woman's fading smile. "You're just a number; one of many that he uses to try to forget me."

"Is that so?" Elisha asked. "Does he usually ask his . . . numbers to move from New York to L.A. to be with him?"

Kimberly's expression stayed frozen. "You're a liar."

"What I am," she responded, "is the number that he needed to finally forget you. What I am, is the creator of the deal that will make him the golden boy to his daddy again. None of those other numbers can say that, can they?"

Kimberly laughed, wondering what this whore would think if she really knew the deal. "Let me guess. You think he's going to divorce me and . . . marry you?"

"Why else would he ask me to change my life for him?"

"Because he's a selfish son of a bitch, and I mean that literally. His mother is a super bitch and she will not let you anywhere near her last name."

"People have a way of warming to me," she responded, looking extremely proud of herself.

"Yes, but what about the ones you don't fuck?" Kimberly asked. She turned her attention back to her sons before saying, "I know there are very few of them, but Janet is one that you don't have what it takes to deal with."

"You don't know me," Elisha said flatly.

"I don't need to." Kimberly continued to focus on the pool. "You don't count, so why bother?"

Kimberly smiled as she heard Elisha huff and push away from the table, but that smile faded in seconds. She didn't give a damn that Janet would eat this slut alive. What she did give a damn about was the possibility that Elisha could be right. If there was anything Kimberly knew about Michael it was that nothing on this planet meant more to him than his father's favor, and he had certainly lost it. Was it possible that whatever he was working on with Elisha could redeem him? If so, he would certainly give Elisha whatever she wanted. He certainly would want to keep her happy until the deal was done, and Kimberly realized that this fact made Elisha very useful to her. Maybe she could be Kimberly's key to breaking free of Michael. But first, she had to find out who Elisha Fisher was and what deal she had brought to Chase Beauty.

Lying out in the lounge chair by the pool at home, Haley had almost fallen asleep before her cell, placed on the table next to her melting margarita, sounded the loud flute that announced a text message. Her eyes flew open and the *People* magazine in her lap fell to the side.

"This better be good," she said as she reached for the phone. She looked at the caller ID and a crooked smile formed at her lips. "Very good."

She flipped the phone open and, as she expected, Sean's message was short and boring.

I know what u did!

She quickly texted back a row of question marks, hoping he would get pissed enough to be more creative.

U stole my files
Ur files? u stole them 1st
Y
Sorry. Have 2 protect myself
How?
If G gets n trouble, so do I. It's a trust fund thing.
Where r files?

Shredded -
FBI has originals
Yes but ur the 1 wants 2 help sis – not FBI
U think u can stop me?
Slow u down while I figure out what 2 do
Do u care re any1 but u?
No, but ur still good in bed
Ur a bitch
Right again.

Haley waited for his response, but there wasn't anything. He gave up so quickly. How disappointing.

As she was grabbing the files and sneaking out of his dingy apartment, Haley had felt a little bit of something that she thought might be considered guilt. But it passed quickly, as did most emotions she didn't have patience for. It wasn't personal really. She'd gone over there to get information and had been willing to sleep with him to get it and hopefully convince him to keep her out of it. She hadn't expected the files, and she imagined the more Sean understood of them, the more determined he would be to clear Taylor, which meant putting her and Garrett in a lie connected to a murder.

Haley just knew that until her business in Australia was taken care of, she needed access to her trust fund. And as things were a little too touchy-feely at home since the plane accident, she didn't want to get shipped off to Europe again.

Whatever it was that Garrett was involved in, she had hastily interjected herself, and she needed it to go away. She figured her best bet was to do as Garrett said, stick to their story. Sean and Taylor were the ones determined to crack their alibis and she had taken away Sean's ammunition. He'd admitted that he hadn't figured it all out yet. Now, he wouldn't get the chance to. As for Taylor trying to help the FBI, Haley would figure out how to deal with her next.

Haley tossed the phone back on the table and reached for her margarita just as two shadows blocked out the sun's rays. She took her sunglasses off and pouted.

"What do you two want?"

Carter reached down and snatched the margarita out of her hands. "This will do."

"Hey!" Haley tossed her magazine at him. "Why are you two always here? You don't live here anymore."

"Did you forget what tonight is?" Michael asked, leaning on his crutches. "Leigh's birthday dinner."

"Mom canceled that," Haley said. "We were forced to go to that funeral instead. Remember?"

"It was just postponed," Michael said. "And you're joining us. This is a family thing, Haley. And we weren't forced to go to that funeral."

"By the way," Carter said, "thanks for not visiting us at all at the hospital or anywhere else for that matter."

Haley rolled her eyes. "I couldn't get around to it. Besides, you two have gotten more than enough attention as a result of your accident. How much longer do you plan on milking that?"

Carter and Michael looked at each other and smiled.

"This is for Mom," Michael said. "So get up and try to act like a human being for one evening."

"You can party without me," she said. "I have a date."

"With Garrett?" Carter asked.

"This would be your business how?" she asked.

"Look, kid, I'm going to give you some advice." Carter's eyes narrowed intently as he looked down at her. "Stay away from Garrett. Whatever is the worst possible scenario going on at that firm, is probably the case. Everyone connected to that place is dangerous."

Haley stood up and placed her hands on her hips. "Carter, if I need advice on how to pretend like I'm happy while the person I love is married to, and having nightly sex with, someone else and that someone else is spending more time with my kid than I am, I'll come to you. Otherwise, stay out of my business."

"Whoa! Ouch." Michael laughed, holding up his hand for a high five. Haley slapped it hard with a satisfied smile on her face. "The kid is harsh, but good."

"Are you two finished having a good laugh?" Carter asked.

"Sorry bro," Michael sighed, still smiling wide. "But even you have to admit that was a good burn."

"You've been warned," Carter said as he pointed to his baby sister.

"Whatevs." Haley turned and walked away.

"She read you well," Michael said.

Carter smirked. "She was wrong. Things are going to change and I have a feeling it will happen sooner than anyone expects."

"So I think I'm going to take it," Anthony said as he slid into bed next to his wife.

Avery was on her side with her back to Anthony. It was this time, right before bed, that was the hardest. It was supposed to be an intimate moment for them; especially now that Connor was officially in her nursery and no longer sleeping in a bassinet next to their bed.

But Avery couldn't look at him. She had hoped to feign sleep, as she had the last few nights, but Anthony was intent on talking.

"Avery, are you listening?" he asked.

"Of course." Avery took a deep breath and sat up in bed. "The job. You're thinking of taking the research job."

Anthony frowned as he observed her. "You don't want me to take it, do you?"

"I want you to be happy," Avery said plainly.

"What does that mean?" Anthony asked. "Avery, what has gotten into you lately? You're acting very weird."

"How?" She smiled at him as if he was being silly.

"I don't know." He grabbed the remote that was between them on the bed and turned the TV off. "Just, very quiet."

"I'm just tired," she lied. "Connor has been crying all day. Her teeth are coming."

"That can't be fun." Anthony placed the remote on the nightstand and turned off the dim lamp. "I'm sorry to bother you with my job stuff."

"You aren't bothering me." She turned to him, feeling horrible that she had made him believe he was annoying her. "I want to hear what you have to say."

"I'm more interested in what you have to say," he said. "About the job."

"Anthony, you don't want the job." She was going to reach out and touch his arm, but couldn't bring herself to touch him. This whole job situation only reminded her of how much Anthony had sacrificed for her. His career was in a shambles.

"It's not that simple," he said.

"We aren't hurting for money," Avery said. "Wouldn't you like to wait until a professor's position comes up?"

"Baby, I've been looking almost every day for six months. It's not happening." His hands rested on his lap. "I think maybe if I just get into the university system, I can work my way back."

"Didn't you say it doesn't work like that?" she asked. "You said that it's very rare for a tenured professor to come back after taking a researcher's job unless it's groundbreaking scientific or medical research."

Anthony sighed, throwing his hands in the air. "Well, what do you want me to do, Avery? I just have to believe that I'll be the exception. Look, baby, I can't be like this anymore. I'm doing nothing."

"You're helping me work at the gallery by watching Connor. You're . . ." Avery couldn't believe it but she couldn't think of anything to say. What was wrong with her?

"Exactly," Anthony said with a disappointed look on his face.

"Listen to me." Avery placed her hand over his. "I need you. I . . . I love you, Anthony. What you've done for me and Connor since the moment I met you can't be measured. The kindness, understanding, and God, all the sacrifices can't ever be repaid."

"I never wanted you to repay me," he said. "Your love is reason enough for me to do anything."

Avery felt his hand turn and grip hers. She thought to pull away, but couldn't find it in herself to do so. She should have just shut up, but she hadn't, and now she felt worse than ever. Or so she thought until she realized that Anthony was moving toward her. He wanted to kiss her.

Avery held a hand against his chest to stop him. The pained look in his eyes was hard to take.

Anthony took the hand she had against his chest in his own. "It's been a while, baby."

Avery tried to remember the last time they had had sex. To her recollection it had been about a week before the plane accident. It seemed ages ago and probably felt so to Anthony.

They averaged sex twice a week and Avery enjoyed it. She had a healthy sex appetite and Anthony was attractive and fit. He never "took her" in the way she dreamed, but he was tender and patient. It was never as it had been with Carter, but there had been no reason for her to think of that. Anthony would be the only man she would make love to for the rest of her life. She was determined to please him and let him know what would make her feel satisfied, and forget everything that had come before.

But there was no doing that now. She had let Carter back into her bed, and not only did she know the comparisons were unavoidable, Avery had never in her life had sex with more than one man at a time. Men did it all the time and she knew a few women who had more than one lover, but she couldn't possibly. She never thought she'd have to deal with it, but then again, she never thought she'd be here.

"I know," she whispered as if speaking quietly would lessen the rejection. "But I really am tired. Tomorrow, okay?"

Avery asked herself why she had just said that. She would just have to come up with another excuse tomorrow.

Anthony slowly let her hand go and leaned forward. He kissed her gently on the forehead before turning and reaching for the remote again.

"I have to change my mind about that damn Museum Ball," he said, his voice unable to conceal his hurt feelings. "The head of the research and development department at UCLA has invited me. Apparently, the university purchased a few tables and he wants you and me to come."

"If you want to go," Avery said, "then we can go." Avery already had her back to him when she heard the television come back on.

"No matter what I do," Anthony said, "I can't escape that damn Chase family. Promise me you'll stay away from him?"

"Him?" Avery asked.

"Carter," he answered. "He'll use something about Connor as an excuse to talk to you, but can you just say no to him for one night?"

Avery bit her lower lip to control the tears that wanted to flow. Could she stay away from him for just one night? She didn't think so.

"Of course," she answered. "I'll pretend as if he isn't even there."

10

"*Lion King!*" Daniel yelled.

"*Prince of Egypt!*" Evan countered.

Kimberly stood in the doorway to the newly renovated media room in the basement of their Hollywood Hills home. It now had eight luxury, plush seats, each with a drink container and pull-out tabletop for placing food. The one-hundred-and-six-inch screen was enormous and the 7.2 surround sound system could be heard on the second floor as if it was turned up all the way.

It was just as Michael and the boys wanted it. Of course it was nothing like what she wanted because Michael never once asked her opinion. Kimberly didn't give a damn. This house that was supposed to be her dream was now her prison. She only hoped that she was on her way to a release without probation.

"Pick one," she said, holding up both DVDs. "You're only watching one."

"We saw his movie yesterday," Daniel said.

"You wanted to watch it too." Evan ran over to the wall near the control booth and began pulling on the dimmers making the room go from dark to only slightly dark. "*Lion King! Lion King! Lion King!*"

"Stop that." Kimberly came over and gently smacked his hand. She pulled him away from the controls. "You'll break it."

"*Lion King* or I'm protesting." Evan stood with his arms crossed over his chest and a pout that would win a contest if there was one.

"I told you about threatening me with protests didn't I?" Kimberly walked over to the player and opened the glass door. "*Prince of Egypt* it is."

"Daddy!" Daniel, apparently not interested in leaving his plush front-row seat, waved at his father standing in the doorway.

"Hey little man!" Michael waved back, taking a second to make eye contact with Kimberly to receive the usual daily contempt. "You guys are gonna get sick of this room. You're in here every day."

"Never!" Evan said. "Daddy, can you make Mommy play *Lion King*?"

"Excuse me?" Kimberly asked. "My decision was made. It's *The Prince of Egypt* and that's that."

To get a break from his crutches, Michael leaned against the wall. "You can watch them both."

"No, they can't." Kimberly turned to him with a determined look on her face. She eyed him intently. Because of the way he treated her, she was losing control over the boys and it stopped today.

Michael was ready to stare her down, but this wasn't worth it. He had something much, much better for her.

"Help me out, Daddy," Evan said in anticipation of an unexpected victory.

"Daddy can't do anything," Daniel said. "He's broken."

"I'm not broken," Michael said. "It's just one leg. I'm still the man of the house. Which reminds me, Kimberly, can I have a word?"

"The movie is starting," Kimberly said. "Sit down and don't get up and play with these controls while I'm gone."

Michael stepped aside as she approached the door and closed it behind her. He'd expected her to stop, but she kept going and it pissed him off.

"I said I need to talk to you!"

Kimberly stopped just as she reached the bottom of the stairs. "I've had enough conversations with kids today."

"Hey, I backed you up in there."

Kimberly had to laugh. "You call that backing me up? You're pitiful."

Michael waited until she started up the stairs to drop his bomb. "I won't take long. I wouldn't want to keep you from the art gallery."

Kimberly froze and it took her a second to compose herself before turning around. She looked him in the eyes with all the hate she could muster, but he only smiled.

Michael nodded to the pool table, which was at the center of the game room.

Kimberly rolled her eyes and walked briskly over to the table. She grabbed the manila folder that was lying on top of the green felt and opened it. There were six pictures of her entering and leaving the gallery through the back door, two for each of three days. The time was written in black marker on the bottom of each picture.

"I had no idea you loved art that much." Michael moved closer to her. He needed to get into the light so he could see the look on her face. "I mean hours and hours a day. And I assume you were parking out back and entering through the alley because you wanted to avoid the press that would surely be in front of the store after hearing that a Chase was a daily visitor."

"What do you want?" Kimberly tossed the folder and the pictures back on the pool table.

"Nothing," he said innocently. "Why would I want anything? I respect that you love art. It's a sign of class. It tells me you've learned something since I took you out of the gutter seven years ago."

"If you insist on playing a game with that idiotic smirk on your face, I'm going to take one those crutches and shove it up your ass." God, how she wanted to do that.

"Threats of violence show you haven't traveled that far from the gutter after all. I guess you're a failed project on my part."

"Your entire life is one failed project after another," Kimberly said. "If you don't know what I'm talking about, ask your father."

Michael wanted to strangle her right there, but waited until she started to leave again before asking, "What is it you love so much about the art there?"

Kimberly kept her back to him. "Fuck you, Michael."

"That is why you're there, right? I mean the private investigator I had tailing you said that he thought you were working there."

She took another step. "Well, I guess he's just as much an idiot as you are."

"Must be," Michael said. "It's a good thing he's wrong because I wouldn't want Avery or her mother to go to jail or anything."

This got Kimberly to turn around.

"If you were working there," Michael said, making certain to keep his voice as unassuming as possible, "then she would have to be paying you in cash. Because I have access to every account you have, and my P.I. would have told me if he saw you at one of those check cashing places. But you wouldn't go to one of those places because you're Kimberly Chase. It would get in the news."

"Avery and Nikki have nothing to do with your sick little vendetta against me."

Michael's expression turned cruel. "That's why it will be so satisfying when I turn them in to the IRS. I'm only the CFO of a billion-dollar corporation, but my money sense tells me they're breaking the law."

Kimberly swallowed hard. "What do you think Carter would do to you when he found out?"

Michael brought his hand to his chin and rubbed it repeatedly. "Let me think. Well, if Nikki goes to jail, he'll buy me a Lamborghini. He hates her. Now, Avery will be a more complicated issue, but Chase blood is thicker than anything else. We'd work it out."

"I wouldn't be so sure of that."

"It would be tough times, but I think it might be worth it to see you lose the only friend you have. She'll hate you. Also, her baby will not be happy you sent her mother to jail. She'll probably try to kill you when she grows up."

Kimberly knew if she stayed in this situation she would be dead well before Connor could ever grow up. She was dying a bit every day. "Are you having fun?"

Michael nodded with a gleeful smile. "The most I've had in a while and that includes fucking you."

When he realized she was coming over to him, Michael braced himself, dropping one of his crutches to free his arm. He wasn't fast enough and she slapped him hard across the cheek before he could stop her.

"You are a sick son of a bitch," Kimberly said.

"I know," he answered. "I really am, but I do have some heart. I mean, I'll forget about the IRS if . . . I don't know . . . maybe you stopped loving art so much and didn't go there anymore."

That gallery was her only link to feeling some form of independence and dignity. But she couldn't put Avery and Nikki at risk. She'd seen what happened to anyone in the path of an angry Chase.

"I hate you! I curse God every night for not killing you in that plane accident. When I thought you were dead, I felt so peaceful and free. I knew you were in hell where you belonged. But I'm not gonna stop praying he'll strike you down one way or another."

Michael tried to hide the sting of her words. If she was just saying them to hurt him it would be fine, but she was telling the truth. "Peaceful? Free? Sorry, baby, but dead or alive, you're never getting away from me."

Michael watched her as she walked away. When would she understand who she was dealing with? He had to teach her that there was nothing she could have that he couldn't find out about and take away from her.

When he turned around to pick up his crutch, what he saw struck him in every bit of what was left of his heart. Daniel and Evan were both standing in the doorway to the media room with a look of devastation on their faces. How much had they heard? What had they seen?

"You're so mean," Daniel said with venom in his tiny voice. "I hate you too."

He disappeared inside the room, leaving Evan standing alone. He didn't seem to know what to do, but when Michael took a step toward him, he turned and slammed the door shut.

Michael stood at the door for probably five or ten minutes

staring at the shiny, fresh black paint. He would make it up to them some way. There had to be something he could buy them. Maybe take them to Universal Studios in San Diego. No, Disneyland would make them forget all about this.

Avery was ready to give up on Taylor. She had agreed to take her sister shopping on chic Robertson Boulevard in Beverly Hills to make her feel better. She was doing it as a favor to her mother, and she was also very concerned that she hadn't seen her sister in a while. But three hours and three-hundred-seventy-five dollars spent in Maxfields, didn't seem to do the job.

"How about The Ivy?" Avery asked. "It's only a few blocks away and maybe you'll see some stars."

"Do you really think we could get a seat there?" Taylor asked in a crestfallen tone.

"We might have to wait a little bit, but . . ."

"I don't want to wait. I'd rather just go to McDonalds."

"Well, there isn't any McDonalds around here," Avery said. She glanced across the street. "Why don't we just go there? Michel Richard Patisserie. I'm sure it's nice."

"Whatever." Taylor shrugged.

"Taylor, you have to help me out here."

"What do you want me to do?"

"I don't know. Talk. Yell. Cry. Do whatever you have to, but do something."

Taylor didn't respond. She only looked at Avery as if she thought her sister was the dumbest person on the face of the earth.

"You're being a brat," Avery said. "Let's get some food in your stomach. I'm sure this . . ."

Avery was speechless as she tightened her grip on the bag in her hand. It took her a moment to recover, but it was long enough to pique Taylor's curiosity.

"What are you looking at?" she asked.

"Nothing." Avery gestured down the street. "Let's go somewhere else."

"Why?" Taylor was staring intently at the restaurant, which had patio seating on both sides of the entry. It was difficult to see who was sitting at the tables because they were under dark green umbrellas the same color as the awning. And there was a screen made of large potted greenery barricading them from the street.

"Let's just go," Avery urged, but from the expression that suddenly appeared on Taylor's face, she could see that her little sister had noticed what Avery was trying to avoid.

"Oh, snap," was her only response.

Carter and Julia were sitting at a table in the middle of the right side of the patio. It was an intimate scene made even more so by the fact that they were sitting beside each other, instead of across from each other like most people.

Avery felt a tightening in her chest as she watched Julia talk on and on, with an expression that told the world she was absolutely elated at that moment. But it was worse to see the way Carter was looking at her and smiling. He spoke once or twice, but not often. He was showing her attention, the kind of attention that a woman needs. Julia felt she wasn't just being heard, but also listened to.

Then Carter leaned in and said a few words before they both broke out in laughter. Julia playfully socked Carter in the arm before tasting some of her salad. Carter leaned back in his chair and placed one arm over the back of Julia's chair.

Avery wanted to cry.

"You are so jealous," Taylor said, watching her sister's reaction to the lovebirds.

"I'm not," Avery lied. "It's just surprising to run into him here."

"Uhm . . . this is like his territory," Taylor said. "We're probably the only non-rich people on this block. Shall we say hi?"

"Stop teasing," Avery said. "Let's just go."

"Jeez." Taylor had to pick up the pace to keep up with her sister, who was almost in a sprint. "Slow down. It's not like they were having sex or anything."

For Avery, it would have been better if they had been having sex. Sex was sex, and Carter was a man. She could imagine Carter having sex with Julia and convince herself it was just to keep Julia happy and not make her suspicious. But that wasn't the case. The scene before her was much worse than a physical release. They seemed so intimate; so close. And the look on Carter's face when he was listening to Julia . . . he seemed incredibly taken with her.

Avery had been foolish to think he would stop caring for Julia. She knew he did. She had caught glimpses of the two of them over the past six months. They would kiss. He would touch her back. She would touch his arm. She would lean into him. He would put his arm around her shoulders. They would leave . . . together.

Avery swallowed the jealousy these scenes inspired inside of her because she had no reason to do anything else. But now that she had shared herself with Carter, revealed her true feelings and rested in his arms, the effect of seeing him connecting with Julia was more than she could stand.

"Where have you been?" Garrett asked as soon as Haley sat down at their table at Gale's Italian Restaurant and Bar in Pasadena.

Haley glared at him. "Where do you think? You want to have lunch five hundred miles from civilization, you have to give a girl a little time to get there."

"It's not that far."

"I hope my car doesn't get broken into." She placed her purse on the chair next to her. She complained about coming all the way out there, but her curiosity about this restaurant was really the only reason she agreed to lunch with Garrett at all. She had heard great things and already liked the Northern Italian décor of the place.

"So what's good?" she asked, reaching for her menu.

"I don't know." Garrett sounded exhausted.

"What do you like?" she asked.

"I've never eaten here before."

Haley ordered a mango mojito when the waiter appeared. "What do you mean? Why did you want to come all the way . . ."

"Honestly, Haley. It's Pasadena. It's not like I asked you to come to Burbank."

Haley was ready to tell him he better check his attitude, but looking at him she realized there was something more to it. Garrett was scared out of his mind. She hadn't really looked at him when she sat down, but now she could see he was breaking out into a sweat and his eyes were red. They were also wider than usual and looking everywhere but where they should be—at her.

"What is your problem?"

Garrett gestured for her to be quiet as the waiter returned to take their order.

"Come back later," Haley ordered. "I might not be staying."

She leaned back in her chair with a judgmental frown. "What have you done now?"

"I haven't done anything." Garrett reached for his glass of water.

Haley could see his hand was shaking a little bit and this made her nervous. "Tell me what's going on or I'm leaving."

"You know why I asked you here," Garrett whispered, leaning forward.

Haley nodded. "You wanted to know what I've heard about the case and . . ."

"Please." He looked around anxiously. "Keep your voice down."

"I'll talk however I please," she said, a little louder than she'd been speaking before. "I can only tell you what I told you over the phone. Nothing. Why would I hear anything? I'm not involved in this."

"Yes, you are. Haley, I need to know I can count on you to back up my . . ."

"You don't need to finish your sentence," she said. "The answer is no. You can't count on me and I'll tell you something else. I'm not the one you need to be worried about. Sean Jackson is determined to extract that idiot sister of his from all this. Taylor is going to help the FBI and there isn't anything I can do for you."

"What have you heard about her?"

"Are you listening to me?" Haley asked. "Just leave me out of all this. And why are you sweating? It's freezing in here."

"Don't turn around, okay?"

Haley quickly swung around in her chair, looking around. She heard Garrett curse before turning back. "Oh, sorry. You shouldn't have said that."

"There is a white man sitting at the bar in a brownish-tan shirt and jeans." Garrett focused on the empty bread plate in front of him. "He's following me."

Haley turned around to look and she saw the man. He was just as Garrett described and stood out, looking a little more rough around the edges than the rest of the guests. "He's more interested in that beer in his hand than anything else, including you."

Garrett was shaking his head. "No, I think I saw him in the parking lot."

"There is no parking lot, genius." Haley picked up her menu.

"The parking lot at my job. Yeah, I'm sure it's him. I came all the way out here to see if anyone would follow me. Yeah, it's him. They have their eye on me. They're following me everywhere. I got bugs in my office, my apartment and my car."

"Cool," Haley said. "It's just like that Tom Cruise movie, *The Firm*."

Garrett looked at her with a grave expression. "It's more like that than you know. I don't understand. I've made it clear to them that I'm not going to tell. They know they can trust me. They've ensured my loyalty, but still."

"How have they ensured your loyalty?" Haley asked, leaning forward.

"They say they have some way to make it seem like I killed Justin. We never really got along and . . ."

"Wait a second." Haley put her menu down. "You're afraid of your firm? I thought you were afraid of the client."

"The client isn't scared of anything," Garrett said. "The firm has assured them they are protected. It's the firm that stands to lose . . . Justin knew about a lot more than his own clients. He'd been investigating."

"And you know this how?"

"I was sort of spying on him," he answered, "but it was the other partners that asked me to do it. Ask me, hell, they didn't give me any choice. They'd suspected him for a while."

Haley had to admit she was a little intrigued. "So what has your firm assured your clients of?"

"That there will be no consequences to them . . . for anything. Velez Holdings is the biggest revenue producer for the firm. They also referred a lot of the other clients we have. If they said so, everyone would bolt."

"So this is about money," Haley said.

"Not just money," Garrett said. "Velez and the firm have been together for a long time. There's a mutually assured destruction situation going on—the one goes down, the other goes right with it."

"And you put yourself in the middle of it."

Garrett's tone was deeply regretful. "Honestly, I thought something was up, which is why I put together my own insurance policy."

"Meaning?"

"I don't think they know about it." Garrett spoke as if he hadn't heard Haley. "I haven't been able to check on it because they're following my every move. I just need to get into that relaxation room at work before I get banned from the building. Or I have nothing."

"So you did know there was going to be a murder?" Haley asked.

He shook his head. "I got the alibi because I needed my bosses to think I was somewhere other than Justin's house, hearing his confessions. When he called me and told me to come to his house that night, he said it was to warn me about something."

Haley smirked. "Warn you? I guess he had it wrong. So you either go down for a murder you didn't commit or you tell the truth and there's a contract on your head."

Garrett gestured for her silence with his hands. "Something like that."

"You could disappear," Haley suggested, taking a sip of her mojito.

"With what?" he asked. "They're monitoring all my accounts. If I take out anything more than two hundred dollars, they'll know I'm on the run. Besides, I don't have enough money to disappear."

"Sucks for you." Haley waved the waiter over. "I'm hungry, and since this might be your last meal, let's go all-out."

Avery moaned out loud as she gripped the headboard. She was lying on her stomach and Carter was behind her. On top of her. Inside of her. She loved the feeling of him rubbing against her as he stroked harder and harder, faster and faster.

She let out a moan as she felt him lean over her and gently take hold of her hair.

"Come here, baby." He gently moved her head to the right so his mouth could meet hers. His tongue went deeper and deeper as he thrust harder. The sounds she was making were driving him crazy.

Avery was caught up by the sound of his heavy breathing and lovemaking moans as he nudged her hair out of the way to lick the back of her moist neck. He'd already made her come once and he was about to do it again.

"Carter!"

"Yes," he responded loudly. The more she called his name, the harder and faster his movements became. He couldn't take it any longer. It was just too good.

He pushed back up using his hands against the bed. He took her by the waist and lifted her butt with him. He didn't want to be outside of her for a second. He held on firmly to her hips as she complied, supporting herself with her knees. He was relentless, unable to do anything but go harder, faster. She screamed his named again as her hair bounced from side to side.

Her body was rocking and she was screaming. The pain was glorious. Avery could hear Carter's frantic moans picking up the pace, and she was about to come. Then she heard a knock; then another. Her mind was gone, her body had taken control long ago, but she was certain she'd heard . . .

Bam! Bam! Bam!

"Carter." Avery said his name, but he wasn't listening to the change in the tone of her voice.

Bam! Bam!

"You fucking whore! I know you're in there! Carter! Carter!"

Carter stopped, wondering if he was imagining things. He opened his eyes and looked at Avery, who was gesturing for him to stop. Confused, he turned to the door just as the banging resumed.

"Carter!" Julia screamed. *Bam! Bam!* "Open this fucking door! I swear to God, I will kick this shit in!"

Carter pulled out of Avery as reality hit him. Julia was at his bedroom door—their bedroom door—trying to get in. At the moment he thought, thank God he had locked it.

"What is she doing here?" Avery whispered in a panic. "You said she was . . ."

"She's supposed to be gone all day." Carter got out of the bed, searching for his underwear.

Bam! Bam!

"Stop it, Julia! I'm coming!" Carter approached the door.

When Avery had called earlier that day to chew him out about seeing him with Julia, he'd hung up on her. He wasn't going to hear this shit. He'd gone back to his home office, trying to get some work done, but less than a half hour passed before Avery was pounding on the door to his penthouse.

She was livid with him when he opened the door and a screaming match began. The sight of her jealousy and the insanity he was effortlessly able to cause within her turned him on. Their worst fights had always ended up in bed. This one was no exception. Avery's only hesitation had been the fear of getting caught, but he had assured her, as Julia had told him, that Julia would be at the museum all day and late into the night. The ball was this weekend and she'd been spending almost every moment there.

So for an hour, Carter and Avery's bodies melted together forgetting the rest of the world and basking in the pleasure that only the other had ever been able to provide.

Too frazzled to even think, Avery reached for whatever clothes she could find and ran into the master bathroom. She slammed the door shut behind her and locked it. Avery had never felt so scared and humiliated. She stood naked in the bathroom, holding her clothes to her stomach and staring at the door. What was happening?

She heard Julia's screaming get louder. She was in the bedroom now. Was she coming to the bathroom? How would Avery get out of this? She listened as Carter and Julia yelled at each other. Julia was hysterical and Carter was angry. What was he angry about? Avery wondered. He was wrong. They were wrong. Avery couldn't decipher the words. Her brain was too scattered. She only heard Julia say her name over and over again.

She was going to tell everyone, Avery just knew it. Everything was going to come crashing down in the worst way it could, and everyone involved was going to be hurt because of her selfishness.

"Anthony," she whispered to herself. He loved her so much.

Avery felt herself calm a little as Carter and Julia's voices began to subside. Neither of them was in the bedroom anymore. But where were they? And where were they going? How was she going to get out of here, past Julia?

Avery realized she had balled up her shirt and pants in her hands. Looking down at them, she was reminded of her naked state. She turned her head to the right and looked at herself in the mirror.

She was shocked. Her hair was a mess and she looked like a guilty woman. She was face-to-face with an adulterer. She was staring down the other woman and it was her.

Avery started to cry as she dressed herself and tried to comb her hair. But nothing she could do could make her not feel like the whore Julia had called her. She had no right to feel sorry for herself, but it wasn't just her she was crying for. Her husband, her mother, her father, and what would this do to Carter when his parents found out?

Another forty-five minutes passed before Carter knocked on the bathroom door. He assured her three times that Julia was not in the apartment at all. He had walked her downstairs and she was gone. Avery finally opened the door but bypassed his outstretched arms.

Carter called her name once, but not again. She was leaving and there was no stopping her. It was a complete disaster. Everything Avery had feared would happen had happened. He knew the only way to keep her would be to compensate for the guilt she felt by making her feel safe. Making her feel that nothing would be exposed before she was ready to do it.

He would deal with Avery later. Right now, he had to get to the café two blocks away where Julia was waiting for him and convince her to not say a word of this to anyone.

11

When Kimberly Chase showed up at the Hotel Bel-Air, she refused to speak to anyone except Lawrence Hardy, the man who handled everything Chase. He would do anything for anyone in their family—even break the rules—and she needed a biggie broken.

The Hotel Bel-Air had several tiny bungalows that looked like summer cottages or guest houses, which you passed on your way to the main estate. The stone walkways led to white picket fences and intimate, ultra-private, tiny houses filled with furnishings that rivaled the best homes in Beverly Hills.

Fortunately, Elisha Fisher was staying in the Chase specialty suite, so Kimberly's excuse that she was there to pick Elisha up for a dinner at Chase Mansion was credible. She knew the room and the occupant. She imagined that Lawrence suspected her of lying when she said she would only wait for Elisha in the room, but he worked exclusively for the highest-end clients of the hotel, including all of the regular celebrities, so a diva fit, which Kimberly showed signs of throwing, was par for course.

Her ploy worked, and as Kimberly reached the bungalow, she sneaked up to the private entrance to the front door. She leaned in, hoping to hear nothing. After several seconds of listening, she was satisfied that Elisha was at least not in the front area of the cottage.

Using her key, Kimberly slowly and quietly opened the front door and stuck her head inside. She saw the Italian furnishings, hand-woven rugs, and the fireplace, but no Elisha. Stepping further inside, Kimberly quietly closed the door behind her. She had purposely worn tennis shoes so she wouldn't be heard walking around.

She only had to take two steps inside before she heard a voice. Elisha was there, and she was talking to someone. Kimberly walked through the living room toward the bedroom. As she got closer she decided that Elisha was talking on the phone because there was no other voice.

Kimberly had not expected Elisha to be there. Because of the way the cottages were secluded from the rest of the world, there was no way to tell if someone was coming or going. Her only clue was Lawrence, who told her he didn't believe Ms. Fisher had returned because she hadn't picked up any of her messages. Now that she turned out to be there, Kimberly would search through what she could, but hoped to get lucky.

A phone conversation could definitely be lucky, and when Kimberly heard the water begin to run in the bathroom, she felt even luckier. Elisha was about to take a bath and that would keep her occupied for a little while. But she wanted to hear the conversation because Elisha's voice was just one octave too loud to be comfortable.

Kimberly was in the master bedroom now, doing her best not to think of how crazy she was to be doing this. She had very little to lose, and her desire to have anything she could use against Michael to gain her freedom and her babies, erased any fear or common sense she might have had in such a situation. She didn't want to get caught, but she honestly didn't care.

Kimberly quickly slid behind the open door to the bedroom so she wouldn't be seen if Elisha came out. She had a slight view of the bathroom, decorated in beautiful marble, and just the edge of very white legs extruding from a terry-cloth bathrobe.

"Keenan, I can't tell you that I . . ." Elisha sighed heavily as she sat at the edge of the tub. "Baby, I know, but . . ."

Baby? So she had another lover besides Michael. Kimberly smiled, relishing the chance to tell Michael he wasn't enough for the girl.

"Why are you so upset?" Elisha asked. "It's done. Your brother is in. Yes, there were some hiccups, but once I convinced Michael, I told you this would happen."

Kimberly couldn't help herself. She risked discovery by tiptoeing across the bedroom to stand against the wall next to the bathroom to hear better.

Elisha stood up and walked around the tub, cradling her cell phone between her neck and shoulder as she began to remove her robe.

"No, I know the ink isn't on the paper yet, but I've gone beyond Michael. I swear to you, Steven will sign by the end of the week. Luxury Life Publishing will be a part of Chase Beauty and . . . Hold on a second, Keenan."

Kimberly froze in the sudden silence and feared that Elisha was on to her, but she was only removing her robe and stepping into the oversized tub.

"You're telling me it's hard to trick Steven Chase?" she asked. "I'm the one that's been dealing with him. I'm the one that's convinced him that this deal is clean and clear. You should be thankful I've come this far. Who else could have tricked both Michael and Steven Chase?"

Kimberly couldn't believe what she was hearing. No one could trick either of them. How had she been able to trick them both?

"Oh stop it," Elisha said impatiently. "I don't care about Michael. I just . . . I wanted to be convincing. You have no reason to be jealous. It was work."

Kimberly knew she was lying. A woman could tell from another woman's voice when she was lying to her man. Whoever this Keenan was, he was right to be suspicious that whatever Elisha was supposed to do with Michael had turned into something more. If it hadn't, Elisha would have reserved her show for Michael. The fact that she came to Kimberly, made herself and her intentions known, meant that Elisha really cared about Michael.

"Baby, there is no chance in hell it will get back to me when this thing blows up in their faces. Do you think I would want

Steven Chase after me? I'm an expert at this. I've positioned my-self to be just as clueless to the disaster as anyone else. Hell, Frist doesn't even know that I know. Steven will blame him."

Disaster? Kimberly realized this was bigger than Michael mak-ing a winning deal. Whoever she was talking to was out to get Chase Beauty.

"I'll be clean as a whistle and you can come in and put the nail in the coffin of Chase Beauty. Yes, dear. Once the contracts are signed, you can break the news and Chase Beauty will be on the hook for everything."

Kimberly hated the woman a few minutes ago. Now she ad-mired her. She was purely evil, and seemed determined to do what Kimberly didn't believe anyone ever could. She was going to bring down Chase Beauty.

"It won't matter," Elisha said with a calm, cool confidence. "Chase Beauty will own Luxury Life Publishing and it will be re-sponsible for everything. The company won't survive. Now, please, let me have a peaceful bath and get some rest. I'm back in the trenches tomorrow."

Kimberly was glad she'd waited a few minutes. After hanging up the phone, Elisha turned the faucet off and it was too silent for Kimberly to make a move. She would certainly be heard, and this was just too juicy to risk getting caught. Fortunately, Elisha reached for her iPod. Once the earbuds were in, Kimberly made her way out of the bedroom undetected.

She spent a few minutes looking through Elisha's things in the study, a room set up better than the average at-home busi-ness office. Nothing made any sense to her, but she found some notes that Elisha had tossed in the garbage for some reason, de-spite the fact that there was a shredder right beside it.

Kimberly unraveled the first sheet and saw the name Keenan written more than once. That was enough. She grabbed all the sheets she could and slipped out just as she had slipped in. She couldn't make hide nor hair of it, but Neil, the private investiga-tor Michael had forbidden her from seeing again, could. He was the only one she could trust to work fast, do a good job, and not let anyone know. She just had to come up with a way to convince him to do it.

She would figure something out. Kimberly saw a light at the end of the tunnel. She was going to be free, and Elisha would somehow be the person who made that happen.

"Carter, are you listening to me?" Steven yelled across the desk.

Carter snapped out of his haze, thinking of Julia and Avery and the mess he was making of this situation. "Yeah, but I thought we were done."

"I'll tell you when we're done," Steven said pointedly, his eyes expressing annoyance at his son, sitting on the other side of the desk in his home office. He had called both boys there for a final powwow before they signed the contracts for Luxury Life Publishing on Monday.

"With the Museum Ball this weekend, there won't be another chance for us to all agree that this is a done deal." Steven turned to Michael, who was standing against the wooden antique Russian bookcase, looking more anxious than usual.

"It's done," Michael said proudly. "All the Is are dotted and the Ts crossed, right, Carter?"

Carter nodded reluctantly. "There is nothing that I can say that would make this a bad deal. It's a steal and it's a great opportunity."

"But?" Steven asked.

"But nothing," Michael argued. "Why are you trying to fuck this up, Carter? Because it's mine?"

Carter tossed him an annoyed glance before turning back to his father. "There is no *but*, Dad. I don't like her. That's it."

"But these are strictly personality issues," Steven said. "I respect your gut, Carter. Tell me."

"Jesus!" Michael couldn't believe this. It would never have gotten to this point if Carter had suggested the deal. He knew his father was doing this just to hurt him.

Carter thought for a second, then shrugged his shoulder. "It's a great deal, Dad. I say we sign Monday and get to work turning that thing around."

"Good." Steven closed the large file on the desk in front of him. He felt satisfied with the deal. Although he assumed it was only to get into Michael's good graces, Elisha Fisher had gone out of her way to meet Steven's needs. "So, after Monday the real work begins."

Steven turned his chair to the right and looked up at Michael from an angle. "Good job, son."

Michael's eyes widened as he stood up straight. "What?"

"You did a good job," Steven offered.

After all that had happened between him and Michael, the grief his choices had cost the family, Michael was still his son, and Steven loved him. Michael was the future of Chase Beauty. Steven had swallowed the bitter pill of Carter's choices. As far as their personal relationship was concerned, that would take time, but professionally, Michael had taken a step forward and he deserved the acknowledgment.

"Thanks," Michael said after a while. He felt stupid for smiling, but he couldn't stop it. This man's approval was more important than bread and water to him, and he hadn't heard that praise in a very long time.

"Is there anything else?" Steven asked.

"The plane accident was officially ruled a mechanical error," Carter said. "The FAA will be sending us the final report next week, so I suggest you get started on your public relations strategy now. Maybe a press conference?"

"No more conferences," Steven said somberly. "I did it before because of the onslaught from the media, but I'll just release a statement. That should be enough. I want to get this whole thing behind us."

"The pilot's family," Carter said grimly. "This will affect our settlement negotiations."

"Nice note to end on, Carter," Michael said. "We have to give his wife whatever she wants."

"I'll be taking care of it," Carter said. "Her lawyers are talking fifty million. We're not doing that."

"No," Steven said. "It was horrible what happened, and we will make it so that she and her children will never want for anything ever again. But that number goes down dramatically, Carter. Do you understand?"

"Yes, sir."

"Good." Steven slapped his hands together, rubbing them quickly. "That's it. I need to talk to Carter now."

Carter stopped in mid-lift from the chair. He had become adept at reading Steven's expressions over the years, and this wasn't going to be nice. He sat back down, bracing himself for whatever was to come.

"What?" Michael said, still reeling from his father's compliment.

"Get out," Steven said impatiently, nodding his head toward the door.

Carter and Michael exchanged glances as Michael passed.

As soon as Michael shut the door behind him, Steven asked, "Are you fucking Avery?"

Carter's entire body tensed up and he was frozen. He looked directly at his father, not moving and not saying a word.

"Stop staring at me like an idiot and answer my question."

Carter took a moment, but regained his voice. "Who told you that?"

"So your answer is yes," Steven said impatiently.

"Did Julia . . ."

"She told your mother she caught you two together." Steven was analyzing his son's every expression. He needed to understand what was going on.

"I don't think my sex life is any of your business." So much for Julia's agreement to not say anything after he put on his best show of the regretful boyfriend.

"Everything you do is my business," Steven corrected. "Six months ago, you boys lost your right to any secrecy. And I thought we had an agreement about Avery."

"And I wanted to stick with it," Carter said. "The plan was working perfectly, but . . . then the accident happened."

Steven had to hold his emotions in check as he watched his son sit silent for a moment. Carter showed anger often, and sometimes joy, but he was rarely this vulnerable.

"It changed everything," Carter finally said. "I'm sorry, but . . ."

"Don't apologize," Steven said. "Unless you're sorry you did it."

Carter took a moment before confidently saying, "I'm not.

Nothing has been clear for me since the . . . Everything has been in a haze. Everything except Avery."

Steven watched his son's head veer a little to the right and his eyes glaze over. It was times like this that he was reminded of everything he lacked as a father. He should do more, give more, but he didn't know what.

"All that other stuff," Carter continued, "like my plans, seemed too small and too arduous at the same time. I could die tomorrow and . . ."

"That's not going to happen," Steven said with a certain tone.

"But it almost did and . . . I did what I felt I had to do and so did Avery." He saw the skepticism on his father's face. "And no, I didn't take advantage of the situation. Avery feels the same way. We were both too scared of what we could have missed."

"I understand."

Carter's head shot up as he looked at his father in surprise. Had he heard right? "You . . ."

"You need to be careful," Steven admonished. "Julia is determined to be a part of this family. You've pushed her to a point you can't return from."

"I know her family is very important." Carter could only imagine how Julia and his mother had planned the next thirty years of their life together already.

"Ours is more important," Steven assured him. "But Julia has the power to make this very ugly and very public, and that is not something I will tolerate. Your mother and I moved this earth to cover up that murder."

"It was an accident," Carter said. "If David had been able to upload that tape onto the Internet, we would never have been able to remove it."

"That's not the point, Carter." The only thing that allowed Steven to deal with the situation was knowing the chaos that David's death had prevented. "With the plane accident and this big acquisition, this family has enough to deal with. If a vindictive girlfriend wants to put our family in the paper, she can do it."

"I can handle Julia," Carter said, even though he wasn't so sure. "She wants me more than she wants my fidelity."

"So what does she do when you dump her to be with Avery?"

Steven asked. "That is your plan, right? You want to be with Avery."

"We're figuring that out," Carter answered.

"You better," Steven said as he stood up. He walked around his desk to Carter and waited until Carter was standing, facing him.

"We were all scared, son." He spoke in a low but emotional tone, rare enough to startle even himself.

Seeing the raw emotion on his father's face, even though it was only for a moment, affected Carter deeply. He never doubted his father's love. It was so much more complicated than that. A kid needs so much more than love from his father. But this touched him and Carter would never forget it.

After a moment, Carter smiled and asked, "Is this where we're supposed to hug or something?"

"That's not necessary," Steven answered. He was already turning back to his desk. "I've got work to do."

"All right," Carter said, understanding that he'd gotten more than he could have expected and he was very, very happy.

"Where in the hell have you been?" Kimberly asked as she rushed into her private bathroom and locked the door behind her. "You were supposed to call me an hour ago."

"It took me awhile to decide whether or not I was going to call you at all." Neil Owen was one of many private investigators the Chase family had used over the years to find out whatever they had no right to know. He was sixty years old and had spent more than half of his life in the CIA before retiring to the private sector.

Over a year ago, Neil made the mistake of agreeing to help Kimberly, behind the backs of the rest of the Chase family. She needed to find Janet's deep, dark secret, and Neil had found it— a rushed abortion and an affair with a French teacher named Paul Deveraux. The disaster that ensued cut Neil off from the Chase gravy train. Kimberly wasn't supposed to ever talk to him again. But she did.

When David began harassing her anonymously, she had gone to Neil to help her figure out what she should do. He found out what he could, and offered to make David regret coming to L.A., but he drew the line at getting rid of David, and Kimberly couldn't settle for anything less.

After this fiasco, someone in the Chase family talked to Neil. He wouldn't tell Kimberly who, but the next time she tried to contact him to help her find a divorce lawyer that wouldn't cave in to the Chase family, he told her in no uncertain terms he wasn't going to work with her.

But Kimberly had her ways. She had her beauty and she had her acting skills. A beautiful woman breaking down in tears while wearing a seductive spaghetti-strap dress could get a man to do just about anything. That and ten thousand dollars in cash she'd gotten from selling three of a her BCBG Max Azria dresses to an upscale designer shop in Malibu.

In exchange, she had promised Neil that Michael would never find out. She was using a phone that Avery had given her a few weeks before, because Michael was tracking her calls. Neil's phones weren't tapped. He was an expert at doing this stuff and was therefore an expert at protecting himself from it, but they wouldn't take the chance. He used an untraceable cell phone.

"You're former CIA," Kimberly said. "What are you afraid of?"

"I'm not afraid," Neil said. "I just don't like clients spreading bad news about me. Your family can cost me a lot of business."

"Well, they'll never know about this."

"Haven't you said that before?" Neil asked. "Like, two times before."

"You took the ten grand," she said, "so speak."

"I can't believe you don't know who this chick's lover is. Keenan? The name doesn't even sound remotely familiar?"

"I know a lot of people," she said, "and it sounds familiar, but I can't place anything to it. Are you saying I know him?"

"Let me put it this way. His full name is Keenan Brady Chase."

Kimberly gasped. "What? Who? Oh my God."

It suddenly hit her, and she had to sit down on the edge of the tub.

"Yeah," Neil said. "Steven Chase's brother. How can you not know him?"

"I've never met him." Kimberly was trying to take it all in as she spoke. "All I heard was that about twenty-five years ago they had a big falling out and they haven't spoken to each other since."

"Must have been some falling out," Neil said, "because I think little brother Keenan is up to something."

"What?" Kimberly was getting more and more excited every second.

"Get this. He's head of the white collar crime division of the FBI." Neil paused a moment. "Speechless, huh?"

Kimberly could barely speak. "So . . . He's what . . . Is he dirty or what? And what does Elisha have to do with it?"

"She's a legit broker and the deal she's doing with Chase Beauty seems to be a clean and clear acquisition of a publishing company. I can't tell you more because it's under wraps."

"Keenan and Elisha are trying to bring Chase Beauty down, and based on what I heard, this deal is going to do it."

"I didn't get an MBA," Neil said. "I can't tell you how and when, but once Chase Beauty finalizes this deal, something bad is going to happen and my guess is that it's exactly as Keenan Chase wants it to be. He's got something going over at the FBI that I can't get to using any of my contacts. He's holding it close to his chest. He knows who he's dealing with."

Kimberly was putting the pieces of the puzzle together. "And he sent his lover, Elisha, to seduce Michael with the prospect of getting back into Steven's good graces so he'd do anything to make this deal happen."

"Yeah," Neil laughed. "That poor son of a bitch Michael is going to end up being the reason Chase Beauty goes down for good. You wouldn't by any chance want to warn him, would you?"

"I love you, Neil." Kimberly could barely contain herself. "I absolutely love you."

12

"Getting an early start, huh?"

Michael turned to see Carter coming toward him in the main ballroom of the National History Museum. He assumed Carter was talking about the glass of wine in his hand. "Hey, brother. Looking good."

Carter smoothed out the arms of his tuxedo. "This is how they look when you don't rent them."

"Fuck you," Michael said. "I own more tuxes than you do."

"Watch your attitude with me. I came over to warn you that Mom is trying to put everyone to work."

"People have already started showing up. She doesn't have enough hired help."

"Well, she's had a lot on her mind with her two sons almost getting killed in a plane accident and all." Carter noticed that Michael replaced his glass of wine with another as the waiter passed. He was using his free hand. The other was holding on to a cane, which he had progressed to after crutches. "It's only seven. How many is that?"

"And I see you showed up with the ice princess," Michael said, ignoring the question. It was number three. "So you still trying to pull that off?"

"Mind your own business," Carter said.

"I take it she doesn't know about Avery," Michael said. "Because if she did . . ."

"She knows," Carter said, before telling Michael about Julia's interruption of him and Avery, and their father's subsequent admonishment.

"So everyone knows." Michael turned away.

"Seems like it."

Carter turned to see where Michael had been staring when he approached him and where he was now looking again. Kimberly was standing on the veranda just below, drinking a glass of wine by herself. She looked breathtaking in a sterling silver Badgley Mischka evening gown. It was impossible not to notice how attractive a woman she was, but Carter also noticed how sad she looked.

"How did you get that to work?" he asked.

Michael didn't turn around. He knew what Carter was talking about. "I didn't. I told her she had to come because it's a family thing and Mom wanted it all to look perfect."

"You've told her that before and she didn't show up."

"She didn't argue for even a second." Michael took a sip of his wine. "She almost seemed eager to come. Considering our interaction just before that, where she told me she hated me and wished I had died in that plane accident, it has me a little . . . curious."

"Curious indeed," Carter agreed. "How can you stand to be with someone who wishes you were dead?"

"Women say that all the time."

"Yeah, but she meant it and you know it. I can feel the poison every time I'm within twenty feet of either of you."

"Enough," Michael snapped. "I'll figure out what she's up to later. Now, I just want to focus on getting that deal done on Monday."

"So you plan to put together the wretched pieces of your family on Tuesday?" Carter asked sarcastically.

"No," Michael responded. "On Tuesday, I plan to take my boys to San Diego and spend two days at Universal Studios."

Carter made a smacking sound with his lips. This boy was unbelievable. "How many of those glasses have you downed, boy? Do you think a couple days at an amusement park will undo the damage you and Kimberly inflict on those kids every day?"

"Didn't you just tell me to mind my own business?" Michael asked defensively. "Don't worry about me. I've got my shit under control."

"Is that so?" Carter asked. He took his brother by the shoulders and turned him away from Kimberly toward the front entrance to the ballroom. "Is this what you call under control?"

Michael hadn't expected Elisha to be there at all, and as she stood in the entrance, wearing a strapless oxblood-red satin gown with bow trim, he knew this could be trouble. His father would not tolerate any scandal touching the upcoming deal. He would see this as Michael throwing a relationship Steven didn't approve of, in his face.

"I told her not to come," Michael said. "She asked me and I said no."

"Got any other women you're sleeping with here?" Carter asked. "Because I'm sure Dad would love to meet them. He certainly seems happy to see her."

Michael looked over Carter's shoulder to see their father standing in front of the stage where the band was playing. He was clearly unhappy to see Elisha there, and when he turned to look at Michael, it made him feel like a kid about to get the punishment of his life.

"So she's here," Michael said. "It doesn't have to mean anything."

"You know how Dad is before a deal. This is the social event of the year for L.A. Big money and all the media are here."

Michael and Carter had heard the speech from their father all their lives. All of these good-old-boy rich cats kissed up to Steven, and their wives kissed up to Janet, but more than a few of them resented having to do so. They would relish the chance to bring Chase Beauty down and put Steven Chase in his place. They couldn't count on the private scandals being made public, because they all had had their own dysfunctional secrets exposed in the tabloids as well. What they wanted was a big, corporate mistake on Steven's part and a social event disaster on Janet's.

Carter took the glass of wine out of his brother's hand. "You should either get her to leave or stay the hell away from everyone in this family, especially your wife."

"This can't be good," Anthony said as he and Avery walked toward the front of the ballroom. "The closer to the front means the closer to the Chases."

Avery checked the invitation in her hand again, given to her by the wife of Anthony's future boss. "They didn't even know we were coming. This was a last minute thing. The invitation only says 'plus three guests.' You said this guy is a very important player on the philanthropic circuit. Of course he's going to be in the front. Look, here we are."

They were at a beautifully decorated table seating eight, just behind the first row of reserved tables. "See, those are the reserved tables. That's where they'll sit."

Anthony didn't seem reassured. "With our luck, this one right in front of us will be . . ."

"Mine," Carter said, smiling as politely as possible as both Avery and Anthony turned to see him.

"Hello Carter." Avery hadn't expected to be so excited to see him again. He looked incredible in his perfectly tailored tuxedo. She wanted him to hold her and wanted him to leave at the same time.

"You look absolutely incredible," Carter said, looking her up and down.

She looked stunning in a royal blue, satin gown with a v-neck to her belly button, revealing her glowing skin. The waist was beaded with rhinestones in the middle. Her cleavage was enticing as the dress hung off her shapely hips and dropped to her feet.

Avery looked down, hoping that Anthony wouldn't see her blush from the way Carter was looking at her.

"Thank you," Anthony said possessively.

"Oh, you look pretty hot too, Anthony." Carter smiled despite wanting to punch the man in his mouth and watch him bleed all over his rented tux.

Anthony responded by wrapping his arm around Avery. "How did you know we'd be coming?"

"I didn't," Carter lied. Anthony would never know how much Carter knew about him even before Anthony did. This entire job offer was a favor to his family, and the extension of Anthony's invitation to the ball was requested during a game of golf at the Los Angeles Country Club.

Easy as pie.

"How could I know?" Carter asked. "You weren't invited, and I'm pretty certain you couldn't afford the ticket. It's five grand a plate and twenty grand a table."

"Carter," Avery admonished him.

"So you just happened to place the UCLA research department head's table behind your family's table?" Anthony asked skeptically.

"That's not my family's table," Carter said. "It's my table. I bought two of them for my firm. You know, that company I own and work at all day with no time to worry about guest lists and seating arrangements."

"You knew," Anthony said.

"He said he didn't." Avery's tone was clearly agitated as she moved away from his grip. "It doesn't matter. He's sitting at his family's table, right?"

Carter nodded. "I'll be an entire three tables away, Anthony. You're safe."

"Safe?" Anthony asked. "What in the hell does that mean?"

"I don't know, buddy," Carter said. "You're the one that seems to think I'm going to . . ."

"Please," Avery said. "Can we not do this tonight? Besides, I don't want your possible future boss seeing you bickering."

"She's right," Carter said, offering his hand. "Tonight is all about the Autism Society of America. Why don't we shake and make friends for the next four hours?"

Anthony ignored Carter's outstretched hand and turned to his wife. "I'm going to go get a drink. You want one?"

"No thanks," Avery answered, even though he was already walking away. She turned to Carter. "You didn't have to do that."

"What did I do?" Carter asked. "It's not my fault he's a para-noid freak. You do look incredible, baby."

"Stop it," Avery whispered harshly as she looked around. No one was looking at them but it felt like everyone was. "Don't do that here."

"Where can I do it?" he asked. "You haven't been answering my calls all week."

"You know why." Avery could feel her body heating up just being near him. How could everyone *not* tell they were sleeping together?

"Yes, and if you actually listened to any of the several messages I've left for you, you would know that Julia isn't going to tell any-one anything."

Avery could see the desperation in his eyes and she felt it too. She missed him terribly and wasn't sure how long she could stay away. "You can't be certain of that. She's here, isn't she? What do you think she'll do when she sees you talking to me?"

"That's not for you to worry about," Carter said. "She's my re-sponsibility and I will control her."

"Why are you even with her?" Avery asked. "I don't want to be your other woman."

"I don't think we want to have this conversation again. You re-member how it ended?"

How could she forget? He left her in the hotel room lit up like a volcanic flame. "It ended unresolved, Carter. She shouldn't . . ."

"When you promise me you'll leave Anthony, I'll get rid of Julia." Carter's expression was starkly serious. "But until you do that, I don't want you to talk about me leaving her again."

"So you're making all the rules?" Avery asked angrily.

Carter ignored her question. "She's staying quiet because she gets to keep me."

Avery huffed. "Do you know how twisted that sounds?"

"What the fuck do I care?" Carter took a step toward her, but Avery backed up. "I know you miss me, Avery. I can taste every inch of you from here."

A little breath of air left her lips as she felt completely drawn to him. She had to hold on to the chair beside her to keep from falling. Every inch of her was on point as she felt a shiver of desire glide from her belly to her breasts.

"You know I want you," she confessed, "but I can't be around you without completely letting go. I'll make a mistake, I know it. Not tonight."

"Then when?" Carter wasn't used to waiting; to not getting what he wanted. Except with Avery. It was always Avery. "When can I see you? When can you get away from . . ."

Carter stopped talking as Avery abruptly turned and walked away. He was clueless as to why she would do that until he felt someone place her arm on his back. He didn't turn around, but waited as she slowly came around to face him.

"You're a liar," Julia accused with angry eyes. "You said you'd stay away from her."

"I meant I wouldn't sleep with her anymore," Carter said. "I'm not going to ignore her. She's Conner's mother."

"So why do I feel safe betting everything I own that Connor wasn't mentioned at all in that little exchange?"

"She doesn't need to be mentioned," he answered. "She's our daughter. She's always there."

Julia looked genuinely hurt by his words, but Carter was too frustrated to care. He needed Avery and he felt like he was dying of thirst having her so close yet being unable to touch her.

"Why is she even here?" Julia asked. "She wasn't invited. Did you arrange this?"

"I had no idea she was coming," Carter said. "But she's here. Just deal with it."

"I am dealing with it," Julia said, "but I swear to you, if you continue to flirt with her I will fuck up this evening for everybody."

Carter's eyes narrowed in anger as he grabbed her by the arm and pulled her to him.

"Are you threatening me?" He looked at her menacingly.

Julia was clearly intimidated, but said nothing.

Carter leaned in close and whispered, "Because if you are threatening me, that would be a mistake. And if you don't like anything I'm doing, you can always leave me. I'm not forcing you to stay."

Julia's eyes swelled with tears as she jerked her hand free and rushed away from him toward the back room. When she had gone, Carter searched for Avery. He needed to get her alone just for a second so he could touch her, kiss her, anything. But when he saw her, she was leaning against Anthony, her arm entwined around his while engaging in pleasant conversation with his future boss and his wife.

Carter wasn't sure he could stand to watch her be wife to Anthony anymore. Not now that she was his again. This was going to be a long night.

"Please tell me we're not sitting at your parents' table?" Garrett asked Haley as soon as they both entered the ballroom.

"Where else would we sit?" Haley asked. "Did you think I was going to spend my own money on this? And God knows you aren't going to fork over a dime."

"I've been here for five seconds and your father looks like he wants to pull out a nine millimeter and do me in."

"I guess he'd have to stand in line for that." Haley thought she was being funny, but Garrett's expression told her that his sense of humor had not joined them this evening.

"Can you cut down on the bitch for one evening?" he asked as he snatched two glasses of wine from a passing waiter.

"I can try." Haley accepted a glass. "But it's not my strong point. Besides, if you want nice you should be doing what I asked you to do."

"I told you, you're not getting that trust fund." Garrett swallowed the entire glass in one gulp. "Your father made sure it was ironclad. You aren't getting a cent more than he wants you to have before he wants you to have it."

Haley wouldn't accept that. "There has to be a loophole somewhere!"

Garrett shook his head. "Even if he died and named your mother, Carter, or anyone else a trustee, they'd still have to follow the conditions he laid out when he started the trust."

Haley looked over at her father with hateful eyes. "He thinks he's God."

"As far as your trust fund is concerned," Garrett said, "he is."

"Well then screw him," she said. "In a few months, I'll have more money in my hand than he put in that trust fund. I won't need it and then I won't need him."

"Where are you planning on getting this money from?" Garrett asked.

Haley shot him a suspicious look. "None of your business. You have your life on the line to worry about."

"Thanks for reminding me," he said sarcastically. "Otherwise I wouldn't have known."

Haley eyed him suspiciously. "What has gotten into you? You don't seem as cowardly as you did the other day."

Garrett tried to manufacture an oblivious expression. "I don't know what you're talking about."

"What have you done?" she asked, finding him interesting for the first time tonight.

Garrett smiled slightly. "I haven't done anything. I'm with you tonight. You and all of these well-respected people."

"If I didn't know better," Haley said. "I would say that sounded like the makings of an alibi."

"Come on, Taylor," Jessica Kramer pleaded with her friend outside the doors of the student union building. "It's only eight."

Jessica was trying to get Taylor to come out for ice cream with a group of girls, but Taylor wasn't in the mood. She wasn't in the mood to do anything, and she had to get home. She wasn't even supposed to be out. Her brother had convinced their parents to put her on lockdown, but Taylor was an expert at sneaking out.

She had met her friends at the student union to hang out in the main lounge near the food court, and they were on their way to a popular ice cream shop right off campus. But Taylor knew she was pushing her luck.

"Sorry," she said as she headed toward the parking lot, away from Jessica and the others. "I gotta get home. Homework, you know."

"Be careful," Jessica said, eyeing the parking lot suspiciously. "That parking lot is not safe."

Taylor waved the rape whistle she had attached to her key chain. "I'll be all right. You guys have fun."

"Call me!" Jessica yelled as she turned and ran to catch up with the other girls.

Taylor didn't need Jessica's reminder to know she had to be safe. She was scared. Her brother had driven home the seriousness of the threat from Cool, Bitton & Klein as well as Roberto Velez. Despite the fact that she knew less than nothing, she was a loose end, and that put her in danger.

Taylor froze in place when she thought she heard a shuffling sound. She looked around the parking lot. It wasn't the best lit of all the campus lots, but it was the closest to the building. She looked around and couldn't see anyone or hear anything, so she started again for her car, which was just one more row over.

But as soon as she started walking again, she heard a noise. It sounded like a laugh, but she had to be wrong. She heard a car start somewhere off in the distance but it was too far away to be concerned about.

She picked up the pace, running for her car, clicking on her remote. As soon as she reached it, she saw a movement out of her left eye. Her adrenaline kicked into high gear as she turned, then came crashing down when she saw what was causing all the shuffling and laughing.

Two kids were going at it, making out as they leaned against the passenger-side door of the car directly across from hers.

When she got in her car, Taylor took a second to exhale and laugh at herself before starting up and taking off. She slowly made her away around the parking lot, which was set up with road bumps, medians, and restrictive lanes to prevent anyone from driving more than fifteen miles an hour.

As soon as she reached the exit, Taylor pressed on the gas and sped out. She saw the light at the end of the block turn yellow and thought to rev up to try to make it, but she knew she wasn't going to, so she stepped on her brakes.

But the car wouldn't stop. Taylor looked down at her brakes for a second as she pressed against them again and again and again. Nothing was happening. She heard a car horn honking, and when she looked up she had already run the red light. She turned to her right and saw a car approaching, its brakes squealing as the driver tried to stop, but there wasn't enough time. It was coming right at her.

When Janet finally reached Steven, standing in the middle of a group of men, she apologized to them all before leading him away.

"Is anything wrong?" Steven asked.

"With the ball, absolutely nothing," Janet said with a smile from ear to ear. "Everything is going perfectly. Can you believe it?"

Steven loved seeing Janet like this. She was beautiful and radiant in her element—the queen of everything. She'd been bred to be a society matron from day one. She hadn't had it easy of late, but she was a survivor, and seeing her running the show to perfection brought him immense joy.

"I never doubted you." He leaned in and kissed her smooth cheek.

"There's the situation with Haley." Janet was focused on making sure the ball went smoothly, but her children were never far from her mind.

"I'm going to deal with Collins," Steven said. "I talked to some of Carter's contacts at the DA and this situation has the potential to get ugly. The FBI has taken over, but don't worry. I'm going to make sure he has nothing more to do with Haley."

Janet knew not to ask more, so she let Steven walk away without a word. She loved her husband and knew that he would always do what was best for the family. He knew how to protect the children and take care of her. Sometimes he would tell her how it was done. Sometimes he wouldn't.

"Janet dear!"

Janet pressed on her perfect smile as Olivia Dexter approached her. Olivia was on that list of people Janet wanted to make certain left tonight's ball with only excellent praise. She was from old

English money; beyond blue blood money. She was a top society matron in Kensington and a friend of the royal family. Olivia and her husband were in L.A. because their teenaged daughter, Heather, competed in international equestrian challenges for a few months during the year.

"Olivia darling." Janet and Olivia shared air kisses on both cheeks as if they were dear friends. They'd only known each other for a month, but women at their level were always friends. "Please tell me you're enjoying yourself."

"Immensely," she answered. "Your taste is impeccable. Glorious. I have to know your caterer. I'm having a party for Heather. She's made the world championships."

"Certainly, and congratulations."

She beamed openly. "We are so very proud of her as you must be of all your lovely children. I spoke with Leigh earlier. She is more than a gem."

"Thank you." Janet was thankful to God for Leigh. She was the saving grace of them all.

"You must go about finding her a husband. She should have so many choices."

"If only," Janet said. "You know young women these days. They don't even think about getting married until they're thirty."

Olivia rolled her eyes as if she understood Janet's frustration. "My son is almost thirty and acts like a teenager when it comes to women. He was taken with your daughter when we were briefly in Sydney."

"Sydney?" Janet asked. "I didn't know you were there when Haley was. Haley loved it in Sydney. She's actually considering buying a condo there."

"Well," Olivia responded, "between your billions and that oil money, she could buy an entire building."

"Excuse me?" Janet asked. "Oil money?"

"She's a very lucky girl," Olivia said before she gasped in excitement at something taking place a few feet away. "Oh, my husband is calling. I will talk to you later, dear."

"Of course," Janet said. She didn't want to seem too eager to know, because she didn't like the idea of someone knowing more about her children than she did. But the second she could get Haley alone, she was going to get to the bottom of it. *Oil money?*

Avery stood hidden by a large column as she seethed, watching Carter and Julia. They were laughing and drinking wine while an older woman told a story that had her hands flailing in the air. He touched her again, brushing his arm against hers. This was the fourth time in the last ten minutes that they had touched. Avery was counting, getting angrier with every second.

"It hurts, doesn't it?" Michael asked as he stumbled with his cane over to her.

Avery knew right away that he was drunk and she wasn't in an understanding mood. "Go away, Michael."

"You think you're hiding it, don't you?" he asked. "You're not. You've been staring at them all night and it's obvious to everyone."

"I don't know what you're talking about." Avery feared he might be right. How could they all not notice?

"I guess you can imagine how he's felt all this time having to watch you with your husband or whatever." Michael waited for a response from Mrs. High & Mighty, but realizing he wasn't going to get one, he went deeper. "And Kimberly won't be working at the gallery any longer." He smiled in response to the surprised look on her face. "Did you two actually think you could keep a secret from me? You're just as stupid as she is."

"Watch your mouth," Avery warned. "Kimberly may let you insult her at will, but I'll make you sorry."

"Ouch." Michael took a step back. "I'm seeing a new you, Avery. Not only are you an adulterer, but these threats are showing me the real Avery Jackson. Not the prim and proper princess you appeared to be."

"Harper," she corrected. "It's Avery Harper."

"Are you reminding me?" he asked. "Or yourself?"

"Go sober up," Avery ordered. "You can barely walk already. You're just going to end up hurting yourself more."

He feigned gratitude. "Are you concerned about me? How

sweet. I guess there's a first time for everything. Any more revelations?"

"What are you bothering her about?" Anthony approached, carrying Avery's wrap in his hands.

"Nothing," Avery quickly answered. "He's drunk."

"So of course everything I say can't possibly be believed," Michael offered.

Anthony looked him up and down with a sneer. "You're drunk and she's tired. We're leaving."

Kimberly had been stalking Elisha all night. She was a social little whore, this one. There wasn't a moment she wasn't sidling up to someone, passing out a business card or flirting away. When she finally found a moment when Elisha was alone and no one was within hearing distance, Kimberly made her move.

"I would think someone from New York would have better fashion sense," she said as she approached.

Elisha smiled as if she was pleased to see her. "I'll have you know this is a Badgley Mischka."

"It doesn't make any difference who made the dress," Kimberly said. "It's two sizes too small, the wrong color, and only brings more attention to your lack of . . . cleavage."

"Thank you." Elisha appeared unfazed. "I'll be sure to make a note of that, but Michael likes me in red."

"He likes all his whores to wear red," Kimberly said. "But he doesn't like them hanging around his family, so I'm thinking he wasn't the one who got you a ticket for tonight."

"I have my ways," Elisha responded.

Kimberly laughed. "That's the understatement of the year. But I am curious, because it's an almost impossible ticket to get. Maybe another Chase helped you out. Maybe . . . Michael's Uncle Keenan?"

Elisha was too caught off guard to hide her surprise. She tried to recover as best she could. "I don't know what you're talking . . ."

"Save it," Kimberly said flatly. "You're quite the pioneer, Elisha. The first woman who can say she's fucking two Chase men at the same time. But I'm wondering how you think Michael is going to still want you after this all falls apart?"

"You don't know what you're talking about," Elisha spat out. "You're gutter trash and you just can't stand that Michael wants to trade up."

Elisha turned to walk away, but Kimberly grabbed her by the arm, pulling her back. "I'm not done with you yet."

"Oh, yes you are." Elisha ripped her arm free and with a threatening tone, said, "And you're going to be sorry if you don't keep your mouth shut."

"Not as sorry as you'll be," Kimberly said joyfully as she saw the panic rise in Elisha. She was about to lose control. "Not only will you have failed your precious Keenan in his plot against Steven, but Michael will hate you, and the entire Chase family will be out for revenge. Do you know what happens to people who try to hurt them?"

Elisha let out a yell as she grabbed for Kimberly, but Kimberly slapped her hands away. She wanted Elisha to lose it in front of everyone to make a fool out of her, but she didn't want to start a fight with the woman. Not here and not now, but it became suddenly clear to her that Elisha had lost it and was coming after her.

Kimberly tried to get out of the way, but Elisha grabbed her by the hair and pulled her back. Kimberly yelled and tried to twist around. *Bad move,* she thought as she felt herself and Elisha tumble to the floor.

"Well you two have a nice, quiet, middle-class evening," Michael said as Avery and Anthony turned to leave.

He thought he heard a yell coming from the other end of the ballroom, but wasn't sure until he saw the look on Avery's face. She had heard it too, and she rushed past him to see where it was coming from.

It sounded to Avery like someone was being hurt and everyone in the ballroom was backing away. That was, everyone except the press, who couldn't take enough pictures of the two attractive women in their formal gowns trying to tear each other apart at the seams. Shocked, Avery was trying hard to see who it was and when she did, she was shocked again.

Michael took awhile to walk toward the ruckus on his cane, but was going as fast as he could. "What's going on?" he asked Avery as soon as he reached her.

"It's a fight," she said. "And you'd better get over there."

"We have security for that." Michael was looking around for someone on duty that evening.

"You still better get over there," Avery said. "Because it's your wife."

Avery reached the fight before Michael did, but others in the family had already gotten there. One security guard had picked Elisha up and Avery rushed over to Kimberly. She was being blinded by the flashbulbs.

"What are you doing?" Avery asked.

Kimberly looked confused. "I gotta get out of here. I can't even see."

"Come on."

Avery rushed Kimberly past a group of people toward the lobby area that lead to the bathrooms. It was secluded and had doors that could be closed, but after helping Kimberly sit down on the plush sofa, it turned out that someone had beaten Avery to the punch.

Steven, who had Michael by the sleeve of his tux, pulled him inside so forcefully that he fell forward. Carter, who had rushed in after both of them, ran to catch Michael before he hit the floor.

"Jesus Christ!" Michael yelled. "Are you trying to break my other leg?"

"I'm trying to kill you," Steven yelled. "Carter, shut the door."

After making sure Michael had his cane and could stand on his own, Carter went toward the door. Before he could close it, Anthony pushed his way inside.

"You don't need to be here," Carter said. "This is a family situation."

"I just came to get my wife," Anthony said. "Avery, can we leave?"

Avery, who was on the sofa trying to help put together the pieces of Kimberly's dress that had been ripped, ignored him. Kimberly was shaking and it wasn't because Elisha had hurt her. She was terrified, and Avery imagined it was because of what Michael would do to her.

"This is the last straw, Michael," Steven said. "Do you know what has happened out there?"

Michael was trying to think, but he could only back up against the wall to stay on his two legs. "I didn't do anything."

"You did everything!" Steven yelled. "This is all your fault. You shouldn't have brought her."

"She's my wife!" Michael screamed.

"Don't start acting like you care now," Avery spat out.

"Shut up," Michael said back to her.

Steven approached Michael with his hands clenched in fists. He wanted to knock some sense into him. "You shouldn't have brought her and you sure as hell should have made sure Elisha didn't come. There were already too many rumors circulating. Now you've confirmed everything and at the worst time. Do you know what this is gonna do to your mother, to Chase Beauty, to the family?"

"Dad." Carter gestured for his father to calm down. "You're overreacting."

"Oh yes, it will be awful," Michael said. "The Chase family is certainly not known for having scandals. We're spotless and not at all dysfunctional. This will be a surprise to the world."

Even though he wanted to, Steven couldn't hit him. "You're too drunk to even know the damage your little affair has caused."

"You're all crazy," Anthony said. "Avery, please, let's go."

"You can go," Kimberly said to Avery. "I'm fine. He can't do anything he hasn't done to me already."

"Come with me," Avery said. "You can't be in this. You can stay at my house tonight."

"The hell she will," Michael said. "This has nothing to do with you, Avery. Get the hell out of here!"

"Stop it!" Carter yelled. "Don't talk to her like that. You've done enough damage. Just shut up."

"Good," Michael said. "You're turning on me too? The only friend I have in the world. My own brother."

Carter stood between Michael and their father, who looked ready to punch anyone he could. "I'm not turning on you. This isn't just about you ruining Mom's reputation. The press is having an orgy out there. Do you have any idea what they're going to do with this? They all know Elisha is part of the deal. We have investors."

"We?" Michael laughed. "You don't work at Chase Beauty, asshole. Who is this *we* you're talking about?"

"Just shut the fuck up," Carter said. "Shut up and go home."

"There's going to be a price to pay for this," Steven warned. "I was clearly a fool to trust you again. I should have put an end to that deal when I first found out about your affair with that woman."

"Yeah," Michael said. "That sounds fair. My sleeping with Elisha is the end of the world, while Carter can fuck Avery all he wants and nobody gives a damn."

Avery gasped as she looked up. Her eyes went straight to Anthony who looked completely shocked.

Carter's fist connected with Michael's jaw in an instant and Michael fell to the ground as fast as a sack of dirt. "You son of a bitch!"

"What?" Michael said, putting his hand on his throbbing jaw. "Everyone knows you're sleeping together and you're still the prize of the family. How is it fair that I get treated differently?"

"Avery." Anthony said her name as more of a question than anything. He made no attempt to hide the utter destruction on his face.

Avery felt a sting in her heart at the betrayed look on her husband's face. "Anthony, please."

"Dammit!" His eyes went cold to her before he turned and stormed out of the room.

Avery couldn't believe this was happening. She turned to Kimberly. "I have to go."

"No, you don't," Carter said, his anger only compounding at the sight of her compassion for her husband. "It's out now."

He reached out for her as she passed him, but she slapped his hands away and ran out. She couldn't think of Carter, Kimberly, or even herself. Anthony was all that mattered now. She had to find her husband.

Carter started after her, but his father called his name.

"No," Steven said. "This family comes first, Carter. You can deal with her later."

Carter felt a second of hope as the door opened again, but it wasn't Avery. It was his mother, and as she stood in the doorway with her eyes tearing up and flashbulbs going off behind her, Carter knew he had to stay.

13

It was six in the morning when Anthony finally appeared in the driveway to his home. He'd been gone all night. Avery had been so scared he wouldn't come back.

After rushing out of the museum, Anthony quickly jumped into a cab before she could stop him. Avery caught the next cab home, calling Anthony's cell over and over again, crying over the phone how sorry she was and how she could explain it all.

How would she explain it? She didn't know and it didn't matter, but she was at home, sitting alone in the darkness of her living room, when he finally answered her call. She said anything she thought would bring him home. She took all his insults. He repeated all the things that she knew already. He had done so much, given up so much for her. He hung up on her several times. She called him back. He didn't answer. She called again. He picked up, called her names and she begged him to come home. That was five hours ago, and Avery hadn't done anything except wait. While she waited, she contemplated what she could do; what she should do. In all her selfishness, she hadn't yet played this conversation out in her mind. She was stupid to think nothing would happen before she wanted it to. But that was only indicative of where she had been this last month. She had answered her heart, but abandoned everything else in exchange. There was often a price to pay for doing that and usually that price was paid by the most innocent involved.

While Avery had been trying to reach Anthony over and over again, Carter had been trying to reach her. She never picked up. He'd left her messages, but she refused to listen to any of them. She wasn't mad at him in the sense that he was to blame, but she was angry that he hadn't controlled Michael better. Part of her believed that Carter wanted the truth to come out.

She couldn't think of Carter or herself. As Anthony made his way sloppily up the stairs to their front door, she knew that she had to do whatever it took to ease his pain.

He didn't look at her as he passed her by and went into the foyer. He tossed his keys in the direction of the console table, but they slammed against the wall and fell to the floor. Avery followed him to the dining room, a room they rarely used. They either ate in the living room or at the kitchen table. Maybe it was the best place to talk. It was the least emotional room in the house.

"I guess I'm not gonna get that job at UCLA." Anthony sat at the head of the table with his head down as Avery sat next to him.

She slid her chair close to him and placed her hand on top of his. He ripped it away and she didn't say anything.

"I don't want to hear any more apologies." Anthony looked up, showing red, tired eyes.

"Anthony, I only want you to know how sorry I am that you were hurt like this."

Anthony laughed. "You say that like you weren't involved in it."

"I meant that . . ."

"You meant that this wasn't the way you wanted me to find out," he said. "So what exactly was the way you wanted me to find out? Or did you plan on making a fool out of me forever?"

"I wasn't trying to hurt you," she said. "Things happened after that plane accident and I know there is no excuse, but I wasn't . . . It wasn't as if I didn't care."

"But not enough. You didn't care enough to stay away from him."

Avery turned her head away, unable to answer.

"Do you love him?" he asked.

She felt the pain of that question sear through her. She should tell him the truth and say she did love Carter, but how could she hurt him more? "I love you. You're my husband and I love you."

"But you fuck him," he said. "You love me but you fuck him."

"It was a mistake." Avery felt sick at his words.

"A mistake?" Anthony slammed his fist on the table as he shot up from his chair.

Avery flinched and backed her chair up. When she looked up at him, he looked as if he wanted to hit her.

"You can't be honest about anything, can you?" he asked. "I saw the way you looked at him. You wanted to be with him again. You were just waiting for something to happen so you could blame it on that instead of yourself."

Maybe he was right, Avery thought. Maybe in her heart she knew that there was no denying what was between her and Carter, but none of that mattered now.

"What do you want me to do?" she asked. "I'll do anything."

"I want you to tell me it's all a lie." Anthony paced the room as his anger seemed to morph into anxiety. "That this is not my nightmare coming true. That I didn't make all these sacrifices for nothing. I gave up everything for you!"

"I know." Avery tried to control her tears. She had no right to cry, but she wanted to badly. "And I can't undo what I've done to us, but I will do whatever I can to fix it."

He stood in the corner next to the painting Nikki had given them as a wedding present. Avery had no idea what he was thinking, but it looked to her as if he was setting emotion aside and achieving some sort of clarity. That was either good or bad for her.

"You want my forgiveness?" he asked quietly.

"I'm begging for your forgiveness," Avery answered.

"I knew this was going to happen when we moved here." Anthony turned to look out the window to the backyard. "Hell, I knew it before. When we were in Florida, you talked about him like he was a scourge on your life, but I could see in your eyes that you still loved him."

"Nothing I said to you in Florida was a lie," Avery said. "I fell in love with you and I wanted this to be forever."

"But when we got here, I knew that no matter how much of an asshole Carter was, there wasn't a chance in hell I could compete with him."

"It was never a competition," Avery said. "It wasn't about that."

"Do me a favor, Avery, and stop lying. Have at least that much respect for me."

Avery believed in her heart that there wasn't a competition, but she wasn't going to second-guess him. She was clearly wrong. "I know things have been hard on you since we moved here and I've made them harder. I want to fix it. I know I can. I made a vow to you and God and I will fix it."

"It doesn't matter what you do," Anthony said, turning around. The look on his face was one of simplicity and decisiveness. He had made up his mind about something. "As long as Carter is around, you'll want him more than you'll want me."

"No," Avery protested.

"And no matter what you promise," he said, "he'll never stop. He has no morals."

Avery suddenly realized what he was going to say and she felt a tightening in her chest. It wasn't possible.

"So we'll have to leave," Anthony said. "I'm going to move back to Coral Gables right away. I'll stay at a hotel until I can get a place."

"Anthony, we can't just . . ."

"You can get things finished around here, but I want you to join me by the end of the week." He had returned to the even-tempered professor again, speaking in pure logic. "We have to look for an apartment."

"Anthony, wait!" Avery stood up, determined to make him understand. "You're forgetting something."

"The gallery? Your mother and Nina can handle that. You can put your sister to work. She clearly needs the structure." Anthony started for the hallway.

Avery rushed after him. "I'm talking about Connor."

"I'm not forgetting her." Anthony stood on the stairs, about five steps up. "Of course she'll come with you. You can get your mother to handle selling the house, can't you?"

Avery wondered if he was thinking clearly after all. "Carter won't let me do it."

Anthony's expression darkened. "You'll do it anyway. You're her mother and you've already signed an agreement that she stays with you."

"But that was when I promised to live in L.A. We've discussed this many times. Neither Carter nor anyone in that family will let me take Connor to another state."

Anthony was clearly unsympathetic. "Do you want our marriage to work?"

"Of course I do." Avery wondered if he had any understanding of how hard it would be to do what he wanted.

"I'm not suggesting this will be pretty," Anthony said, "but you should have thought about that before you fucked him."

Avery bristled at his harsh language, but kept her composure. "I can't lose my baby."

"Then don't," he said. "Do whatever you have to do and I'll help you, but if you want our marriage to work, this is what has to be done. I've given up everything for you and I'm getting some of it back. It's always been about you, Avery. That's why you thought you had a right to do this with him in the first place."

"I never thought I had a right," she argued. "But this isn't about me. It's about Connor. We lied to them, Anthony. We forged documents and tried to keep her away from Carter. If they bring that to court, with the power of their name and money, I'll lose her. And if I lose her, I'll die."

"He owes you this, Avery." Anthony looked at her with pity in his eyes. "Look at what he's made you into. Would you ever have thought you would cheat on me? I don't recognize you. Moving back to Florida isn't just about getting our marriage back. It's about you getting yourself back."

Avery didn't respond as Anthony turned and headed upstairs. There was nothing left to say.

Getting herself back? Avery didn't know what that meant,

because though she knew what Anthony thought it meant, her heart continued to tell her that getting back to herself meant being with Carter.

No matter how painful it would be, Avery knew she could give Carter up. She could move to Florida and still want him, ache for him, and dream of being with him. She could live with that torture because she had made her bed. But she couldn't and wouldn't live without her baby. That was too high a price to pay for anyone—Anthony or Carter.

No one was going to take Connor away from her.

Haley was determined to stay in her room all day. After the fiasco at the ball last night, both of her parents had gone nuts and continued to be walking volcanoes. Whatever had happened in that room that night, it was certainly more than two idiots fighting over her brother. There was poison throughout the house and she didn't want anything to do with it.

So when her mother knocked on her bedroom door before trying to open it, Haley got a bad feeling in her stomach.

"Haley." Janet called out her daughter's name in that same smooth, controlled tone that told everyone that she was about to take control of a volatile situation. "Let me in. I'm not going to tell you again."

Haley hopped off her bed and kicked the clothes on her floor out of the way as she walked to the door. "Whatever is going on, it doesn't have anything to do with me, so just leave me out of it and go away."

"Haley, I have no time for your bullshit today. Open this damn door, now!"

Haley didn't hesitate to open the door now. Her mother found cursing low class, and whenever she was reduced to it, it meant that she had reached the end of her own civility and all hell was about to break loose.

Haley opened the door slightly and blocked the entry with her body.

Her mother did not look good. Even in the worst of times, Janet always looked perfect. Image was everything and appearances were her specialty. She maintained her dignified look and immaculate manners under circumstances when the average woman would be unable to hold it together.

But not today. She looked tired, and Haley wondered if her mother would start drinking again. She wasn't an alcoholic, but she had had an episode with valium that had gone too far and she had sworn off all potentially addictive substances.

"What is it?" Haley asked.

"Detective Jackson called this morning." Janet barely had a mind to deal with her real problems. The last thing she needed to hear was that Haley was inviting more danger her way. "He told me everything."

"That asshole." Haley rolled her eyes. "Well, those files were only copies and he didn't have a right to have them anyway."

"Do you have information that can help the case?"

"Don't you have something better to do than harass me?" Haley regretted her words as soon as she said them. Her mother was about to smack her in the face. "Sorry. Look, I just don't want to get involved anymore. I thought that was what you'd want."

"I told him you would meet him at the station tomorrow afternoon at two o'clock and give him, and the FBI, any information you have. Kenya Austin will meet you there as your lawyer."

"Is that what you told him?" Haley asked with a sarcastic grin.

Janet's expression was gravely serious. "Taylor Jackson was in a car accident last night. Her brakes failed and her car was almost crushed. She could have been killed. Detective Jackson said it was confirmed that someone had tampered with her brakes."

"But she's not dead." Haley said the words more as more a question than a statement.

"She's scared, but fine."

Haley didn't bother to protest any further. "Will you come?"

"No." Janet gave her daughter one last look to let her know that she meant business and from the expression on Haley's face, the message was received.

"Dad, I can fix this," Michael pleaded as he leaned over his father's desk in his home office. He'd expected to get a reaming when he showed up this afternoon, but he hadn't imagined Steven would cancel the deal altogether.

"You can't fix anything," Steven said. "Look in a mirror. You're a mess."

Michael didn't need to look in the mirror to know what he looked like. If it was even half of how he felt, he had to look like death. "Too much has been invested in this to just dump it."

"Hundreds of thousands of dollars," Steven offered. "And I'm still canceling. If you . . ."

Steven stopped as Carter entered the room. "Where have you been?"

"I had things to take care of," Carter said. He could feel Michael looking at him, but he ignored him. "I'm here now."

"Well, thanks," Steven said sarcastically. "So nice of you to come by."

"I'm here!" Carter yelled.

Steven stared him down for several seconds before speaking again. "I was telling your brother, who at least had the respect to show up on time, that the publishing deal is dead. I'm not signing the contracts."

Carter finally looked at Michael and, as angry as he was, his compassion for his brother was unavoidable. This had to destroy him. He had bet everything on this deal. "I don't think that's necessary."

"You don't think?" Steven asked. "Okay, Harvard lawyer. You tell me, what options do you think I have after last night's fiasco? Have you read the papers?"

Carter nodded. "It's ugly, but it's not fatal. If you can talk to your investors and hold off on the deal for another six months, I think we can jump right back into it."

"Six months?" Michael asked. "Elisha isn't going to wait that long. Other bidders aren't going to wait that long."

"Do you think I give a shit what Elisha wants?" Steven asked. "You put all the contracts together, Carter. How much is pulling out going to cost compared to a six-month delay?"

Carter couldn't provide those numbers right now. His mind was ten miles away in View Park. "I don't know, Dad. There will be several thousand in penalties and possibly a few hundred thousand in restoration for money spent on labor to prepare the warehouse and everything to your specifications. They've done a lot of work."

Michael couldn't believe this was really happening. "What about the compensation for losing the other companies that had put in bids but pulled out because they thought we had it?"

"There's that," Carter said, "but that's workable. If we delay, it could cost us less or more. It depends on what happens to the company between now and then. If competition jumps up again, we'd probably lose the deal and everything we've invested."

"There goes that *we* again," Michael said, meeting Carter's glare with his own. "You still get your legal fees for all the work you've done."

"Shut up," Steven said. He sat back in his chair and placed his hands over his face. Sighing heavily, he felt a hundred years old. "I have to think of your mother."

"Mom has nothing to do with Chase Beauty," Michael said.

"But she has everything to do with me," Steven answered. "And I'm tired."

It was difficult for Carter and Michael to see their father like this. Steven was a god to them, he always had been. A tyrannical and occasionally merciful god that assured them that he loved them despite everything. He was a titan and impenetrable. He was a king and he was always stronger than the both of them combined. But now he looked tired, like he said, and Carter and Michael knew that they were the reasons why. They had put a chink in the armor of their king.

"She's tired," Steven continued. "I don't think either of you really understand what the toll of these last six months has done to us. That murder cover-up and the plane accident have exhausted our emotions. We don't blame you for the accident, but we thought you were dead and it almost killed us. Putting out your sister's fires is one thing. But this is just another mess that I'm not willing to fix. I could, I'm sure, but I don't want to. It's over. You two deal with this Monday."

"Dad," Michael protested.

"It's over." Steven gestured finality with a flat wave of his hand. "The tabloids are one thing, but the business papers are questioning our integrity and holding us to a higher standard than they place on anyone else. For whatever reason you let Kimberly stay in your life, get over it."

"That's not as easy to do as you might think," Michael said.

"I don't care," Steven said. "I have tried to understand that you love her, but whatever this sick thing you call a marriage means to you, you need to choose. Her or Chase Beauty. You can't have both."

Michael was stunned as his father stood up and walked by him without another word. Steven left the room with haste, leaving his sons to contemplate his surrender to the trouble they had caused him.

Michael came face-to-face with his brother. "I'm sorry. I . . . I didn't mean to hurt you, Carter. I just . . . I was so angry and fucking sick of being the brunt of his venom. Maybe it's best this way. No matter what I do, Chase Beauty won't give me what I want."

"You don't mean that." Carter placed a hand on his little brother's shoulder.

Michael looked up at him. "I don't know what I mean anymore."

Carter was just about to bang on the front door of Charlie and Nikki Jackson's home for a third time when Nikki finally answered the door. She met him with her usual disapproving stare and Carter responded with his usual I-don't-give-a-damn stare.

"You're early," Nikki said. "Connor isn't ready."

"What do you mean she isn't ready?" he asked impatiently. "She's six months old. Does she have to pack? Is she on the phone or something?"

"Don't give me your attitude," Nikki said. "Avery said you were coming by at five. It's only three-thirty."

"Can you just go get her?" Carter ordered more than asked.

Nikki didn't move an inch. "Look, boy. It isn't my fault that you ruined everyone's life."

Carter tried to calm down. "I just want my daughter and I want to know where Avery is."

Avery hadn't returned any of his calls. She'd sent him a text asking him to pick Connor up at her mother's and keep her for a few days. She would talk to him when she got back. Back from where? He stopped by the house, but no one was there.

"I'm going to be a moment." Nikki took a step back, opening the front door all the way. The baby was in the living room, fast asleep on the sofa, guarded in by pillows. "I don't want to wake her up."

"I can find out easily where she is," Carter said.

"Carter, she isn't trying to hide from you," Nikki said. "I just found out this morning about your affair. You two have really screwed things up."

"I'm not looking for your opinion."

"Well you're going to get it. Whatever hold you have on my daughter, it's almost ruined her life. But she's a strong woman and she is going to save her marriage."

"She said that?" Carter believed that Avery was trying to calm things down with Anthony, but she was certainly not going to make him any promises.

"She's in Florida, Carter. She went with Anthony to help him settle in at his hotel."

Carter saw a ray of hope. "Anthony is moving back to Florida?"

"They all are," Nikki said, approaching the sofa and gently picking up Connor. "As soon as she clears everything up here, she is taking Connor and she is going to make things work with her husband."

"She wouldn't do that," Carter fumed. "She wouldn't leave me and she wouldn't take Connor away from me."

"She's not taking her away." Nikki carefully offered Connor to her daddy, followed by the baby bag. She might have put up more of a protest but she needed to be freed up to deal with Taylor. "There's breast milk and formula bottles in there. You'll work something out. She knows you're Connor's father and she wants you to be just as much a part of Connor's life as she is. But you two will not be together."

Nikki leaned in and kissed Connor on the cheek. "Now, I have to get back to my other daughter."

Carter wanted to believe that Nikki was only saying this to hurt him because she had never liked him. But he also knew that

Nikki told the truth. Avery had said she did so, to a fault, when it came to the serious things. If this was true, then Avery had betrayed him, and he wasn't going to wait until she got back from Florida to know. He had to find her now and remind her that her heart, body, and soul belonged to him, just as his belonged to her. And Connor belonged to both of them.

"You have to save this, Michael," Elisha pleaded over the phone. "You can't let this die. You have to."

"I don't have to do anything," Michael said. "You and Kimberly put an end to that."

Standing in his living room, Michael took the last remaining sip of scotch from the glass in his hand.

There was a short silence before Elisha spoke again. "What did she tell you?"

"She would have to talk to me to tell me something," Michael said. "Why?"

"She was talking crazy, Michael. There's something really wrong with her. You can't believe anything she says."

"I never have." Michael looked at his empty glass before tossing it into the fireplace, and smiled at the blaze. "You're both crazy. All women are."

"You're drinking," Elisha said. "You don't mean this. I know you care about me, Michael. And I know you'll do anything for your father."

"Not anymore," Michael said. "No, that boat has sailed and so has yours. You can cancel the ceremonial signing at Chase Law tomorrow. Of course if you want to watch while we draft and sign cancellation papers, you're welcome to join us."

"You can't do this. You've come too far."

Michael could tell from the tone of her voice she was about to get emotional and he didn't have the stomach. "You'll have no problem selling it, Elisha. Good-bye."

He hung up before she could respond and made his way back to the bar to get another glass. He could hear Kimberly's high-heeled shoes walking his way. When she appeared in the archway to the living room, he could swear she had a smile on her face.

"How nice of you to show up," he said. She had slipped out of the back room while he was defending himself from his brother and father's onslaught of accusations. He hadn't seen her since. "Where did you go? And don't say Avery's."

"Avery's," she answered with a vindictive smile. "It's none of your damn business. I wasn't going to come back here for more of your abuse."

"Were you hoping I would have calmed down by now?" Michael asked. "Because you'd be right. I have."

Kimberly nodded to the glass in his hand. "Still drunk I see."

"Not at all." Michael put the glass down. "I am possessed with a sound mind."

Janet shuffled both of her grandsons into the house. They had managed to fall asleep in the car during the drive from Chase Mansion to their home, and now she could barely get them to walk. She didn't even want them to be here, but Michael demanded to see his kids, and she had promised to bring them home as long as Marisol was there.

"Go on upstairs to bed," she said sweetly as they both looked up at her. She loved them desperately and hated every time she had to walk away from them.

As the boys set off for the stairs, Janet turned her attention to the voices she was hearing. She was certain she'd heard a woman, and it wasn't a woman with an accent. Kimberly must be home. When he called this morning for his kids, Michael told her that he hadn't seen Kimberly at all.

Janet took a few more quiet steps toward the living room and peeked in. She didn't have the strength to confront Kimberly at the moment, but couldn't help but care about what was happening between her and her son.

"What you're possessed with is a great deal of liquor," Kimberly said. "I'm actually enjoying this, watching you turn into an alcoholic. Daddy Chase will be so proud of you."

"Shut up!" Michael took the glass in his hand and threw it against the wall.

Janet jumped as the glass exploded into little pieces and the liquor stained the rose-colored wall. She noticed that Kimberly didn't even flinch. He'd clearly done this before.

"You win, Kimberly." Michael raised his hands in surrender. "You ruined the deal and now my father hates me."

"I knew Steven and I would eventually find something in common."

"You'd better shut your mouth about my father right now!" Michael ordered as he approached her.

Kimberly stepped aside. "You want to hit me? Go ahead, but you better not ever go to sleep again, because you won't wake up."

"Are you threatening to kill me?" Michael laughed. "I ought to hit you just to see you try."

"Go ahead," she teased. "Make sure that what little ounce of pity your father had left for you goes up in smoke. He's already covered up a murder for you."

"And he can cover up another one!" Michael backed Kimberly against the wall. Her lack of fear startled and angered him. He wasn't going to hit her, but it looked as if she didn't even care if he did.

"What are you going to tell the twins?" Kimberly asked. "Mommy slipped and fell? Maybe I ran into a wall."

"I'm not going to tell you again to shut up."

"It won't matter what you say to them because they already hate you."

Michael slammed his fist into the wall right next to her head, making a huge dent in the wall. Kimberly flinched, but she didn't try to move.

"My boys love me," he said. "And I've been doing you a big favor by allowing you to stay in their lives. That's over. You're never going to see those boys again."

Kimberly was tired of this diatribe. "Well, now you're going to have to kill me because I'm not leaving this house without my children!"

"You will leave without the children," Michael yelled. "You'll leave without them and without even half a penny. You'll be back in the gutter in no time!"

Janet took a couple of steps away from the archway because she just couldn't take it anymore. It was beyond pitiful and heartbreaking. Since the first day she met her, Janet had always known Kimberly would only be bad news for the family, but she never imagined it would get this bad. This was completely unaccept-able. For the sake of her grandchildren, Janet had to . . .

She swung around at the sound of sniffling. To her horror, both boys were sitting on the bottom step and both were in tears. They hadn't gone upstairs like she told them to, and she'd been too caught up with Kimberly and Michael to notice.

Janet rushed over to them, not bothering to ask what they had heard. She knew they'd heard everything, and from the tortured looks on their faces as they wiped their tears, she knew that they had heard many other hateful exchanges between their parents.

"It's going to be okay," she whispered to them both. She kissed their cheeks and helped them stand. Without saying any more, she quickly led them outside and into the car, instructing her driver to go back to Chase Mansion.

For these boys, Janet knew she had to put a stop to this. It had to end now.

14

When Garrett opened the door to his office, Haley wasn't surprised by the confused look on his face. She hadn't been returning his calls since the ball, and she had never been to his office before.

Garrett nodded to the assistant he shared with the part time associate who occupied the office when Garrett wasn't there. She looked a few years beyond retirement age and didn't seem to appreciate Garrett getting a social visit.

"What are you doing here?" Garrett asked as he shut the door behind him.

"You've been calling me, haven't you?" Haley positioned herself on the firm leather sofa against the wall of his small office.

"Yeah, but." Garrett looked around nervously before joining her on the sofa. "I'm just really busy."

"Why are you even still working here?" Haley asked. "You think these people . . ."

Haley was shocked when Garrett quickly covered her mouth with his hand to silence her. She slapped his hand away. "Are you crazy?"

Garrett leaned in and whispered. "They're listening."

Haley looked around before asking, "Are they watching?"

Garrett shook his head before returning the volume of his voice to normal. "I want to work here. The firm has supported me through all this."

There was a knock on the door and Haley thought that was rather quick, until she realized it wasn't Garrett's assistant. It was a young man of Middle Eastern descent carrying a stack of papers.

"Hey, Garrett." The kid waved with his free hand as he smiled at Haley. "Girlfriend visiting, huh?"

"Are those the files?" Garrett was up and grabbing the files quickly. He placed them on the desk.

"All of them." The kid stood in the doorway, his gaze moving back and forth between Garrett and Haley.

"You can leave now," Garrett said.

Disappointed, the boy shrugged and left.

"He wanted you to introduce me," Haley said.

"He's an intern." Garrett sat down at his desk, sorting out the folders in front of him. "He hasn't earned introductions yet."

"Aren't you an intern?" Haley asked.

"I'm a law clerk," Garrett corrected. "One step up from an intern."

"Whatevs." Haley walked over to the desk and sat on the edge. Her short skirt lifted up, revealing her shapely, smooth cinnamon legs. "Are you going to take me to lunch?"

"I can't," Garrett said. "I want to, but I had to wait for him to bring me these files and I'm running late."

"Why didn't you get them yourself?" she asked.

Garrett frowned at her, tossing the file in his hand on the table. "Let's talk about something else."

"You can't access files, can you?" Haley leaned in, but she didn't whisper. When Garrett didn't respond, she knew she was right. "They've cut you off."

"It's a precautionary thing," he said. "If any of the members of the firm are in legal trouble, their access is limited. What's important is that I'm still here."

"For now." Haley reached behind her and tugged at the drawer right beneath her. Locked. Of course. Where in the hell was that garage guy anyway?

As if on cue, there was a knock on the door before the disapproving assistant stuck her head in. "It's Joe in the garage. He says something's up with your car."

Finally. Haley was ready to get this thing started.

"Great." Garrett pressed the flashing red light on his phone and then the Speaker button. "Joe, please don't give me bad news."

"Sorry buddy, but you're out of luck." Joe sounded like a mobster from Jersey. Haley could only imagine what he looked like. "All four tires, buddy. Someone is pissed at you."

Garrett looked confused. "Who has been down there?"

"No one that I saw," Joe answered. "I can call the shop that the firm has on retainer and they'll take care of it, but I need you to come down and fill out the request."

"Can't I just send Alana?" he asked, looking up at his assistant still standing in the doorway. She frowned her disapproval of his offering of her services.

"She can fill out the form," Joe said reluctantly, "but she'd need all your driver's license info and stuff and you'd still have to sign it. Plus, she's kind of mean."

Haley laughed as Alana huffed and closed the door.

"Shit," Joe said. "Was she there?"

"Yeah," Garrett reached into the drawer to his right and pulled out his car keys. "I'll be down in a second."

As he stood up, he turned to Haley. "You want to come with me?"

"Are you serious?" Haley asked. Inside she was screaming *just get out of here.*

"Of course." Garrett headed for the door. "Just wait here. I'll be back in five minutes. And don't touch anything."

"Take your time," she said sweetly as he closed the door behind him.

Haley immediately hopped off the desk and began her search. She needed to get that locked drawer open. Reaching into her purse, she pulled out her silver nail file.

This was her part of the deal. It was a deal she'd made with

Sean and no one else knew about it. He was in his car, across the street from the office building in downtown L.A. where Garrett's firm owned two floors. She was to go in and get Garrett out of his office so she could look for the insurance policy he had mentioned while they were at lunch in Pasadena . . .

Despite her complete hatred of Taylor Jackson, Haley did not want the girl hurt. Happy to know she had gotten out of the wreck with a few scratches and bruises, Haley had made her way to the station to tell the investigators everything Garrett had told her. The FBI said it was helpful, but Sean wasn't satisfied.

Haley wasn't that concerned with him, considering he was the one who had sicced her parents on her, but then he reminded her of how she felt when the Chase jet had gone down and they didn't know if her brothers were dead or alive. That was how he'd felt when he was told that Taylor's car had been crushed in an accident. He'd thought she was dead. His parents thought the worst as well. Haley couldn't ignore the effect those moments of not knowing the truth had had on her, and on Sean. And she also couldn't ignore Garrett's behavior on the night of the ball. She was his alibi that time.

So she told Sean what she didn't tell the FBI. She told them that Garrett had a hidden file on a USB memory stick that could blow the firm apart, an insurance measure he wisely took as soon as he realized the criminal element his firm represented. He'd read too many John Grisham novels not to first think of protecting himself. What she didn't tell the FBI, but she did tell Sean, was that she might know where Garrett's insurance policy was.

It was likely on a USB stick in his office, hidden somewhere no one would suspect.

The FBI needed more information. They had already executed warrants for both Garrett and Justin Ursh's offices and homes. The homes turned up nothing, and the office searches were so limited, due to the power of the firm and the confidentiality of the information, that they were unable to seize anything that wasn't obvious. The murder had not yet officially been tied to the law firm, further limiting their scope.

If Haley could identify the hidden file, then they could get another warrant and seize it. What she had needed was an excuse to get in—she was seeing her boyfriend—and an excuse to get him out of the way—his tires were slashed.

Excited by her own genius, Haley hurried out of the office. She ignored Alana's request for her to wait so she could be escorted out. When she reached the front desk, she leaned over the counter with an impatient expression that urged the girl on the phone to put her conversation on hold.

"What can I do for you?" she asked.

"My boyfriend, Garrett Collins?"

"Yes, I saw him leave just a few minutes ago. He was going to the garage, right?"

Haley nodded. "He just called me and said he can't find his car keys. He said he was getting a massage or something this morning. Is there somewhere you guys go to get massages?"

"I think he's talking about the massage chairs in the relaxation room," she said, looking around her desk. "The actual masseuse only comes every other Tuesday."

"Where is that room?"

She pointed to her left, the opposite of the way Haley had come. "Down the hall this way. It's at the end so you can't miss it. It says Harmony Room."

"Thanks."

"Wait," the girl called after her just as she started off. She reached out and offered a tiny card. "There aren't any files or anything in there, but it's still locked. You'll need this key, but bring it back before you leave."

"Thanks." Haley snatched the card and rushed down the hallway.

Although there weren't cameras in the offices, she knew there were cameras in the hallways, and someone would see her go into the room. She only had a moment to be right, and get it done.

When she reached the room, she quickly slid the key card through the slot and opened the door. She saw three massage chairs and two long sofas. There was a gray marble table in the middle of the room with a tiny fake fountain for sound effects. But most importantly, the room was empty.

Haley rushed over to one end of the first sofa she reached. The sofas each had four pillows. Two tiny, cylinder-shaped pillows situated next to the arms and two larger pillows against the back that people would use to rest their heads. She pulled and tugged at the small pillow, but felt nothing but cushion. She went to the other end of the sofa and grabbed that pillow. She squeezed and pulled. Nothing. She rushed to the sofa on the other end of the room and grabbed one of the small pillows. She squeezed and felt nothing, but when she pulled, she saw a seam peek out at her. You had to stretch the pillow, but it was there. A tiny seam made of thread just one shade darker than the pillow fabric itself.

Haley dug in with her nails as hard as she could. She finally opened the seam just as she heard voices outside the room. She was terrified and excited at the same time. She reached further and finally felt something just as she heard the sound of a key card inserted into the lock.

When the door opened, Haley tried to play it cool. That was hard, considering one of the two men that entered the room she immediately recognized as the man that Garrett tried to convince her had been following him in Pasadena. Their eyes made contact and Haley felt certain he knew she recognized him.

She tried to recover by smiling at him with her best vixen look.

"Ma'am." The other man was middle-aged and Asian. "You aren't supposed to be in here. How did you get in?"

As the men approached, Haley remained in the position she had been in when they opened the door. She had jumped onto the sofa and had lain down, and when they entered the room, it seemed as if she was trying to relax by positioning the tiny pillow between her head and the sofa arm. She wasn't positioning it so much as she was trying to return it to its original condition so they couldn't see the seam.

"My boyfriend told me to meet him here." Haley acted as if it was her room and they were the intruders. "Do you mind?"

"Yes, we do," he answered, approaching her. "Please, ma'am, give me the key card and get up."

The man from Pasadena just stood at the door, saying nothing.

"What is this?" Haley slowly sat up. She had to hope that the pillow looked normal. She couldn't look to see because the second she looked, she would be giving the men a clue that something was up. If they inspected the pillow, she was toast.

"We're with security." The man held his hand out as if to offer Haley help. "And non-employees are not allowed in the Harmony Room."

"Then why would he tell me to meet him here?" She accepted his hand and stood up. "And why would your desk girl give me the key?"

"Those are both good questions I will find out the answers to." As soon as he let go of her hand, he held his out again. "The key card, ma'am."

Haley rolled her eyes, annoyed, as she offered him the key. "You guys have some communication problems in this office."

She again locked eyes with the Pasadena man and felt that she would only arouse his suspicion if she pretended not to recognize him. She was a good liar; one of the best.

"Do I know you?" she asked innocently.

"No," he answered in a deep voice.

"Yes, I do." She grabbed her purse off the hook. "You work security at the L.A. Country Club too, don't you?"

"No," he repeated.

"Well, you look just like one of the guys that drives old ladies around in the golf carts." She made a move for the door. "Excuse me, please."

"Your purse," the man behind her said.

Haley realized that Pasadena man wasn't going to move, so she turned around to the other man. "I beg your pardon?"

"I'm going to need to search your purse."

"What for?" Haley hugged her purse to her chest. "Are you going to say you keep confidential information in the massage room?"

He seemed unfazed, and Haley tossed the purse at him, pushing it against his chest. That sufficiently pissed him off, as did her purposeful, snotty-nosed stare as he searched through the purse. Being a bitch was a good distraction and it made people want to get rid of you quick.

"Can I have it back now?" she asked. "Or are you thinking you like it and might want to keep it yourself? You look like the kind that owns a few purses if you know what I mean."

Without speaking, the man handed Haley the purse back. She thought she was home free as Pasadena man stepped aside, giving her the clear to leave. But just as she did, she noticed the other man walk over to the sofa. Her heart jumped into her throat. He was going to inspect the sofa!

Haley sped past Pasadena man and walked as fast as she could without looking as if she was doing so, down the hallway and to the elevators. She showed no signs of the frayed nerves she was feeling, knowing that there were cameras in the elevators as well.

When she reached the lobby, Haley sprinted toward the door. The security desk was to her right. Haley glanced quickly that way and saw one man talking with a woman on the other side of the desk and another on the phone.

There were no metal detectors on the way out. Just that last revolving front door. Haley was almost there when she heard someone yelling "Ms.! Ms.!" but she didn't stop. She ran across the street and hopped into Sean's waiting, running car.

Sean sped off immediately. "Did you get it?"

Haley took a breath for the first time since exiting the elevator. She reached into her blouse and the lining of her bra. She pulled out the tiny USB stick and waved it in front of Sean.

"Piece of cake," she answered, although she had a feeling that Garrett was in more trouble now than ever.

"What else did he say?" Avery asked her mother over the phone.

She had taken a short break from Anthony and was on her way to the hotel bar when her cell phone rang and her mother told her about Carter's behavior yesterday when he'd come to pick up Connor.

"I've repeated the entire conversation, sweetie." Nikki paused. "He has Connor, Avery. He won't believe that you're trying to take her away."

"That's good," Avery said. "Have you called him this morning? I know you're busy with Taylor, but I need to know how Connor is."

It had been two days since she kissed her baby and handed her over to her mother. She ached to hold her and kiss her. She came to Miami with Anthony alone because she didn't want Carter thinking she was trying to take Connor away from him and she wanted to focus her attention on Anthony.

But nothing was working. It had become painfully clear to Avery that there was not going to be a resolution to this. Anthony's anger only seemed to increase with time and, even worse, her need to be with Carter only increased as well.

She was trying desperately and making promises, but Anthony knew she didn't want to stay with him. He knew better than she did. Avery was intent on healing her marriage, but Anthony seemed intent on making her admit that she was fooling herself. He loved her, he said, and he would give his life for her, but she would betray him again. Whether Carter was in California or Guam, Anthony told her, he knew she would find a way to be with him, and Carter would continue to use Connor to keep her near.

Avery tried to placate him, but when he suggested that she give up custody of Connor, it was the last straw. Anthony seemed convinced that the only way their marriage could work was if Carter was out of it completely, and the only way to assure that was to take Connor out of the equation. Avery wanted to believe he was caught up in irrational anger, but he suggested it again later and Avery lost her temper.

To keep from making things worse, she left the hotel room for some air and a drink. What she really wanted was Carter. She just couldn't deny it, no matter what she told herself.

"Taylor is all right," Nikki answered with a heavy heart. "She's just scared, but barely a scratch. And yes, I spoke with Carter over the phone this morning. He was short and curt, but I could hear her cooing in the background. She sounded very happy. He said he was taking her to his parents' for dinner."

Avery stopped just at the edge of the lounge, noticing all the people sitting alone at the bar or at the tables around it. They all looked miserable and lonely and made her rethink her need for a drink. She turned and headed back through the lobby toward the front entrance. Air would do her better.

"I think I'll be home tomorrow," Avery said, eagerly awaiting her mother's response.

"With or without Anthony?" Nikki asked.

"Without," she answered reluctantly. "Mom, he keeps suggesting that I give up custody of Connor to get Carter out of our lives."

"He doesn't mean that, baby. He loves Connor."

"I know, but . . . I think he hates Carter more." Avery felt her stomach rumbling. When was the last time she'd eaten? "Mom, I need you. I can't believe how horribly I've messed up my life and now Anthony's and Connor's."

"Connor will be fine," Nikki said. "I can hear the pain in your voice and I wish I could be there with you. You should come home. Come home and stay here."

Avery wanted so badly to do that, but she couldn't hide in the comfort of her safe childhood. "I have to deal with this and I have to do it today."

"Do what?" Nikki asked.

Avery sighed. "Mom, I'm going to end my marriage."

"Avery, please wait before you do that. You love Anthony and he loves . . ."

"Mom, I love Carter. And please don't lecture me. I know it's wrong."

"I haven't lectured you once, have I?" Nikki asked. "Marriage is sacred, baby. It needs to be real and pure and . . . if yours isn't and you don't believe it ever can be, then you should end it. But you might feel differently after things have calmed down."

"No, Mama." Avery knew in her heart what had been true all along. "I won't feel differently about Carter. I never will. I love him and he is Connor's daddy. I'm not going to stop wanting to be with him."

There was a silence on the phone that lasted several seconds before Nikki said in a very quiet voice, "Come home, baby. We'll deal with it. Just come home."

The only reason Avery wasn't crying when she hung up the phone was that she didn't have any tears left. She'd been doing a lot of crying these past few days, but she was done. She was done crying, begging, promising, and pleading.

But now maybe she was hallucinating.

Avery assumed as much when she saw Carter walking through the glass doors of the hotel. He was in a pair of jeans and a faded purple polo shirt, looking like he stepped out of a magazine advertisement. It had to be her hunger, or maybe just her aching heart, but she swore that Carter was walking right toward her.

Carter's relief at the sight of Avery immediately caused his anger to lighten. He was happy to see her and concerned by the way she looked. She looked tired and miserable. But none of that was enough to make him forget the main reason he dropped his baby off at Chase Mansion and caught the first flight to Miami.

"You can't take Connor away from me," he said as soon as he reached her. "No matter what happens, you can't . . ."

"I would never do that," Avery said, before flinging herself at him and wrapping her arms around him. She dug her head into his chest and squeezed him tight. Just touching him felt like jumping into a freezing lake after years in the desert. "I would never take her from you."

By instinct, Carter wrapped his arms around Avery. He loved her and he would never turn from her if she needed him. "Your mother said you wanted to be with Anthony."

Avery looked up at him. "I thought I did. I wanted to be a good wife. I'd caused so much pain and I just wanted to do what was right."

"What could be more right than us being together?" Carter asked. "You, me, and Connor. Nothing; no matter what anyone else says, is more right than that."

When he kissed her, Avery felt, for the first time in the longest time, that everything was going to be okay. When their lips separated, she took his hand and led him off to the side of the main lobby for some privacy.

"How did you know I was here?"

"I had Anthony's credit card traced." Carter saw the look on

Avery's face and he felt bad, but he didn't regret it. "I'm sorry, Avery. I know that upsets you, but I wasn't going to let anything keep me from you. I wasn't going to wait while Anthony guilted you into staying with him."

"You can't do that stuff," Avery said. "Carter, I love you, but you can't."

"I know." Humility had never come easy to Carter, but Avery was his exception to everything. He couldn't be proud when it came to her. "I've always expected you to accept who I am with no demands, but I was wrong. I expected you to adjust to my life, my family, and look the other way when I used my money or my name to manipulate lives and situations. I've always thought I had a right to be who I am, but I know that I only have a right to be what you need."

Avery felt a warmth in her heart that threatened to overwhelm her. He had never said anything like that to her, ever. "I just need you. I just need you and Connor."

"And you have us." Carter embraced her tightly, never wanting to let go. "I'm sorry that I made this happen. I know that it was my lies and deceit that made you leave me. I gave you no choice."

Carter could have said that a million times to make her feel better, but this time he knew in his heart and soul that he meant every word. She deserved a better man and he had to be that for her. She was willing to give him another chance and he would make it worth it.

"I should have stayed," Avery admitted. "I should have tried to work this out with you, tried to forgive you and make it work. I knew I was pregnant and I let anger and fear turn me into a coward."

Carter was already feeling more grounded than he had in a long time. He was frustrated and angry over everything that was going on in his family and had been holding it all inside because he knew that Avery was the only person that could make him feel better.

"Anger and fear are very common emotions my family evokes in others," he said.

"They'll be angry with you," Avery said. "You know how your parents are about the way things look and there is no way this won't get out."

"Do you care?" Carter asked.

Avery smiled as she shook her head. "I don't think I could make your parents angrier at me than they already are."

"No," Carter said. "I mean at all. Do you care at all? Not just my parents. We're going to upset other people."

Avery looked away as thoughts of Anthony tugged at her heart. "I do care about Anthony. I have to find the strength to tell him it's over. I owe him that. I owe him much more than that, but at least that."

"You could just come with me now," Carter said. He felt her separating from him and didn't want to let her go. "Just come, and leave everything. I'll take care of you and . . ."

"I can't," Avery said. "I can't run away anymore. I've been doing it for so long. Running from you, your family, the way I feel. I've hurt him enough. I've got to do this."

"I'll wait for you," Carter said.

"No." Avery pulled away from him reluctantly. Now that he'd held her, she'd gotten her second wind. She could handle this. "Go back home and be with Connor. I'll deal with Anthony and come home tomorrow."

"Avery," he protested.

She pleaded with him. "Carter, I've done so much wrong with this marriage. Let me at least end it with some dignity for me and Anthony."

"You do what you feel you have to do." Carter didn't want to leave at all, but he wasn't going to fight her. He could see the light at the end of the tunnel and would have to be happy with that for now. "But come home as soon as you can. Connor and I will be waiting for you at . . ."

"Julia still lives with you."

"I'll take care of that," Carter said. Julia would have to leave, but it might take more than a day to make that happen. He couldn't expect Avery to come live there until it was all done. "Your house?"

"No," Avery said. "That's not right. We have to be somewhere else. Not in a hotel."

"No more hotels." Carter smiled. "Look, Connor is at Chase Mansion. I'll go there and you come there as soon as you can. We'll find somewhere to be alone and we'll talk."

"Sounds good." Avery couldn't wait.

Carter kissed her softly on her lips and smiled. It wasn't a passionate kiss like all their others, but it was pure and sweet. It was a kiss that said everything would finally, after what seemed forever, be all right.

"I love you," he whispered in her ear.

"I love you too," she whispered back, feeling a sense of peace she hadn't thought she'd ever get back.

They embraced for a long time, but it was still painful for both of them when they had to separate. As Avery watched Carter walk out of the hotel, she knew that the pain wasn't over. There was a lot to do and deal with and it would all be painful. But it would all end with her and Carter and Connor being together. Her family, the one she'd always wanted but had given up hope of having, was going to be real.

Steven wasn't happy if his wife wasn't happy, and Janet was very unhappy. As he stood in the doorway of the bathroom, looking into their master bedroom, he observed her beauty. In her mid-fifties, Janet looked ten years younger, and flawless. He appreciated the care she took with her appearance and body. She still turned him on after all these years with her magical smile, silky skin and generous curves. She had been a patient wife, accepting that he would not be home as much as he should, for the sake of Chase Beauty. When he had fallen short as a father because of his quest for an empire, Janet had been mother and father to their four children. He would be grateful to her forever for that.

He tried to show that gratitude as often as he could. Even when he was out of the country, he called her every day, reminded her that he loved her, complimented her appearance and taste.

She could have anything she wanted, and he saw to it that she had everything she didn't even know she wanted. While being executive director of the Chase Family Foundation was her day job, Janet's life was the family, and when the family wasn't working, she was miserable.

Steven watched her, sitting up in bed, slowly turning the pages of an art magazine without really looking at any of them. It had been like this ever since the Museum Ball. There was no comforting her, despite his several attempts. No one seemed happy these days, and that was what this was all about.

Janet looked up and managed a smile as she saw Steven come toward her. "You're looking very handsome in your new nighties."

"I have asked you several times not to call my pajamas nighties." Steven slid into the bed of their massive suite, next to her. "I was hoping you'd get a little frisky."

He leaned in to kiss her, but she turned her head. He pecked her on her cheek before pulling the covers up to his waist. "Janet, please talk to me."

Janet closed the covers of her magazine and laid it flat on her lap. "Have you handled the situation with Haley's boyfriend?"

Steven didn't want to bother his wife any more than she already was. "I was told the boy never showed. My man waited for an hour. He called him, went to his apartment. Nothing."

"That can't be good," Janet said. Great, another thing to be worried about.

Steven agreed. "Where is she now?"

"In her bedroom," Janet said. "I want her to have protection."

"I'll take care of it tomorrow." Steven reached over and placed his hand gently over hers and squeezed. "Baby, I know you're upset. The ball was . . ."

"I don't care about the Museum Ball," Janet exclaimed. "It was a disaster, but I can ease my way out of it. The only thing that matters is Michael."

"I don't want to talk about him." Steven turned away. "He hasn't shown up to work at all."

"Can you blame him?" Janet regretted having to send the twins back home into that madness, but both Kimberly and Michael were demanding their return. "Steven, we have to do something."

Steven reached for the remote, but Janet snatched it away before he could get it.

"Our son." Janet took hold of Steven's chin and turned him to her. "My baby is broken. No matter what he's done or caused, we have to let it go. He is lost and we have to save him."

Steven knew she was right, but facing the reality of who was really to blame for all this was hard. "Everything he's done ultimately leads to trying to please me. I've been too hard on him since David's death, but I thought after the plane accident, he understood that I still love him."

"He was already spiraling before that," Janet said. "The accident probably made it worse. Whatever the case, if we don't save him, we'll lose him forever. And the twins."

Steven wrapped his arms around her comfortingly. She was right, but he wasn't good at this. Janet was the heart of this family and although it had been an unspoken agreement that he would guide his boys and she would take care of the girls, Steven didn't believe he could reach Michael alone.

"That marriage is poisoning him," Janet said. "We have to end it for him."

"That will only make him hate us more." Steven had objected to Janet's earlier request to intervene in Michael's marriage, which she'd been repeating for more than a year now.

"For now," Janet said. "But he worships you, Steven. He'll do what you want and he'll only stay mad at you for so long. Until then, we'll deal with it. What's important is that he and the boys get a new start."

Steven nodded. "I'll call a lawyer."

"Don't ask Carter," Janet said. "I don't want him to interfere."

"Why are he and Connor here?" Steven asked.

"Just let that go," Janet said, reaching for the phone on the nightstand. "I know how to get this done quickly."

Kimberly was in the media room setting up another movie for her boys when her cell phone rang. She usually turned it off or put it on vibrate when she was home, but had forgotten. She had no idea where Michael was, so she wasn't worried about him overhearing a phone conversation she wasn't supposed to have. She hadn't seen him since he stormed out yesterday after yelling at Janet over the phone to bring his kids home.

She didn't recognize the number, so she answered with caution. "Hello?"

"Mrs. Chase." Neil's deep, scratchy voice was immediately recognizable. "Do you have a moment?"

"Hold on." Kimberly pressed the DVD button and turned down the lights before rushing out of the media room. "Go ahead."

"I found out more about Mr. Chase's brother."

Kimberly started upstairs. "Well, the whole plan is squashed, so it doesn't matter much, but go ahead."

"Does it have something to do with what I read in the papers last week?"

"My little melee at the ball?" Kimberly felt her stomach turning just at the thought. "Not how I planned it all, but it worked out in the end."

"You actually saved your husband from a big disaster," Neil said. "I have a contact at the FBI who snooped around. It took him a long time, but he found out that Luxury Life Publishing was involved in several double-subscription billing schemes. They also violated several privacy laws by selling off its subscriber lists' personal information. There is an unusually high number of people who were victims of identity theft within three months of subscribing to a Luxury Life publication. This has been going on for about two decades."

"Two decades?" Kimberly heard noises in the foyer. Marisol was talking to someone and she thought it might be Michael.

"Keenan Chase's department had been investigating the publisher for three years. They were ready to pounce as soon as they found out he was selling. They wanted to get him before he could get rid of the company. Then Mr. Chase found out that the publisher was in negotiations with his brother, Steven."

"So this was revenge." Kimberly stopped at the edge of the foyer as she saw who Marisol had let in and shuffled into the living room. Her in-laws.

"Yes. He must have contacted Elisha and convinced her to help him."

"No," Kimberly said. "They were lovers. That's how he found out about the negotiations, because I'm sure it wasn't public at the beginning."

"Whatever the case," Neil said, "he was going to go after the company, and although Steven wouldn't be criminally liable, he could have been fined tens of millions."

Kimberly didn't speak as Janet and Steven turned to see her. They had very serious looks on their faces and she was worried. She hated them both and they hated her more. So why were they here?

"I have to go," she said. "I have company."

"Just one more thing," Neil said. "I imagine that Keenan was going to get Elisha to testify that Steven knew all about the fraud or create some documents to support the idea. Either way, Chase Beauty would have been fined millions and then would have been sued by thousands of customers for hundreds of millions. It would have destroyed the entire company."

"Thanks," Kimberly said before hanging up. Someone hated King and Queen Chase more than her.

Kimberly placed the phone back in her pocket and walked casually into the living room. "What are you two doing here? And if you think you've come here for the boys, I will . . ."

"No," Steven said. "We've come here because of Michael."

Kimberly felt a slight panic in her chest. "What happened to him?"

"You happened to him," Janet replied.

Steven placed a hand on Janet's shoulder. She had promised to keep this civilized and quick. "He's not here, right?"

"You know he's not," Kimberly said. "What do you want?"

"We want you to leave." Steven took a few steps toward her and offered her the manila envelope in his hand. "You can offer that to any lawyer. He or she will look it over for you and verify everything."

"And everything would be what?" Kimberly reached into the folder and pulled out what looked like a contract because of the blue backing. On the cover of the first page, it read *Dissolution of Marriage* . . .

"You've been wanting to divorce Michael for a long time," Janet said. "Well, we're going to make that happen."

"The contract is very generous," Steven said. "You file for divorce and we will not let Michael stop you."

Kimberly couldn't believe this. "You can't make him give me a divorce."

"Kimberly," Steve said in an admonishing tone. "You've been a part of this family for too long to doubt what I can make happen."

"We covered up a murder you committed," Janet reminded her.

"I didn't murder him," Kimberly retorted. "It was an accident."

"The point is," Steven interrupted, "this time the divorce will happen. The contract offers you a one-time settlement of twenty million dollars."

Kimberly knew something was up. "If I do what?"

"Leave the state of California," Steven said. "Go anywhere you want, but never come back here."

Kimberly tossed the contract on the table. "You expect me to believe that you would be fine not seeing the twins at all?"

"No," Janet said. "We expect you to be fine never seeing the twins at all."

Kimberly wanted to lunge at her and slap that superior expression off her face. "You still expect me to give up custody of my children."

"Yes we do," Steven said.

"My babies that I carried inside of me and gave birth to."

"They're Chases," Janet said, "and they belong with Michael and with us."

Kimberly laughed bitterly. "How can you possibly ask . . ."

"We aren't asking," Steven interrupted. "We're giving you a choice. Stay this way and ruin those boys' lives or go away and be rich for the rest of your life."

Kimberly was so enraged, she felt near tears. "I am not ruining their lives! Your son is the one that is ruining everyone's life. I won't leave them with him."

"We will take care of Michael," Janet said. "And we'll make sure that he gets it together for the children. But you have to go. That's the first step to saving those boys."

Kimberly swallowed hard, feeling the insistent stares of both of them on her like a magnifying glass reflecting the sun onto an ant. "This isn't really a choice at all, is it?"

"We'd like to think it is," Steven said. "If this doesn't work, then we'll have to do what is necessary to protect Michael and the boys."

"From me?" Kimberly asked. "I'm the villain here?"

"We have compassion for your situation," Steven said, hoping that Janet would stay quiet. "Michael's obsession with you, his need to do . . . whatever this is supposed to be, is wrong. It's hurting you and the boys."

"And separating them from me would make everything better?"

"This is a painful situation," Janet said. "But we will make sure the boys deal with not having you around anymore."

"Can I at least call them on the phone?" Kimberly asked.

"You will be out of their lives for good," Steven said. "There is no in-between here. If it is ever possible that things change, we'll contact you."

"Because you'll always know where I am, right?" Kimberly asked. "You want me gone, but you'll track me everywhere."

"You've both left us no choice," Janet said.

"You still have the choice of minding your own fucking business," Kimberly said. "But you think everything is your business, don't you?"

"Everything that affects our family is our business." Steven stepped aside as a gesture to Janet that it was time to leave. "Think about it, Kimberly. There really is no other choice. You will not get these children, and this situation you have here cannot continue."

Kimberly took a moment to make sure she could maintain her composure. "How can I know the lawyer I show this to isn't going to lie to me for you."

"Because we want this," Janet said. "And twenty million dollars is nothing compared to the sanity of our son and the emotions of our grandchildren."

"You have twenty-four hours." Steven was already guiding Janet out of the room.

"Or else?" Kimberly asked.

"Twenty-four hours, Kimberly."

Kimberly stood in the living room for a while after they were gone, letting her rage build up. They were paying her off—thinking that twenty million dollars was worth never seeing the two people in the world that she would kill and die for.

Kimberly reached down and picked up the contract. She was all set to rip it up when a thought came to her. Steven was right. Michael was obsessed with her. It was twisted and hateful, but it was obsession. All wasn't lost yet.

15

Her television blaring a celebrity dance show, Haley was sitting at the vanity in her bedroom, trying to see if she could make her hair look like the girl on the cover of *In Style* magazine when her cell phone, settled in between brushes and hair clips, alerted her to a text.

She leaned over to see who it was and tossed her brush on the table to grab it.

We can't use it

She knew Sean was talking about the USB stick.

Y not?
2 much 2 text. Call me

Haley dialed his number and he picked up immediately. "Why can't you use it?"

"The law firm flexed its muscles." Standing outside the BHPD headquarters, Sean stepped further away from a group of cops that had just gathered near him. "They got the plates on my car and traced it to me and then the police department. They called the mayor and the chief of detectives."

"But you didn't do anything," Haley said.

"They threatened to go after Chase Beauty as well."

"That's just great." If Haley thought she was in trouble before, she would be in deep shit now. She just needed to hold on for a few more months. Then it wouldn't matter what her parents wanted. "Are you in trouble?"

"I think my personal involvement in the whole thing cushioned my fall. The chief knows how upset I am about my sister's accident. He's pissed, but I think he understands. It's the FBI we have to worry about."

"You shouldn't have waited for me."

"I wasn't going to leave you," Sean said. "I wasn't going to let anything happen to you."

Haley hated herself for feeling so affected by his words. After everything she had done, he still cared about her. "Will the FBI be able to use it?"

"As of now, they don't want anything to do with it. You were right, they discovered the pillow and I guess they grilled Garrett."

"Where is he?"

"No one knows, but we have to find him. He's in danger."

"Everything is worse now, isn't it?"

"No," Sean answered. "It's just more complicated—delicate."

"There has to be . . ."

Haley turned around on the satin vanity bench she was sitting on, in response to the sound of her last name. The gossip reporter on the local news station was discussing a new charitable initiative the Chase Foundation was launching, scholarships for minorities to private preschools and grade schools. It was Janet's latest genius idea to deflect some of the bad press from the Museum Ball and it gave Haley an idea of her own.

"Do you still have a copy of the USB?" she asked.

"Yeah, I made it before I handed the original over." There was a short silence. "Why?"

"If the cops aren't going to do anything with it, I think I know who will."

* * *

When Michael stepped out onto the back patio of Chase Mansion, he saw his father in the outdoor kitchen, drinking a glass of wine while standing in front of the large, stainless steel barbeque, grilling assorted chicken parts and steaks.

In that moment, Michael thought of turning around and leaving. His father had been trying to reach him for days. He hadn't showed up at Chase Beauty and he only went home to spend time with the boys for a short while and disappeared again. But one can only feel sorry for themselves so long, so he decided to come out of hiding and heed his father's request to come to Chase Mansion to talk.

Was he going to fire him? Bump him from the board of directors? Demote him? Or maybe he would just disown him. Michael knew there was a potpourri of reactions his father could have, and for the first time in his entire life, he really didn't care.

Just as he was about to leave, Steven turned around and saw him. He waved Michael over. Michael slowly made his way over there, trying hard to decipher what that look on his father's face meant.

Steven put his glass of wine down. "Where have you been, son?"

"Around."

Steven didn't think it was worth it to demand a better explanation. "You look better than the last time I saw you."

"A shower can do wonders." Michael leaned against the wooden column. "What did you want, Dad?"

"Your mother and I have been talking."

Steven pushed the last piece of meat to the edge of the grill so it wouldn't burn, and closed the lid. He placed the fork on the table and focused all his attention on Michael as he told him about their plans for him and Kimberly. Steven had hoped Janet would be around to do this with him, but she wasn't home and Steven didn't know when he would see Michael again. His son appeared to be in a state of disbelief through most of it, but as it seemed to settle in, he became furious.

"Who do you think you are?" Michael demanded, standing up straight. "God? You think you're God?"

"No son, I'm your father, and your mother and I are . . ."

"Deciding that my marriage is over?" Michael asked.

"Your marriage was over a long time ago," Steven said. "Son, we are doing this because we love you."

"Bullshit!" Michael slammed his fist into the column. "You're doing this because my marriage has become inconvenient for you."

"Look at where your life is, son. You cannot tell me that this marriage is good for you anymore. Most importantly, it isn't any good for the boys. You have to get over this poisonous obsession you have with Kimberly and do what is right for them."

Steven took a step toward Michael, who seemed ready to break down, but Michael stepped back.

"Stay away from me," Michael warned. "I won't let you take her away from me."

"She's gone, Michael. She's been gone a long time and you know it."

"She'll never go for it." Michael was vigorously shaking his head. "She won't leave the boys."

"She's agreed to do it," Steven said. "For the children's sake. She is putting what's best for them ahead of what she wants. She called the divorce lawyer this morning. Now all you have to do is . . ."

"No!" Looking for the first thing he could find, Michael grabbed the heavy steel wok and threw it. He couldn't believe that Kimberly would do this. He had always known that no matter what, she wouldn't leave the boys.

"Get a hold of yourself, boy."

"I'm not your boy," Michael said. "I won't go along with it, and since neither your or Mom's names are on that marriage certificate, you can't do this without me."

"Even if she has to fight you, we will support her."

Michael laughed. "That will look great in the press. You and Mom siding with my ex-hooker wife against me in a divorce."

"We will go through anything to help you see the light and get your life back together." Steven paused, wishing he could find the right words to make it okay. He knew it would take so much more. "We are doing this for you. Nothing else matters to either of us. Not the family's image and not Chase Beauty."

"Well, we all know that's a lie."

Steven had initially thought to use Michael's position at Chase Beauty as leverage to get him to comply, but changed his mind. He was going to get Michael to agree, but he wasn't going to threaten him or bully him.

"It's not," Steven responded. "I love you more than Chase Beauty and you are the one that will take it over when I'm gone."

Michael was shocked to hear his father say such words, when he expected the complete opposite. He searched his father's face for a telltale sign of a lie as he came closer, but he couldn't find it. As Steven came face-to-face with him, placing a hand on each shoulder, squeezing tight, Michael believed him.

"I have done everything for you," Michael said.

"I know, Michael." He looked into his son's eyes and the pain he saw dug right into him. "And now I'm going to do everything for you."

"I want to keep her," Michael whispered.

Steven shook his head. "She's not a toy or a pet. She's not your property. She's a person and she wants to be free."

"No." Michael reached up and shoved his father's arms away. "I won't be without her. Not even for you."

"Michael!" Steven called out as Michael turned and left. He called his son's name a few more times, but Michael was gone. It was okay. He wasn't going to give up. He loved his son and had made a promise to his wife.

Avery's phone rang the second she plugged it into the car adapter. In her haste to get to Miami with Anthony, she had forgotten her charger and the phone had been dead all day. Once she arrived at LAX and reached her car, the first thing she did was plug it in. As a mother, she didn't have the option of being unreachable. And this was why it bothered her when she saw her mother's name on the caller ID.

"What's wrong, Mom?" Avery asked as soon as she answered. "Is Connor okay?"

"Connor is fine," Nikki answered. "Where are you?"

"I'm at LAX." Avery could tell something was wrong with her mother's voice. "It was ugly, but I ended things with Anthony. I just got back. What is it?"

"I've been trying to reach you all day."

"It's an eight-hour flight. My phone was dead. Are you sure Connor is . . ."

"It's not Connor," Nikki said. "Baby, it's Anthony."

"What?" Avery braced herself for the worst.

"The Miami police were trying to reach you and they couldn't, so they called us."

The police. "What happened, Mama?"

"Anthony was in a very bad car accident."

"What?" Avery's hand came to her mouth in shock. "Is he . . . What is . . ."

"He's alive, but he was hurt really bad. When they called a couple of hours ago, he was in critical condition."

Avery tried to soak it all in. What had she done to him?

"Avery, are you there?"

"Yes." Her voice was shaky. "What else did they say?"

"They say he was drinking, but that was all."

"I have to go back." Avery grabbed her purse from the passenger's seat. "I'll call you when I get there."

She hung up, grabbed the charger and jumped out of the car. As she ran back toward the airport, the world started to cave in around her. This was her fault. She shouldn't have left him alone and now look what had happened. Avery didn't know what she'd do if he died and she prayed to God to let him live. She would do anything if he could just survive.

Michael stood outside Kimberly's bedroom for a few minutes before knocking on the door. She didn't respond to his knock, as usual, but as he gripped the door knob, he was at least grateful that she hadn't locked it this time. When he stepped inside, Kimberly was delicately placing some of her very expensive clothes in a suitcase. She didn't look up, but Michael had gotten used to that.

"When are you leaving?" he asked.

That caught Kimberly's attention. "Steven told you."

Michael approached the other side of the bed as she gently folded a pair of jeans and placed them in the suitcase. "How could you leave the boys?"

Kimberly felt her chest tighten at the question. She couldn't, she wanted to scream. She never would. "You've given me no choice."

"It seems more like my parents have given you no choice."

Kimberly placed her hands on her hips and tried to manage the most resolute expression she could. "I would like to spend some time with them before I go."

"When are you . . ."

"I'm just moving into a hotel room." She reached around the suitcase and zipped it closed. "As soon as you sign the contract, it is filed, and the money is deposited into my account, I have to leave. It will take a few days."

"What will you tell the boys?" Michael felt almost overcome with a sense of loss. He didn't understand it, but it was undeniable.

"I haven't decided yet," Kimberly answered. "If you're willing to behave we can come up with something to tell them together."

"It will kill them."

"I know," Kimberly said. "But we're killing them now. You and I both know that what we're doing is damaging them in ways that can't be fixed if it continues. I'm doing this for them. As much as it will kill me, it's better for them to have one parent who loves them and is at peace with themselves than two parents who poison the air every day of their lives."

"Kids need both their father and mother." Michael stood still as she came around the bed and placed the suitcase next to an already-filled suitcase, against the wall next to the bathroom.

"In eleven years they'll be adults and they can do whatever they want." Kimberly went over to the drawer where she was placing her jewelry in a secure case. "I imagine you and your family will fill their heads with hateful things about me, but those boys love me and I know they'll want to see me."

Michael wrapped his arm around the bed post. How could she be so nonchalant about it? Did she hate him that much? Yes, he told himself. Yes, she did and he deserved every bit of it. But his children didn't.

"You're right," Michael said. "We've . . . I've fucked everything up and the boys are paying the price."

Kimberly turned around to try to figure out what he was up to. Did he mean it? Was this actually going to work? "We all are."

"But they'll just keep paying if you leave."

Kimberly sighed. "I can't stay."

"Not with me," Michael said. He swallowed hard, feeling the impact of what he was about to say. "We shouldn't be together."

Kimberly stopped and watched him intently. She was waiting and staking everything on what he said next.

"I'll give you a divorce," Michael said. "I won't contest anything. I can't give you twenty million dollars, but I can give you ten million, alimony, this house, child support and . . ."

"Child support?" she asked.

Michael nodded. "Joint custody and they can live with you, here. Here, or anywhere else you want to live as long as you don't leave."

Kimberly took a moment to find her voice. Her babies. "What do you mean by joint?"

"I won't become a weekend daddy, but they can live with you."

"What will your parents say? The contract . . ."

"Is invalid until I sign it," Michael said. "And I'll never sign it. I want you to stay."

"I won't be yours," Kimberly said. "Never again, Michael. Divorce or no divorce. You can't have me."

"I know," Michael said after a moment. "But the boys can, and that's all that matters."

Kimberly had to dig her nails into her palms to keep herself from showing the effect of Michael's emotion. What had Steven said to make him do this? "They'll be angry that you're letting me keep them and stay."

"Then they'll be angry." Michael shrugged. "You can unpack. I'll call a lawyer to put the contract together as soon as I can."

"How do I know you'll keep to it?" Kimberly asked.

"Because I love the boys," Michael said. "And I don't want you to leave. You know that. If there is anything you can know, it's that I don't want you to leave."

Kimberly knew that Michael still didn't comprehend that she was leaving him, even if she stayed in L.A., but that wasn't important now. He would understand soon enough. Right now, all that mattered was getting her kids and getting her divorce.

"I'm still leaving," she said. "I have to get out of here. But if you can get me the contract, I'll get a lawyer to look it over to make sure it's valid. After that, I'll move back in and you can move out. The boys can stay here."

"So you'll stay?" Michael asked.

Kimberly nodded. "This is good, Michael. This is much better for everyone. I would have been miserable the other way and so would the boys."

"So would I," Michael added.

Kimberly waited until he was gone to fall to the ground on her knees. She started crying right away, feeling the stress and build-up inside of her begin to subside. She held her hands to her chest and leaned against the dresser. This was how she had planned for it to go. Despite all his venomous threats, Michael had some sick need to have her around and he assumed, through the kids, he always would.

It was a risk, but one she had been willing to take. Because the Chases could have given her two hundred million. She still wouldn't leave without her babies. And now she wouldn't have to.

Avery was tired beyond belief, emotionally and physically, but she tried to carry on. She took a deep breath before pushing open the door to the room Anthony was in at the hospital. When she entered, she gasped at the sight of him. He wasn't awake or conscious and his entire face was bandaged.

"Oh my God." Avery rushed to the side of the bed and raised up the bed sheets. One of his arms was in a cast and his midsection was in bandages as well. She looked down further. His legs weren't in bandages, but they were bruised all over and full of scratches.

"Mrs. Harper?"

Avery hadn't even seen the doctor who had been in the room the whole time. She looked very young and tired, as if she'd been seeing frantic wives all day.

Avery nodded. "Is he going to make it?"

The doctor smiled. "Yes, he's just sleeping. His condition has improved over the last five hours."

"So he will recover?" Avery hesitantly reached out to touch him. She laid her hand flat on his chest.

"That's what I need to talk to you about, Mrs. Harper." The doctor's expression turned extremely serious.

Avery kept her focus on Anthony. "Just come out with it."

"Your husband was driving under the influence and he ran a red light. The oncoming car hit him from the driver's side. All of his air bags deployed, which is the only reason he's still alive. But his body was jolted very badly. He sustained spinal injuries."

"Oh no." Avery stepped away from the bed, backing up. "Please, don't say . . ."

"I'm sorry, Mrs. Harper."

"Avery."

Avery watched with horror as Anthony reached his arm up only to have it fall because he was so weak. When she came back to the bed, she took his hand in hers and squeezed, looking into his eyes. She could barely see them through the bandaging.

"You . . . You came back."

Avery bit her tears back. "Of course, Anthony. I'm here."

"You're my . . . wife."

Avery nodded. "Yes, I am your wife and I am so sorry."

"I need you." Anthony tried to lift himself.

"Don't," Avery said. "Be still. I'm here."

"You won't leave me?"

Avery couldn't bring herself to say the words because it was too painful. She just shook her head and squeezed his hand tighter.

16

"Haley! Haley!"
Lying out by the pool at home, Haley couldn't hear her sister Leigh call her name, but she could see her, standing in the doorway to the Florida room, waving her over. She assumed it was a waste of her time, but since she wasn't doing anything, Haley removed the iPod earphones and placed her laptop on the table next to her drink.

She took her time walking from the pool, through the Florida room and into the kitchen, where Leigh was looking at the television mounted against the wall, right next to the door that led to Maya's room.

"This better be good," Haley said. "Neiman Marcus is having a Gucci handbag sale."

Leigh's brows narrowed. "Since when did you shop sales?"

Haley made a smacking sound with her lips. "Since Mom and Dad took back the credit card they gave me. I'm stuck with my own card, which, disgusting as it sounds, has a limit."

Leigh feigned her pity. "Poor baby. But look, your boyfriend is on the news."

Haley proudly looked up at the television where a reporter was discussing the latest in the Cool, Bitton & Klein scandal.

"Based on information revealed by our own Channel Four news team, which we received from an anonymous source, Beverly Hills police and the FBI arrested several partners at the firm earlier today."

"Did you know about this?" Leigh asked. "Garrett works there, right?"

"I had no idea," she lied. "He used to work there, but I don't think anyone's going to be working there anymore."

The reporter's voice continued as the screen offered pictures of men in expensive suits being led out of a business building, the same building Haley had run out of just days ago. Only they were in handcuffs.

"While the murder of Justin Ursh has been the primary focus of law enforcement, a spokesperson for the police department said that the arrests were made as a result of this station's release of several documents showing a pattern of obstruction of justice, which is not protected by the client-lawyer confidentiality rule."

"Mom and Dad aren't going to be happy about this." Leigh grabbed an apple from the fruit basket in the middle of the kitchen table. "I have to go to the clinic."

"Have fun with the hookers and drug addicts," Haley called after her before returning her attention to the screen.

"The Beverly Hills Police Department has scheduled a press conference an hour from now, but sources tell Channel Four that a witness has come forward with new information about Justin Ursh's murder."

"So Garrett did come forward," Haley said. "I thought he'd be dead by now."

Haley jumped three feet into the air as, unexpectedly, a very large Hispanic man walked into the kitchen. He was dressed in a tight black T-shirt that revealed muscles that were so bulging they seemed ready to bust out, and black jeans. He was looking directly at her.

"Who in the hell are you?" Haley asked.

The man didn't respond and Haley was ready to hightail it out of there screaming at the top of her lungs. The law firm had sent someone to kill her!

"Do you know who I am?" she asked. "Do you know who my father is?"

"Yes, he does."

Steven Chase, a man of substantial size himself, was completely hidden until he came out from behind the mammoth creature, his wife right behind him.

"What is this?" Haley asked. "You scared me to death. Who is that?"

"This is Tony," Janet said, and gestured for him to sit down, but he shook his head. "He doesn't talk much."

"But he's a skilled bodyguard." Steven reached up and turned the television off. "And he's your bodyguard until I decide he's not."

"You've got to be kidding me." Haley looked Tony up and down. "I don't need this walking steroid cautionary tale following me around. If you haven't noticed, the whole thing with Garrett's firm is over."

"It isn't over yet," Steven said. "And the fact that you were scared as hell just a moment ago is all the proof we need to know putting him on you is the right decision."

"Putting him on me?" Haley laughed. "How dirty of you, Daddy. Matchmaking for your little girl."

"Stop it." Steven had no patience for Haley's foolishness, but he was trying to fulfill his promise to Janet. He needed to put up with it to reach his children, but he didn't think anyone could reach Haley.

"Don't be disgusting," Janet said, as she stepped forward as if to tell Steven she would take over from there. "The news is encouraging, of course, but it's far from over, and until we're confident it is, Tony is your new best friend."

Haley leaned back against the kitchen island with a sarcastic smirk on her face. "Remember the last time you tried to put bodyguards on me? I recall I eluded them quite easily and one of them was drugged while sitting outside my bedroom door. Oh yeah, and they played no role at all in saving me from the attempts on my life."

"Garrett is missing," Janet said. She watched as her words

reached her daughter. Haley was crazy and mostly a fool, but she wasn't stupid. "Your father tried to pay him to get him out of your life. He offered him five million dollars to disappear completely, and Garrett accepted."

Haley glared at her dad. "Great. You give him $5 million and I have to beg for five cents. Sounds fair."

"The point is," Steven said, "he never showed up. No one can find him, not even the FBI, and I checked."

"But the news said that a witness . . ."

"Garrett called the FBI, told them what he knew, and agreed to come right to the police station if they could guarantee his safety."

"Well that was his first mistake," Haley said. "Thinking the local FBI could do their job."

"He never showed," Steven said.

Haley shrugged. "Well, what do you want me to do? It's not my fault."

It probably was, Haley thought, but there was no going back now. "Are you going to try to lock me in the house again as well?"

"No," Janet answered. "That never worked before, but Tony will go with you everywhere, including class."

"Fantastic." Haley said.

"Excuse me."

Everyone turned to see Maya standing in the archway with a perplexed look on her face.

"There's a young man here to see you, Haley."

Haley's eyes widened. "Is it Garrett?"

"No," Maya answered. "He said his name is Peter."

"Peter?" Haley was drawing a blank.

"Peter," Maya repeated. "He also says he's your husband."

"Peter!" Haley's memory was immediately jogged and she was stunned. What in the hell was he doing at her house—or in the country, for that matter? "Oh yeah, Peter."

"What is going on?" Janet asked.

Steven walked over to Maya. "What did you say?"

"Let him in," Haley said, trying not to show her shock, as both of her parents turned to her. This certainly wasn't how she wanted this to happen.

"Haley?" Janet's stomach was already hurting.

"I forgot to tell you," Haley said with an innocent tilt of her head and a sweet smile. "When I was in Sydney earlier this year, I kind of got married."

Carter was standing at the top of the mansion's massive staircase that set off in two directions. He was expecting Avery, and with every visitor to the Chase Mansion that wasn't her, he was getting more and more concerned. He had been trying to call her all day, but was unable to reach her.

Returning to the baby's room, he looked down at Connor as she slept peacefully in her bassinet. It was then that his cell phone rang. Hoping it wouldn't wake the baby, Carter grabbed it off the changing table quickly. When he saw who it was, he rushed over to the window, the farthest spot from Connor, and spoke in a quiet voice.

"Avery, where are you?"

"Carter." Avery almost wept his name. "How is Connor? Where is she?"

"She's fine," he said. "She's with me, but she's only got one bottle left."

Avery didn't need to be told that. Her breasts were killing her. "You know how to make formula."

"Yes," he answered. "At home, but I'm not at home. Remember? I'm at Chase Mansion, where you're supposed to be, and I don't even think Mom keeps a supply of formula."

"Ask Maya. She can . . ."

"Avery, forget about the formula. What in the hell is going on?"

"I'm in Miami, Carter."

Carter paused to let the words, and what they might mean, sink in. But they couldn't mean that. "When are you coming home?"

"I . . . I'm not sure. Anthony was in an accident."

"Oh." Carter assumed he should care. "I'm sorry. Is he gonna be okay?"

"No," she answered. "He's alive, but he had a spinal injury and he can't walk. Carter, he can't feel anything from his waist down and it's all my fault."

Carter took it all in. "Jesus, Avery. I'm sorry. I . . . What happened?"

Avery repeated everything she knew from the doctor and waited to hear Carter's response.

"This isn't your fault," he said. "He was driving drunk."

"But he was doing that because I left him. He begged me to stay, but I left him."

"You didn't have a choice," Carter said. "I wish I could be there for you, hold you. I think I should come."

"No," she said. "You can't be here for me or hold me. Carter, I am so sorry. You know that I love you."

Carter ignored what the voice in his head was telling him she was trying to say. It wasn't possible. "I know what you need. Connor. I'll bring her with me. Just holding her will make you feel better."

Avery wanted to hold her baby more than ever before, but she would have to wait a little longer. "I'm so sorry, baby. I know I promised you, but . . ."

"Avery, don't." Carter's voice caught in his throat. "You're upset and scared and confused. You aren't thinking clearly."

"He's paralyzed, Carter. Do you understand that? He can't take care of himself anymore."

"Then you'll find someone to take care of him," Carter said. "It won't be you."

"I can't leave him!"

"I'll pay for everything," Carter said. "He'll have the best care."

"No, I . . ."

"Avery." Carter's tone was tinged with a warning. "You can't do this. You can't do it to me or us or Connor."

"We'll work something out," she said, even though she knew that wasn't going to happen. "It will take awhile, but . . ."

"No," Carter said bluntly, doing all he could to keep his emotions in check. "No more working anything out. I'm sorry, Avery, but I won't do this. Not anymore."

"Please, baby."

"When that plane was going down, I only saw you. I only saw you and Connor and I will not wait anymore. I will not!"

Avery cringed at the sound of his voice. "I just need more time."

"No more time." Carter's voice was suddenly cold, the way it went when he refused to invest any more in the conversation. "Choose right now, Avery. Anthony or me."

"Of course I choose you," Avery cried. "But I can't be with you right now. Look at what we've caused!"

"Him or me." Carter waited for a few seconds but it seemed like more than an hour of silence. "Then it's him."

"It's not him," Avery said. "It's this situation. He can't . . ."

"I don't want to hear anymore," Carter interrupted. "This is it, Avery. There is no going back. It's over."

He tossed the phone across the room and it fell apart when it hit the wall. Sitting down on the window sill, Carter didn't try to fight the rage that was building inside of him. How could this happen? Didn't things always work out for him? If nothing else, Avery was the one thing that he knew would be his. The one thing he wanted more than anything, and once again, she turned him away.

Carter sat there for a long time feeling nothing but anger and resentment. In one instant, the life he thought was about to really begin had disappeared and he was back in the life he'd had before. Waiting and wanting something he couldn't have.

Not anymore.

Carter stood up and walked over to a chair near the door, taking a second to look down at Connor, who was still sleeping peacefully. He reached into the pocket of his jacket and pulled out the tiny, blue velvet box.

He was flooded with emotion the second he opened the box and looked at the ring inside. He remembered the way he felt, the way Avery reacted when he had proposed to her on the balcony in Hawaii. He was so hopeful, and even though he was holding the secret of what he had done to make her leave Alex, the man she was engaged to when he fell in love with her. he had believed that it would be the first day of them planning their life together forever.

Before she left him, she'd given the brilliant-style, high-cut

Lucida diamond with a center rectangular stone of about five karats and two bezel-set side stones, back to him. He held on to it because he knew that they would work their way back to it. He thought they had.

How could she do this to him? Again.

Carter clenched his fist around the stone, finding comfort in the pain it caused him. He wanted it, and he wanted more. He'd thought at first he would throw the ring in the garbage, but then again . . .

Opening his hand, Carter looked down at the ring and in an instant, he knew what he was going to do.

Kimberly waited as the lawyer sitting on the other side of the desk read the last page of Michael's divorce contract. The woman, one of the best divorce lawyers in California, hadn't said a word since she started reading an hour ago. This was the same woman who initially refused to take her case because, like most of the other top divorce lawyers, Michael had contacted her first and placed her on retainer. Kimberly wondered how many hundreds of thousands of dollars he had spent on this ploy alone.

The lawyer, Sarah Bunting, removed her glasses as she placed the contract on the desk. She looked up for the first time in an hour, but her face was undecipherable.

"Well?" Kimberly asked.

"What did you do?" Sarah asked.

Kimberly frowned, confused.

"Do you have pictures of him naked with a horse or something?"

Kimberly smiled. "So it's good. The settlement, the custody is good?"

"Good?" Sarah laughed. "That damn thing is great. Hell, there are rich men all over California that would kill your husband if they saw this."

"I just want to know that it includes everything Michael promised." Kimberly reached forward to take the contract back.

"It does," Sarah said. "You can sign it, Kimberly. You're a multimillionaire. You got the money, the house, a few cars, guaranteed alimony until you marry again, and primary custody of your sons in a joint custody deal. Hell, all Michael retains is his investment in Chase Beauty, his trust fund and control of the twins' trust funds."

"You make him sound destitute," Kimberly said. "He's got many more millions than I'll ever see. His trust fund alone has more than twenty million and his interest in Chase Beauty is almost a hundred million."

Sarah nodded. "But all your other accounts were split in half. Do you think you can manage on ten million dollars with an additional hundred and fifty thousand every year in alimony and two hundred thousand a year in child support? Considering you don't have a mortgage, and Michael has taken responsibility for the boys' expenses, including forty thousand a year in private school tuition, I think you might be okay."

"I'll be free," Kimberly said. "I'll be free and I'll have my boys. That's all that matters. I would have done that for nothing."

Sarah appeared skeptical. "Well, good thing for you and the boys, you don't have to. What's next on your agenda?"

"As soon as I leave here, I'm calling a travel agent. I've got some business to handle."

Avery sat in her rented car in the parking lot of the hospital in a haze. She hadn't eaten or slept in what seemed like forever. All her tears had dried up and she felt as if she was dying without the sound of her baby's voice. All she could think of was Carter's angry last words.

She understood he was angry and he had a right to be. Hell, she was angry too. She'd made a promise to Carter and herself to embrace their love and make a family with Connor. Avery wanted nothing more than to keep that promise, but right now she simply couldn't. After spending the day with the doctor, who explained to her all Anthony would need, she felt overwhelmed, like she was drowning.

She would just have to make Carter understand. He was mad, but he loved her as much as she loved him. She would figure something out, something that allowed them to be together without deserting Anthony at the lowest point in his life, a point that she had led him to.

Having sat in silence for almost an hour, Avery jumped at the sound of her cell phone ringing. Anthony was in surgery again and the nurses promised to call her when it was over. But when she retrieved the phone, Avery noticed it was her sister, Taylor, and not the hospital.

"Taylor, what's going on?"

"Are you in front of a television?" Taylor asked.

Avery could hear the apprehension laced throughout her words. "No. I'm at the hospital. Why?"

"It wouldn't matter," Taylor said. "It's an L.A. station anyway. You wouldn't get this in Miami."

"Get what? Taylor, don't play with me."

"Well, you're going to find out, so I'll tell you. I'm sorry, sis."

"Sorry for what?" Avery just knew this was about Carter. Something told her it was. "What happened?"

"I'm watching the gossip segment of the afternoon news and the anchor lady just said that Carter Chase and Julia Hall have publicly announced their engagement."

Avery felt like a brick had dropped on her head. "What? What do you mean? He can't . . ."

"She was holding the press release in her hand," Taylor said. "Apparently it was faxed less than an hour ago."

"No." Avery couldn't, wouldn't believe it.

"I'm sorry," Taylor said. "With everything that's happening with Anthony, you don't need to hear this, but it's out and you should know because everyone else will."

"No," Avery repeated.

"Can you believe this?" Taylor asked. "The nerve! The Chase family sent a picture along with the press release and they put it on the screen. What an asshole."

"What is the picture?"

"It's a picture of him and Julia cuddled up together at some picnic thing or something and guess where Connor is."

"Connor?"

"Julia's holding her on her lap."

Avery took a deep breath. "That was on purpose, Taylor."

"Why include Connor?" Taylor asked. "She's your baby and . . . it just seems odd."

"It's not," Avery said. "It was a message to me."

"What?"

"Carter is showing me his new family. He's letting me know I have a fight ahead of me. A fight over Connor."

Kimberly thanked the waiter for bringing her the recommended lobster beluga pasta, one of the many starters Citronelle restaurant in Washington, D.C. was famous for. Taking in the glorious smell, Kimberly sat back comfortably in her seat and looked around the place.

"So this is supposed to be the finest restaurant in all of D.C.?" she asked her dinner companion. He remained silent, seeming unwilling to indulge her. "It's okay, but kind of dated looking. Are you sure you aren't going to eat anything?"

He sighed impatiently. "Can you tell me how you found out about me?"

"How hard can it be to find out about you?" she asked, reaching for her fork. "This looks almost too pretty to eat."

"Mrs. Chase, please."

Kimberly could see that this was painful for him. She imagined it had been ever since she contacted him earlier that day. "Forgive me. Even a first class flight from L.A. to D.C. is taxing. But again, you're so important at your office, of course I would find you."

"What about Steven?"

"Your brother?" she asked. "No, he doesn't know . . . well, he knows about you, Keenan, of course, but he doesn't know about this."

"This?" Keenan Chase, a less impressive version of Steven Chase, not as strong or demanding, raised an eyebrow but otherwise stayed as still as a statue in his chair.

"Have you dumped Elisha yet?" Kimberly brought the fork to her mouth. "Because you really should. She totally fucked everything up."

"Do you really think I'm going to talk to you about that?"

Kimberly expected more of a resemblance between Keenan and Steven. Speaking to him on the phone, he had been harsh and cold, very much like his brother. He was angry she had called, but as soon as she mentioned she wanted to talk about Luxury Life Publishing, he'd agreed to meet her.

Upon seeing him, Kimberly realized he looked nothing like his brother. He was handsome and fit and looked younger than he was, just like Steven. But he didn't have the presence Steven had. People noticed him because he looked like he was ready to beat the crap out of anyone who came within a foot of him, but he was no Steven. Maybe that was why he hated Steven so much.

"Oh my God." Kimberly closed her eyes as the food exploded in her mouth and moved down her throat. "This is delicious. I can't even imagine what the next course will taste like."

"Elisha was a bad choice," Keenan finally admitted. "She became too attached to Michael and I could no longer trust her."

Kimberly nodded in understanding. "My soon-to-be ex-husband has that effect on women."

"Ex?" Keenan seemed intrigued.

"Thank God." Kimberly dabbed at the corners of her mouth with her napkin. "Yes, I am soon to be free of the Chase family to a certain extent. No one really gets free of them, you know?"

"What does this have to do with me?" Keenan asked. "I take it this isn't a nice-to-meet-someone-in-the-family visit?"

"You're smart," Kimberly said. "Smart, but not smart enough. That's why your attempt to destroy Steven failed. You're lucky he never found out about you, because if he had, you'd be toast."

"Is this blackmail?" Keenan asked. "You've come for money in exchange for not telling Steven I plotted to bring his company down."

Kimberly shook her head. "I don't know why you hate him so much."

"There are many reasons too complicated to go into now."

"Now yes, but you'll have to tell me one day. I mean, if we're going to work together."

Keenan laughed disbelievingly. "I'm working with you? On what?"

"I'm not eager to rehash the past either." Kimberly paused to take a drink. "But to summarize, I want Steven and Janet Chase to lose everything. They tried to buy me and steal my children away."

"Do you know why?"

Kimberly waved a dismissive hand. "Oh, no bother. It has to do with a murder and other stuff, but my point is, you and I can do a lot more than you and Elisha ever could."

"How do I know I can trust you?"

"Do you still want Steven to hurt for whatever it is he's done to you?"

Keenan's expression darkened and that was all the answer Kimberly needed.

"I think you're willing to take the chance." Kimberly leaned forward. "You see, you and I want the same thing and together, we can make Steven and Janet Chase wish they were never born."

A PRICE TO PAY

ANGELA WINTERS

ABOUT THIS GUIDE

The questions and discussion topics that follow
are intended to enhance your group's
reading of this book.

DISCUSSION QUESTIONS

1. What do you think about the way the plane crash affected Steven, Janet, Carter, Michael, Avery, and Kimberly?

2. Do you blame Sean for letting Haley trick him by sleeping with him, or is he just a victim of her evil ways?

3. Do you blame Michael or Kimberly for the disintegration of their marriage, and whom do you blame for the damage to the children?

4. Did you think Steven and Janet were right to interfere with Michael's marriage in the way they did, by forcing his hand in a divorce?

5. Were you surprised at Michael's offer to Kimberly at the end of the book?

6. Did you think Avery should have resisted Carter more, or was their reunion inevitable?

7. Why do you think Haley still has it in for Taylor Jackson?

8. Did you believe Carter wanted to change his ways, or was it all still more trickery and manipulation to get Avery?

9. How do you feel about the way Carter treated Julia?

10. Do you think Haley's offer to help Sean by stealing the USB stick from Garrett's law firm was genuine, or just a way to save herself from her father's wrath?

11. What were the dynamics of Michael and Steven's relationship in this novel? Was Steven being too hard on him? Why does what their father think matter so much more to Michael than to Carter?

12. Was Avery right to stay with Anthony in the end?

13. What do you think Carter has in mind with the engagement to Julia? Do you see a custody battle in the future?

14. What did you think about Haley's surprise announcement of her marriage at the end? There were very few hints in the book of something important about Sydney. What do you think she's up to?